Champions of the Scarred Lands

Tales of Fantasy and Adventure

Editor: Stewart Wieck
Cover Artist: Vincent Dutrait
Copyeditor: Melissa Thorpe
Graphic Designer: Aaron Voss
Art Director: Richard Thomas

Copyright © 2002 by White Wolf, Inc.

All rights reserved.

No part of this book may be reproduced or transmitted in any form or by any means, electronic or mechanical — including photocopy, recording, Internet posting, electronic bulletin board — or any other information storage and retrieval system, except for the purpose of reviews, without permission from the publisher.

White Wolf is committed to reducing waste in publishing. For this reason, we do not permit our covers to be "stripped" for returns, but instead require that the whole book be returned, allowing us to resell it.

All persons, places, and organizations in this book — except those clearly in the public domain — are fictitious, and any resemblance that may seem to exist to actual persons, places, or organizations living, dead, or defunct is purely coincidental. The mention of or reference to any companies or products in these pages is not a challenge to the trademarks or copyrights concerned.

The trademark White Wolf, is a registered trademark.
ISBN: 1-58846-808-9
First Edition: January 2002
Printed in Canada

Distributed for Sword & Sorcery Studios by
White Wolf Publishing
735 Park North Boulevard, Suite 128
Clarkston, GA 30021
www.swordsorcery.com

Champions of the Scarred Lands

In Sunlight and Shadow	5
Anthony Pryor	
Journey to the Past	41
William R. Prohaska	
Feast or Famine at Burok Torn	71
Gherbod Fleming	
Three Dreams of Belsameth	95
James Stewart	
Merrin's Tale	139
Keith Sloan	
A Game of Silk and Mirrors	157
Eric Griffin	
Love Incarnate	177
Stewart Wieck	
Tie Your Own Rope	187
Brian Williams	
The River's Flow	217
Alejandro Melchor	
Thief's Mark	241
Carl Bowen	

In Sunlight and Shadow

By Anthony Pryor

The morning sun reflected off bloodstained waters. On the bluff above the crimson sea, atop a great stone tower, an armored man stood, cradling an infant in his gauntleted hands. A priest in white robes stood beside him, bearing a silver chalice filled with water, pure and clean in contrast to the bloody waters below.

"Have you chosen a name, Edaron deBronis?" the priest asked. He was a lean and slender man with a firm jaw and dark, intense eyes.

"I have, Brother Emili," the armored man replied. "He shall be named Barconius."

The priest let a single drop of water fall onto the infant's head. The child did not take it well, and immediately began to squirm and cry.

"I name you Barconius deBronis," said the priest. "On this, Mithril's founding day, the most auspicious of naming days, I invoke Corean the Champion, Madriel the Merciful, Tanil the Huntress, and Hedrada the Just, and ask that they grant you're their blessings. May your life be one of faith and righteousness. Praise be."

"Praise be," said Edaron.

The men stood in silence for a moment, contemplating the rising sun.

Edaron looked down at his child. The infant had calmed, and now simply looked sleepy.

"My son," he said, softly. "Barconius. One day you will be greater than all of us."

"So let it be," said Emili Derigesh. "In Corean's name."

In Sunlight and Shadow

***

Forty-six years, and today I stand at that same spot, clad in my own suit of paladin's armor, gazing out across the same sea. And the same sun still shines on the same bloody waters, and we still pray to Corean for salvation.

Champion Barconius stirred from his reverie, and focused his attention on High Priest Emili Derigesh. He was no longer the vital young priest who had christened him that day so long ago, but the spark that drove him, the unshakeable faith that sustained him, were still visible in the old man's bright, intelligent eyes. Emili Derigesh's body had grown old, but his heart had stayed young and true.

Regrettably, he had grown no less long-winded. He faced away from the bloody waters now, gazing down on the assembled multitudes who crowded the public square below, addressing them with a strong, vibrant voice. He spoke of the great city of Mithril, its history, its promise, and the assurance of eventual triumph.

And he had been doing so for nearly two hours.

"Though the titans were defeated a century and a half ago, their minions continue to lurk in shadows and plot against the forces of the Divine, against our champion Corean, and the other gods of good. It is our duty and our responsibility to stand firm against them, and show them that their masters have truly passed from this world, and that the day of the titans shall never return."

Derigesh gestured expansively, pointing south, to the heights above the harbor, where a huge, motionless giant stood, its silvery skin glinting in the morning sun.

"There stands the promise, the symbol of Corean's eternal strength. The Mithril Golem, tool of the gods, that held the tail of the mighty titan Kadum as he was chained and confined beneath the ocean, where he lies today in eternal torment, his lifeblood pouring out to stain the waters of the seas around him, an eternal reminder of his defeat and his endless punishment."

The Golem... yes. That titanic construct, crafted by the gods themselves as their chosen avenger, their surrogate in battle, the monstrous beast that fought for them and scattered entire armies of titanspawn in its wake. The tireless machine that chased down Kadum himself and held him, despite terrible damage, and now stood as a sign of the gods' endless power.

Or, some would claim—though never within earshot of a priest or paladin—their impotence. The golem stood now where it had stood 150 years ago, motionless and by all evidence lifeless. Its battle with the titan had left it with scars—dents and welts, scrapes and gaping wounds. One of its vast shoulders bore the impression of a gigantic hand, its fingers dug deeply into the shining metal. Did it stand as a promise, the skeptics asked, or as a symbol of the limitations of the divine?

The priests admitted to no such doubts. Yet now and then even Barconius himself, anointed Champion of Mithril, paladin and knight of the Order, felt the tiniest stings of doubt. What if the Golem was nothing more than a machine? And a

In Sunlight and Shadow

broken machine at that? Was the faith of the city wasted? Were its founders wrong? Was the promise of Corean nothing but a sham, and was the power of the gods truly finite?

No, he thought. I am Barconius. I am the Champion of Mithril. I am a paladin, as was my father before me, and his father before him, back to the days of the Divine War when my people stood proud and strong at the right hand of Corean.

I am Barconius. My faith is strong.

"And so it was, nearly three decades ago, when the dark powers of the Penumbral Lords threatened our city. The will of Corean was invincible, and in the person of the youthful knight Barconius, and his companions, the Avenger struck back at those dark forces who used our own sacred catacombs as their base of operations, and sought to corrupt this holy city from within..."

Barconius drew a deep breath, as the high priest's words triggered memories, and for a moment he was 18 again, a newly made knight, listening to the fearful tale of a frightened man...

***

The engineer was visibly shaken, his face pale, his eyes wide.

"Paladin," he said, voice rushed and agitated. "We were in the catacombs performing a routine survey, and we found... we found tunnels... tunnels that were on none of our maps... It was terrible... You must help..."

Barconius gently put a hand on the man's shoulder.

"Calm yourself. No one can hurt you here. Tell me what you saw."

"The tunnels were very old, my lord. They contained old tombs and chapels. But they... They were desecreated. Horribly desecrated. There were strange sigils painted on the walls, and there was blood. So much blood my lord..."

"Fresh blood?"

The man nodded. "Varro went down with some others to map the tunnels. I told him not to, that it was evil and we needed to tell the paladins, but he didn't listen. He hasn't come back, lord. I fear the worst."

"Can you find the place again?"

"Yes. I can at least show you the entrance. That's as far as I dared go."

Barconius considered the man's words. Plainly, someone needed to investigate. But who? He himself was newly promoted to command, only slightly more experienced than his squad of six paladins. After a moment's hesitation, he summoned a page.

"Go tell High Priest Derigesh what this man has said," he told the young man. "And tell him that I have taken my squad into the catacombs to investigate."

The boy nodded and dashed away.

Barconius turned to look at his paladins, standing at the ready a few paces away. Like him, they wore shining plate armor, their shields and breastplates

In Sunlight and Shadow

inscribed with the sigil of Corean—four swords in the shape of a compass rose, points outward. Gelban, a half-elven ranger of the Behjurian Vigil assigned to assist the squad stood with them, clad in light leather armor and a brown cloak.

"This engineer has found something that we need to look into," Barconius told them. "We must go into the catacombs."

Dutifully, and without comment, ranger and paladins fell in step behind Barconius as he followed the engineer.

***

Barconius awoke from his reverie. Emili Derigesh was still speaking, and the crowd was growing restive. Barconius had heard the old priest's exhortations a thousand times before, with only the smallest of variations, and knew that he was capable of droning on for another hour if he felt the need.

But even as Barconius steeled himself for another long speech, he felt the touch of an armored hand on one shoulder and heard low, hushed words.

"Barconius. Look."

It was Ingunn, Warden of the Towers, a grim-faced, gray-haired woman in paladin's armor. She pointed urgently westward. As Barconius looked, he felt a cold dread sweep over him.

Red as blood and bright as the sun, the holy beacon ascended. A moment later, it was joined by a second, rising into the sky, miles distant, a silent cry for help from a paladin in danger.

Every instinct in Barconius' soul urged him to run, gather paladins, and chant the words of the holy beacon's reply, the spell that would instantly transport him to the stricken one's location. But moving calmly and deliberately, he turned to Emili Derigesh and whispered softly.

"Please conclude quickly, your grace. A holy beacon has been sighted."

Derigesh's eyes widened imperceptibly, but he continued with scarcely a pause.

"And with those holy thoughts in our minds, and the memory of those ancient heroes in our hearts, I wish all citizens of Mithril a joyful Founders' Day and bid you spend it in joy and happiness. Praise Corean, and honor the names of all the gods for the great victory that they have brought us."

Thunderous cheering greeted the high priest's words, though Barconius could not tell whether the crowd shouted out of piety or relief that the speech was at last over.

"Gather your paladins, Barconius," Derigesh said, his voice tight with concern, "and do what you must do. Corean be with you."

Barconius saluted and turned to where Ingunn and the other Mithril knights were gathering. They moved with deliberation, knowing the urgency of the moment, but did not rush or panic for fear of alarming the crowd below. All knew, however, what the beacon signified—one of their number was in peril.

Overhead, the holy beacons burned, motionless heralds of dread.

In Sunlight and Shadow

***

Mithril's catacombs were not considered places of death; rather, they were for quiet contemplation, veneration of fallen heroes and silent adoration of the gods.

But this, Barconius thought grimly, gazing at the defiled chamber, this was something different.

The room had once housed a small chapel, its walls graced with delicate frescoes depicting Corean and the other gods comforting mourners and escorting virtuous souls to paradise. Many scholars and priests would have given anything to see it in its undisturbed state.

But now it was a nightmare. The walls were daubed with necromantic and demonic symbols, the frescoes defaced with blood and filth, the altars overturned and defiled. Foul magics had been cast here; Barconius could feel it. The very air reeked of evil and perversion.

"This is as far as you went?" Barconius asked the engineer, who stood beside him, trying not to tremble.

The engineer shook his head. "Yes, sir paladin. Varro and his team were foolhardy and chose to go on, but I fled to warn you."

"That was wise," said Gelban, his soft eyes dark with revulsion. "The ones who did this were here, bare hours ago."

"You can track them?" Barconius asked, and the ranger nodded.

"Very well." He gestured to one of his paladins. "You, escort this engineer back to the surface, and tell the high priest what we have seen."

The engineer, visibly relieved, followed the paladin from the chapel.

"I'll not expose him to further danger," Barconius said, partly to himself, partly to Gelban and the others. He waved a gauntleted hand at the defiled shrine. "Those who did this are down here still. We will follow and make them pay for their blasphemies."

Grimly, the six paladins followed the ranger from the chapel.

***

A small group of armored men and women stood on the battlement, staring with worried gazes toward the beacons. There was Ingunn, chief of the Beacon Knights, who had first seen the distress signal. Beside her stood Valtanon, a square-jawed paladin with an ugly scar across his neck, a memento from a murderous blood reaper. He was speaking to a handsome, blonde-haired knight. Barconius struggled to remember his name.

A woman stood nearby. Clad in silken robes and a wizard's staff in one hand, no one would ever have mistaken her for a paladin. Milk-white skin and violet eyes betrayed her half-elven ancestry, and Barconius knew that slightly pointed ears hid beneath her cascade of pale hair. Her name was Nabila Silverheart, list mistress of the Guild of the Shadow, the wizards and sorcerers who helped defend Mithril.

In Sunlight and Shadow

"There are two beacons," Barconius said. "Above the Plains of Lede. Who is it?"

"Deranthus and Natalya were leading a patrol near the Highfort Ruins," Ingunn said. "It's probably them."

Barconius nodded. "Who is on duty in Titanswatch Tower?"

"Lady Karina," Ingunn replied. "One of my best."

"I have contacted her with a scrying crystal," Nabila Silverheart said. "Her beacon's answer spell is prepared, and she will cast it when you dispatch your paladins."

"Very well." Barconius turned his gaze back toward the beacons. They still shone strongly. Good. It meant that the two paladins were incapacitated as a result of combat, but were still alive. "I will send my paladins. But I will go as well."

Ingunn seemed taken aback, but said nothing.

Nabila Silverheart was not as reticent. "Champion, you must stay in the city. This could be a trap, and we can ill afford to lose you."

Barconius felt an iron hand grip his heart. There was more than mere concern behind her words, but he could not afford to think of such things now. "I know, sorceress. Yet, I must go. Deranthus and Natalya are paladins—my brother and sister in Corean. I've let others face danger long enough. It is time that I faced it as well."

"It is not your task to face such dangers," Silverheart said. "That is a task for others. Send me. I will help your paladins."

15

"No," Barconius said. "It is for me and my paladins alone. Corean wills it."

Silverheart nodded, a trace of sadness and resignation in her deep violet eyes. "I hear and obey, Champion, though I cannot agree with your reasons."

Barconius forced a smile. "No one is asking you to, sorceress. Know, however, that your concern and kind words are not lost on me."

Silverheart returned the smile, her face almost supernaturally beautiful. "Corean keep you safe, paladin."

Barconius nodded, and for a moment an image flashed in his mind, of sweeping the woman up in his steel-clad arms and pressing his lips to hers.

You do not need this life. You need not be a knight. You have served your people well, and none would condemn you if you put your sword down and lived the rest of your life as an ordinary man.

Harshly, he forced the thoughts away.

I am Barconius. My faith is strong.

***

The tunnels were unadorned, their stonework rough-hewn. They had lain undiscovered for decades, and now something lurked down here. Something foreign and hostile.

They had been traveling for nearly an hour when the shadows came alive.

Gelban was the first to fall, inky black hands twined around his throat. His torch fell, plunging the corridor into darkness.

In Sunlight and Shadow

Shouts of alarm erupted behind Barconius, then he felt a cutting, icy chill as lifeless fingers clutched him and clawed at his face.

"Corean!" Barconius forced the word out. "Corean, give me strength!"

With a mighty heave, he slashed upward with his sword. When it touched the unearthly flesh of his attacker, its blade burst into hot, silvery flames, illuminating the corridor. The shadow-thing fell back, its substance draining away like foul black water. It truly looked like a man's shadow, but twisted, animated by foul magic.

Barconius swung his blade again, cutting through the creature, and it vanished into tattered wisps.

The shadow that had attacked Gelban stood atop the still body, dark hands wrapped around the ranger's throat. It was an unliving thing, a creature of hate and fear, and Barconius knew he could cause it to flee. He thrust his sword toward the monster, shouting.

"Begone!" Barconius shouted. "Corean wills it! The power of Corean compels you!"

The strength of the god flowed through him, and the creature shuddered, hissing in agony. It turned its black, featureless face toward Barconius, then vanished, melting back into the darkness. Gelban lay motionless, but behind them, the paladins fought for their lives.

Barconius turned, sword on guard. Two of his paladins were down, but the others belabored the insubstantial monstrosities with their shining weapons. He hewed at one of the shadows that stood over a helpless paladin.

Walking shadows, he thought. Creatures of unlife. Only a necromancer or powerful spellcaster could have summoned such things. They faced magic in its darkest and most evil form.

The fight was short and furious. When it was over, Barconius surveyed the carnage, panting heavily, his sword's light fading as the threat receded.

"Gods," he muttered. Only three paladins remained on their feet; the others lay motionless.

"Help them if you can," he ordered, then turned back toward the fallen ranger. "I'll see to..."

He stopped, biting his words off in utter horror and disbelief.

Gelban stood there. He was still wore his armor, but was wreathed in shadow, his once-gentle hands transformed into black claws crafted of unliving darkness, reaching toward Barconius.

***

Valtanon, Ingunn and the blonde paladin stood beside Barconius, their collective gaze focused on the shining beacons. In unison, they chanted the beacon's reply spell.

Great Corean, your children call out to you.

Barconius forced all thoughts from his mind save the beacons and the plight of his paladins.

Lord Corean, greatest and most powerful, help us to vanquish our enemies as you did vanquish the titans and scatter their legions like dust. Carry us to aid your children in their need.

In Sunlight and Shadow

So often, he had heard others utter the words. Now, for the first time in long years, Barconius uttered them, feeling the hand of Corean reach out and carry him aloft, bearing him toward the stricken paladins. Even as he traveled, however, Barconius felt fear and doubt that lurked in his soul... and once more he was in the catacombs, lost in darkness.

***

The others were gone, fallen to the shadows. Alone, Barconius fought his way through the labyrinth, guided only by the light of his sword. Again and again they came at him, deathly silent, clawing at him with icy fingers.

And again and again he cut them down, moving like a man in a dream. Soon, he almost believed that he had died in the corridors, and now dwelt alone in a hell of his own making, beset by the souls of those he had slain.

Gelban lay twice slain behind him—the elf who had been his friend, taken by the inky black shadow of nightmare, then risen and killed once more on Barconius' blade. In death, however, Barconius had felt the ranger's soul slip away almost gratefully, bound for the embrace of the gentle goddess Tanil, where he would dwell in peace for eternity.

Now, Barconius fought darkness, struggling to escape from its clinging touch. His very presence was enough to drive the creatures away, but they were many and he was only a single paladin, human and imperfect, fighting the shadows with ever-growing weariness. But still he fought, Corean's sigil burning in his mind, his soul unbending even as his body grew weary.

I am Barconius. My faith is strong.

At last, after a lifetime in darkness, Barconius saw light. Faint at first, it grew stronger, driving away the shadows. Then he was back in the outer catacombs, limping, weak and near collapse. He stumbled forth into the light of morning, his armor battered and rent, his holy sword notched and discolored.

"Barconius!"

It was a blessedly familiar sound. The world was ablaze—hours in darkness had robbed Barconius of his day vision, but when he squinted, shutting out the terrible light of the sun, he saw the solid jaw, the dark eyes and the now-balding visage of the man who had named him before Corean.

"High Priest Derigesh," Barconius said, shocked at how weak and thin his voice sounded. "Your Holiness. Please... The catacombs... They are all dead..."

Barconius fell into Emili Derigesh's arms, his tale tumbling urgently from his lips.

***

The four paladins stood in an endless wind-swept sea of golden grass. A moment later, a flash of silvery light heralded the arrival of a fifth, the Beacon Knight Karina. Her face was surprisingly soft and gentle, her raven-black hair, shot with silver, blowing in the stiff wind of the plains.

In Sunlight and Shadow

"Welcome, Lady," Barconius said. "I'm glad you could join us."

Karina looked him up and down, and spoke with obvious surprise.

"My duty and my pleasure, Champion," she replied, blinking. "To what do we owe the blessings of your company?"

Barconius smiled wanly. "The will of Corean, Lady."

A huddle of ruins stood nearby, surrounding a hazy hemisphere of pure black magical energy, nearly three hundred yards across. Directly above the black dome's center, the two beacons burned.

"It's wicked as Vangal's armpit," Valtanon growled. "I can smell it."

"So can I," Ingunn replied. "Whoever created that is well prepared. As if..."

"As if we were expected?" Barconius finished her thought. "I'm not surprised. Very well, then. They are prepared for us. So shall we be prepared for them. You all know what to do. Invoke the Body of Corean."

The five paladins stood in a circle, heads down. After a moment, each spoke in turn, invoking the five sacred spells that formed their most potent defense, the armor of light.

As they chanted, a luminous web of light began to form around them, weaving into a bright, shimmering circle.

"Corean arm and armor your servants," Barconius said. "We invoke your body and don your armor."

Now the five were clad in shining armor that seemed crafted of living light. Barconius had seen these spells in action a thousand times, but they still filled him with awe.

He pointed toward the ruins and the ominous black hemisphere.

"In Corean's name," he said. "Advance."

***

Barconius told his story as two priests prayed over him, calling up the healing power of their god. He felt strength return to his limbs, and lost vitality flowing back into him.

"We have detected a great nexus of evil beneath the city," Derigesh said when Barconius finished. "I have summoned my paladins to root it out. I bid you lead them into the catacombs and destroy this evil before it can spread farther."

Barconius stared in disbelief.

"You can't be serious, your holiness. I'm not yet even a Mithril knight. I can't lead your paladins."

"Corean wills it," Derigesh said. "You know the way. My knights will aid you. But you must help us find and defeat whatever lurks in the catacombs."

Barconius swallowed hard. He knelt before Derigesh, holding out his sword, hilt first.

"In Corean's name," he said, "I will do my best."

To his surprise, Derigesh gently pulled the weapon from his hands, then gestured to a nearby acolyte, who approached, bearing a long, cloth-wrapped bundle.

In Sunlight and Shadow

"Paladin Barconius," Derigesh said, unwrapping the bundle and drawing forth a great, gleaming sword, "take this weapon. It is called Titansbane, and it was borne by your father, and by his father and grandfather before him. He bid me give it to you when you were old and strong enough to bear it, and tell you that, though he could not be with you, he loved you nonetheless."

Barconius felt his eyes widen and a sting of unfamiliar emotion as he accepted the weapon.

"This..." he began, and felt his voice break. "This is a Mithril knight's sword. I'm not worthy to bear it. I must forge my own."

"And so you shall, Barconius. But I must keep my promise to your father. Now, his love will guide you through the darkness below."

Barconius swallowed as the strange mixture of sorrow and joy swirled through his mind.

My father.

He has barely known the man. A paladin and commander of the elite Order of Mithril, Edaron deBronis had spent most of his time at his duties, seeing to the city garrison, patrolling beyond the walls, serving as a Beacon Knight and aiding paladins in danger. When at home, he had been a loving, doting father, ever proud of his son. But he had been home so rarely. For Barconius, his father had been little more than a loving stranger.

Edaron had died while doing his duty. The storm hag Ukla'tha had captured two paladins. Edaron came in response to the holy beacon's call, bringing a handful of powerful knights with him and given his life to save the two captives. Ukla'tha herself perished at Edaron's hands, but not before she had dealt the knight a mortal wound. Even the high priest could not save Edaron, for his wounds were too great, and his very soul had departed.

He serves Corean now, Derigesh had said at the memorial. *In death as in life, and in anticipation of the glorious day when all of the Champion's servants shall be reunited with their loved ones, when Corean's great destiny is achieved, and the darkness of the titans is finally vanquished.*

Barconius had been six years old, but the words still echoed in his mind.

Blinking back tears, he took the sword and stood up.

"Thank you, Your Holiness," he said. "I shall try to honor my father's memory."

Derigesh smiled. "You honor it already, paladin."

***

Darkness receded before the five paladins, falling back but lurking at the edge of their radiance, a black beast waiting to spring.

"I don't like this," Valtanon said. "We should be dispelling this, not just pushing it back."

"Be wary," Barconius said. "There's terrible magic here."

"Tell us something we don't know," said Karina with a dry smile.

***

In Sunlight and Shadow

The battle raged for days beneath the streets of Mithril. Paladins, city guard, Behjurian Vigilists, wizards from the Guild of the Shadow, and others descended into the catacombs, joining the fight against the shadows and their mysterious masters. There were other creatures, too—undead, demons, aberrations that had no name—but slowly, step-by-step, at a fearful cost, Corean's legions pushed them back.

Always Barconius was there, Titansbane blazing, cutting through the enemy like a scythe cutting ripe wheat. The enemy perished or fled at the sight of him. With the armored holy warriors of Mithril behind him, and the spells of its wizards to support him, Barconius fought the enemy to his lair.

There were five of them—the Penumbral Pentagon they called themselves. Masters of shadow magic, they had hidden in the catacombs for years, building their power controlling the forgotten places of the city, scheming to eventually overthrow the high priest and the paladins, and create a terrible new city of darkness.

The Pentagon chose a vast, domed chamber for their last stand. Barconius suspected that it was not part of the original catacombs, but instead the work of some ancient race, and that the members of the Pentagon had simply taken it as their lair.

They had turned the chamber into a place of death, full of traps and living shadows. The Pentagon saved their most fearsome spells for last, summoning up even more powerful shadow-creatures, vengeful spirits, undead and demons.

Their leader was the worst. Dar'tan was his name, and he seemed a creature of shadow every bit as much as his minions. He had the delicate features of an elf, but his skin was jet black and his hair shone like silver. When he raised up the power of shadow, dozens of his foes died or fled screaming, and for a time it seemed that he alone would turn the tide against the folk of Corean.

But he had not reckoned with Barconius. Through the nightmarish whirl of light and shadow, of blood and steel, Barconius fought, his resolute gaze fixed upon the black-clad penumbral lord, struggling inexorably toward the dark elf.

Dar'tan gave ground, seeking to slow or stop the paladin's advance with spells and more bestial minions.

"Dar'tan!" Barconius bellowed, hacking down a rot-fleshed zombie. "I bring Corean's justice!"

Something like fear flickered in the elf's eyes, but it was instantly replaced by steely defiance.

"It is a false justice, paladin!" He raised his hands and a skein of shadows grew around him like a shield. "You think you know the truth, that the light will shine forever. But darkness and shadow are never banished, and in the end they always triumph."

Barconius struck at the shadowy shield. Titansbane flared blindingly, and he felt the shield give slightly.

"Never, sorcerer! Corean is great. The struggle against shadow never ends!"

In Sunlight and Shadow

"Neither does the shadow," Dar'tan hissed. "The darkness always returns. The darkness always finds its way."

Dar'tan retreated and another penumbral lord stepped into Barconius' path, arms spread, black shadow-fire bursting from his fingertips. It struck Titansbane and vanished like smoke. Barconius hacked down, and the penumbral lord fell, his head and shoulders nearly severed from his body.

Dar'tan's eyes widened.

"You feel fear, dark one?" Barconius bellowed. "Your allies are slain, your minions flee!"

"*No!*" Dar'tan's voice was a shriek of anger and hatred. A whirlwind of darkness burst from his hands, enveloping Barconius and the paladins near him. Feeling the same terrible cold as when the shadow had touched him, Barconius stumbled to his knees, fighting the urge to collapse and let the cold consume him.

But even as it grew, the chill shadow flickered and died as a wave of warmth and courage spread from the sword and into Barconius' body.

My son, echoed a voice. *Barconius. One day you will be greater than all of us.*

The darkness fled and Barconius felt a gentle hand touch his.

Father?

Then he was on his feet, swinging Titansbane with all the strength he could muster. Dar'tan gasped as his shadow-shield broke, then the terrible blade cut into his shoulder, cleaving flesh and bone, sending his left arm spinning away. Black blood pumped from the gaping wound, and the dark elf fell to his knees.

Barconius advanced, sword raised for a killing blow.

Dar'tan looked up, his face drawn, his eyes wide with terror. His lips trembled as he spoke a single, quavering word.

"Mercy?"

Barconius hesitated, sword drawn back. One motion and Dar'tan would die.

But he paused, Dar'tan's plea hanging in the air, protecting the dark elf like his web of shadows...

Dar'tan fumbled at his neck with his one good hand, seizing a tiny bead that hung on a chain. His fingers closed around it, his lips moved silently, eyes reflecting not fear and contrition, but smug arrogance and triumph.

Barconius swung Titansbane downward in a flashing silver arc, aimed at the dark elf's neck...

Titansbane met only shadow.

Overbalanced, Barconius stumbled and fell, clattering heavily to the floor. He rolled to his feet, sword at the ready.

Dar'tan's severed arm lay in a pool of blood, but the penumbral lord was gone.

***

And so it was that the Penumbral Pentagon was driven from Mithril, and the young paladin Barconius was proclaimed a hero.

In Sunlight and Shadow

It was, of course, only a matter of time before Barconius took his rightful place as Champion of Mithril. Under his leadership, the Order of Mithril grew in strength and influence, and the city itself became increasingly powerful and prosperous. And with each passing year, Barconius' fame spread and his legend grew. The great knight. Son of the great Edaron deBronis, grandson of the paladin Retarius, who had battled the hags in the Bryndor Hills, and great-grandson of Toren, who was said to have stood at the side of Corean's avatar in the battle with Thulkas, the Iron God. The perfect paladin. Champion of Corean.

But something had changed. Barconius was no longer the brave young paladin who had led Mithril's legions against Dar'tan and the Pentagon. True, even two decades later he was still brave and vital, his gaze steady, his sword arm strong. Titansbane still rested at his side. Yet, like a caged tiger, Barconius paced, tested his boundaries, and longed for the freedom of battle and the joy of risk.

But battle—so Derigesh and the others told him—was for younger, less important individuals. It pained Barconius, sometimes fiercely, to send the young and the strong and the noble into battle time and again, never knowing if they would return. More times than he cared to count, Barconius had seen corpses, clad in bloody armor once so bright and flawless, or witnessed the return of a once-proud knight, now crippled and humbled, because he, Barconius, had sent him to his fate.

And how they fought, those shining defenders of Corean, confident that when their time came, the god would scoop up their souls and bear them to paradise to stand at his right hand, and return once more to the mortal world, along with the other celestial hosts, if and when the tides of evil rose.

And Barconius was their leader. Stern, powerful, ever-faithful Barconius, the finest paladin and most perfect knight of this age or, some claimed, any other.

He was Barconius and his faith was strong.

But how strong can a man be, he wondered? How long can one maintain the fight against evil before realizing that evil is limitless, and you are just one man?

He'd seen the looks of adoration and love in the eyes of the people. Children gazed at him in awe. Men looked at him with gratitude. Women cast loving glances at him, hoping against hope that he would respond, and that they would be the ones who finally brought the perfect paladin to the altar.

Even Nabila Silverheart, wise and old as she was, was not immune to such feelings, though sometimes Barconius thought her the only one who saw him as a man and not Corean's living avatar.

And the worst of it was, Barconius thought, he knew the truth—that he was not an avatar, not a paragon, not the right hand of Corean. He was a man, flesh and blood, life-sized and imperfect, cursing himself for his doubts, fearing that his faith was weak, and that sometimes even he did not truly believe in the eventual triumph of Corean.

In Sunlight and Shadow

Was he like the Mithril Golem, he wondered? Gleaming and heroic, but empty and broken inside?

When at last the two beacons rose from the Plains of Lede, Barconius knew that the time had come to at last test himself, and to confront his doubts firsthand. As had his father before him, Barconius would step into the jaws of the dragon, and see if he could withstand its fire.

***

In the center of the dome, the darkness receded, hollowed out like a cavern, but still deep in shadow. Ahead of them rose a weathered pile of stones, the remnants of an old platform or dais.

"Gods," whispered the blonde paladin.

A figure stood there, tall and spare, clad in black, wreathed in shadowy tendrils like curling, twitching vines. At this distance he looked human, but unnaturally thin and pale. And behind him...

Barconius suppressed a sudden rush of anger. Two poles stood, each topped with horned skulls. His paladins hung motionless by their chained wrists, heads down. Their armor was battered and bloodstained, hacked by fierce blows.

"They're alive, Barconius," said Karina. "I can feel it."

Barconius grimaced and stepped forward, brandishing Titansbane. It shone brightly, as if aware of the evil that surrounded it.

"I am Barconius, Champion of Mithril!" he shouted, but his words seemed swallowed up in the gloom. "In the name of Corean the Avenger, I demand you release your prisoners to me!"

The man's words echoed back to Barconius as if borne on night-dark wings.

"Welcome, Champion. I allowed these knights to send out their beacons in the hope that others would come to save them. We never thought to summon the great Barconius himself."

The words resonated chillingly in Barconius' mind, and he strode forward, his gaze fixed on the dark figure.

"We?" he demanded. "You are not alone in this. Who is your master, dark one? Who bid you take my people?"

The man's reply oozed contempt.

"I have no master, paladin. But the chief of our order is known to you. He would like you to know that he has replaced the arm that you took from him."

Barconius faltered.

"Dar'tan." It was not a question. "He lives still."

"Yes, paladin. And he has grown strong."

Chaotic thoughts spun through Barconius' mind. He had always known that this day would come, when he finally learned the fate of the penumbral lord. Now, at last, he knew.

"You are Dar'tan's minion?"

The man laughed. "As I said, I am no minion, paladin. I am Lord Mortus of the Penumbral Pentagon, and I am nearly Dar'tan's equal. Come and test me, paladin. You will see." He waved an arm at the gray void that surrounded them. "This is a small

In Sunlight and Shadow

portion of the realm of shadows, paladin, brought to Scarn by my magic. Your god is weak here, where my kind hold sway."

In the instant that Mortus' gaze shifted to the shadows beyond Barconius' circle of light, the paladin was in motion. Titansbane whirled in a flashing silver arc, cutting down two living shadows, then reversing to demolish a chaotic thing of bone and sinew that lurched out of the darkness.

"For Corean, paladins!" he shouted as above him Mortus gestured, arcane syllables flowing from his lips. "Strike!"

Shadows and other things emerged from the black void to assault the other paladins. Grimly, they held their ground, shining beings of pure light, weapons moving with blinding speed, sundering or dispelling their foes.

Darkness leapt from Mortus' fingertips as he flung his spells at the paladins. Some found their mark, but the armor of light was strong, and the knights fought on.

A creature that might once have been a steppe troll rushed at Barconius. Now a shambling mass of bone and rotted flesh, it hammered him with a great rusty axe. He blocked the blow, feeling shock jar through his arm as his shield exploded into fragments.

He stepped into the creature and chopped savagely, severing its thick forearm. As the axe and arm tumbled to the ground, Barconius backhanded his blade into the creature's unprotected neck. The huge head spun away, the body tottered and fell, and

Barconius leaped clear, only to face the cold, clawed hands of two more shadows.

Above him, Mortus shouted an incantation, and black fire burst forth from his fingertips, enveloping Barconius in a dark inferno.

"Feel the touch of the black flames, paladin!"

The flames seared Barconius, drawing strength from his limbs, even as they consumed the two shadows that he was fighting. Fire flowing in his veins, Barconius forced himself forward, toward the rocks, toward the figure of Mortus and his helpless captives. Every step was like a thousand miles, but the armor of light held back the worst of it, and in his mind, the image of the Avenger burned, strong, proud and unyielding.

I am Barconius. My faith is strong.

Then the glow of the armor of light flickered and began to fade. Mortus' words echoed in Barconius mind.

This is a small portion of the realm of shadows, paladin... Your god is weak here, where my kind hold sway.

The armor of light vanished, and the pain increased tenfold.

The image of Corean grew dim. Barconius reached for the power that had sustained him, the goodness and light of the Champion, but it slipped away, swallowed up by the shadows.

Barconius fell to his knees, feeling his life slipping away, borne like smoke from the black flames. He looked up, meeting Mortus' triumphant gaze.

In Sunlight and Shadow

"You have failed, paladin." The words echoed hollowly. "Dar'tan will be pleased."

Still wreathed in ebon flame, Barconius hauled himself painfully to his feet, dragging himself along, step by agonized step. He still had strength left... strength to heal himself, and move the last few paces toward Mortus.

The shadow-mage seemed amused. "You're strong, knight," he said, stepping back toward the two unconscious paladins. From his belt he pulled a wickedly curved dagger. "But not strong enough to save your brother paladin."

With that, he seized Deranthus by the hair and yanked his head up, exposing his neck. The dagger flashed, seeking out the unprotected flesh.

"No!" Barconius shouted, and the words of a sacred invocation sprang unbidden to his lips. "*Corean! Let your mercy be our shield!*"

The dagger pierced the helpless paladin's flesh...

Barconius reached forth, the healing energies that he had been about to use on himself now flowing into Deranthus.

He felt the touch of the blade against his own throat, felt his own flesh give way before the cold metal, felt his own lifeblood burst forth, staining his silver armor crimson...

As Corean shields me, let me shield you, brother...

Mortus cursed in frustration, glaring as Barconius again fell to the ground, blood gouting. Contemptuously, he drew back the dagger for a second blow...

Behind him, a sphere of white light appeared, and at its center, clad in swirling robes of white and indigo, a staff clutched in her hands, stood a woman, pale-skinned, silver-haired, violet eyes hard, lips set in a grimace of concentration...

"Nabila..." Barconius gasped, strength fleeing from his limbs.

Flames leaped from Nabila Silverheart's staff, striking Mortus, sending him tumbling, his robes burning with clean bright fire. He cried out and tried to rise, but Nabila held out her hand and shouted. A swarm of tiny daggers burst forth, stabbing into Mortus' flesh, darted away then stabbed again.

Somehow, Mortus was able to get back on his feet. Burning, screaming, beset by the cloud of daggers, he fled blindly, missed his footing, then fell from the stone platform, his body striking a rock, and finally crashing, lifeless, to the ground a few feet from Barconius.

The black flames faded, but Barconius' blood still flowed from his wounded throat, and with the last of his fading strength, he looked up at the woman, who picked her way down from the cliff toward him, her bright with concern.

"Nabila..." Barconius said, weakly, and reached out toward her, but the shadows were too strong, and closed over him.

***

Barconius stood bathed in light. The chill of death was gone from his limbs, and he felt once more like the young paladin who had entered the

In Sunlight and Shadow

catacombs. He was clad in his armor—unmarred, shining plate and chain—and Titansbane rested at his hip.

A voice echoed in the vastness.

"My son."

Barconius fell to his knees as a tall armored figure appeared before him, sword in one hand, shield in the other. Its face shone like the sun, but it did not hurt Barconius' eyes as he looked at it.

"My Lord Corean," he said softly. "I have fought in your name, and tried to be humble and merciful." He swallowed, and felt the same rush of emotion that he had felt when Derigesh gave him the sword. "Yet I have felt doubts, and I have... I have even questioned your will, great Champion. I give myself up to your mercy and await judgment."

The armored figure approached, and a gauntleted hand reached out to touch Barconius' bowed head.

"You have done well, my son. But you must return. It is not your time."

Surprised, Barconius looked up. A gentle voice spoke.

"My son. Barconius. One day you will be greater than all of us."

The light of the being's visage faded, and Barconius looked upon a face much like his own. A face from long ago.

Barconius felt tears on his cheeks.

"Father?"

"Go, my son. In Corean's name."

And the vision faded, blurring and receding as if down an endless tunnel, while his father's words echoed softly in his ears.

"I love you, my son. I will always be with you. In hope and despair. In triumph and defeat. In sunlight and shadow. Always, my son."

***

"Barconius?"

Nabila Silverheart's face had replaced his father's, and she gazed down at him, a look midway between hope and despair on her elfin face.

Barconius felt tears on his face. He lay on the plains now—the shadow realm was gone, banished by its creator's death. Nearby, the others were busy applying healing to each other and the two freed captives. Mortus' corpse, a crumpled black bundle of broken bones, lay untouched and unheeded.

The blonde paladin knelt beside Barconius, his bare hands resting on the older paladin's armored chest. Barconius felt warmth spread out across him, driving off the pain and stiffness of his wounds.

"You came like the herald of Madriel, sorceress," Barconius said. "To strike the foe and save your people." He forced a smile. It didn't hurt much. "Though I distinctly told you that this was a task for me and my paladins alone."

"Oh, Barconius." Silverheart sounded as close to tears as he had ever heard her. "You know that the faithful of Madriel aren't good at taking orders."

In Sunlight and Shadow

"And thank all the gods for it," said the blonde man. "Else we'd have lost our greatest champion."

Barconius suppressed the urge to roll his eyes. Carefully, he sat up.

"Care, Champion," said the blonde man. "I've healed all I can, but your wounds were severe."

"It's all right," Barconius said. "I've seen worse."

"You could have healed yourself, Champion. Healed yourself and slain the shadow-mage. But you saved Deranthus instead." His voice was hushed. "You would have given your life for him. You show us the way, Champion, and we can only follow."

Barconius felt vaguely uncomfortable at the young man's adoration, but spoke gratefully. "My thanks, knight. But we all follow as Corean leads. I must humbly apologize to you, but I'm afraid that I've forgotten your name."

The paladin looked sheepish. "I understand, Champion. There are so many of us these days…"

"Never mind that. Tell me your name, paladin."

"Edaron, sir. I have the honor of being named for your father."

Barconius smiled. It didn't hurt at all now.

"A fine name, Sir Edaron. Bear it proudly."

Edaron flushed and looked even more embarrassed.

"Thank you, Champion."

With help from Nabila, Barconius rose unsteadily to his feet.

"Come on," he said. "Let's go home."

***

Two men stood atop Titanslayer Citadel as the sun set behind them, and the Blood Sea faded to black. It had been a long day.

Edaron looked down at his son, sleeping in his arms.

"Duty will keep me away from him, Emili. I will never be able to show him the love that he deserves."

"He will know," Derigesh said. "I will make sure of it."

"Give him my sword when he is old enough, Emili, if I am not able. And tell him that I love him."

Derigesh nodded gravely. "It will be as you ask."

Edaron gently touched the slumbering child's brow.

"He will not be alone, Emili, I swear it." Edaron spoke softly. "I love you, my son. I will always be with you. In hope and despair. In triumph and defeat. In sunlight and shadow. Always, my son."

Journey to the Past

By William R. Prohaska

William R. Prohaska

The city of Provark sat quietly in the cool night air. Aria looked out of the window in her room at the Soaring Falcon Inn, and saw that besides the town's guard, very few people were out tonight.

She stepped back into her room, making sure she didn't disturb her companions. She could just make out each in the darkness.

Aria had met all of her current companions at the Phylacteric Vault, up north. The Phylacteric Vault was an academy of the arcane, where virtually every facet of it was researched, except for the black art of necromancy. Aria had lived at the Phylacteric Vault for eleven of her thirty-one years, and studied there for six years more.

The three friends she traveled with now were from the Phylacteric Vault as well. Shinara was the closest to her. A bard out of Shelzar, Shinara had come to the Phylacteric Vault to get help controlling certain sorcerous powers, which had been manifesting in her. Since arriving, she'd learned a great deal, only losing control when she or a friend was in emergency need. She was the smallest of the four of them, at just over five feet tall and less than a hundred pounds. Her hair was long and brown, silky to the touch.

Her eyes were brown as well, big, like a deer's. Even sleeping, she radiated sensuality.

On the cot next to hers was Linora Davenport. Linora and Aria had been friends since as long as either could remember. When Aria had moved to the Phylacteric Vault, they had both come to tears. Then, Aria had lost contact with her oldest friend. Then, just as suddenly, about five years ago, she

Journey to the Past

showed up at the Phylacteric Vault. Aria was surprised by subsequent events, which led to an archmage's death. Linora had subsequently stayed with Aria, and they often traveled together. Aria was shocked when Linora revealed some martial training from a monastery outside of Ghelspad, of which Linora would say nothing. She was just over five and a half feet tall and weighed a hundred and twenty five pounds, the same as Aria. Both had long hair, but that was where the similarities ended. Linora's hair was golden blond to Aria's raven-black locks. Linora had soft, sky blue eyes and skin just slightly tanned by the sun. Aria, on the other hand, had eyes as green as emeralds, with skin was the color of fresh cream.

The third cot contained the sleeping body of Delmon Farwalker, an elf Aria had known for many years. He'd come to the Phylacteric Vault to study the art of wizardry, though he had never really excelled at it. But Aria had never seen any one who was better with a bow. He stood just over five and a half feet, though he was still a bit shorter than Aria and Linora. He was very thin, around a hundred pounds. His hair was black with silver streaks throughout it. His eyes were dark blue with silver specks. His tan skin had a silvery sheen to it. He didn't look any older than Aria, though she knew him to be over a hundred and twenty years old.

Together the four of them had traveled all over Darakeene, and occasionally out of it as well. They had discovered a balance that had carried them well in the internal politics of the Phylacteric Vault. Now, they were venturing where few would even think of: the ruins of Skykeep in the Kelder Mountains.

Aria went to the far corner of the room and knelt down on the floor. She reached into a small pocket in her sash, and pulled out a bit of chalk. She began to chant softly, letting the arcane syllables roll off her tongue. Slowly, the room and everything in it disappeared.

In its place was utter darkness. Aria had come here before many times. This was where her mistress lived, if you could call it that. Aria watched as a spark of light appeared and grew. It was about six feet in diameter, and pulsed in rhythm with Aria's heart.

Aria had found this place by accident, while studying the multiverse. She still wasn't sure if she hadn't been pulled here, and in all reality, it made no difference. She'd made a pact with this entity, even though her studies told her the entity had to be lying about its identity. Little by little though, she was beginning to believe it just might be possible. This entity certainly knew things that no other could know.

Aria heard a voice in her head, faint and definitely feminine. 'Greetings, young one. Are events proceeding as planned?'

Aria smiled. A year ago, her mistress had told her of an ancient temple which had been in Skykeep. When the city fell, the treasure and lore had been presumed lost. But her mistress had told her where the temple was, and how to get in. The only stipulation was that Aria had to use all her abilities to give her mistress a second chance at life.

Journey to the Past

"All goes as planned, Mistress Miridum. We are about to leave Darakeene. We await only your blessing," Aria replied.

'That is good. I have arranged for you to receive some aid that you will need. Be well, young one. Speak with me again before you venture into the Kelder Mountains.'

"Yes, my lady."

A portion of the light split itself, about half an inch in diameter, and floated over to Aria. Aria let it rest against her forehead, and felt her mind expand as it was filled with arcane secrets and ancient lore.

Slowly, Miridum drifted away and then disappeared. Aria then watched as the inn room faded back into view. She immediately grabbed her journal and began writing everything down, before she could forget.

As the sun came up everyone started to wake. Aria looked at the others and said, "I think we should get ready to leave Provark."

Delmon asked, "And where are we to go from here?"

Aria pulled a map out of her backpack, and the others crowded around. "We'll head east to Murmur pass, then go north. We'll then continue east until we reach the Kelder Mountains. I'll contact my source again there."

Shinara shook her head, and said, "I really wish you'd tell me who your source is."

Aria shook her head. "You wouldn't believe me if I did."

Everyone just chuckled, mostly due to the fact that this conversation had happened so often in the past, always whenever Miridum sent Aria on a journey to discover some arcane secret or a unique spell component.

This time though, Shinara just sighed. Aria knew they wondered, but she hadn't told anyone about Miridum, and wouldn't until she knew whether this was the real Miridum, or not.

Aria let the silence last only a few seconds, then said, "Delmon, see to the horses. Shinara, see if you can find out anything about the trails we'll be taking. Linora and I will see to our provisions. Any questions?"

No one said anything. They'd done this a hundred times before, and gods willing, would do it a thousand times again.

Delmon quietly walked over to the window and stared out at the sunrise, giving the ladies a semblance of privacy to prepare themselves.

Aria slipped a silk skirt on, then two silk sashes, which fell from her shoulders, across her breasts, and attached to the top of her skirt. She then pulled a silk cloak around her shoulders. All of her outfit was silver with black edges. Each was also enchanted to provide her with special protections.

Shinara wore light blue breeches, which had slits running from her hips to her ankles. She wore a white blouse, which showed a lot a cleavage, and a vest just a shade lighter than her breeches. Aria had enchanted Shinara's clothing in much the same way as she had her own.

Journey to the Past

Linora wore gray breeches, a gray blouse and a gray cloak. No embellishments, no frills, just solid practicality, enchanted as everyone else's was.

When the women finished dressing, they left Delmon. They went downstairs and asked the innkeeper if he served food in the morning. They'd eaten here the night before, and hadn't been disappointed. The innkeeper brought out a tray of fruits and sweetmeats, as well as a flagon of Veshan morning wine.

When Delmon came walking down the stairs, all three women smiled appreciatively. Though they had all agreed that anything beyond friendship would be a bad idea, all three thought him very handsome.

He wore dark green leather breeches, with elven chain mail over his chest. His long hair was held out of his face with a headband the same color as his breeches. Aria hadn't needed to enchant his clothing. The elves of Vera-Tre had seen to it.

He joined them at the table and they broke fast together, as they did almost every morning. Then one by one, they went about their duties. They agreed to meet back at the inn at high sun.

As Aria and Linora walked around town, they noticed a man following them. As they were discussing what to do about it, he walked up to them and said, "Excuse me. I am Jak Tarvinish. I'm looking for Aria of Weyside. Would that be one of you?"

Weyside was the town Aria had been born in, so she said, "That depends on why you're asking."

"I believe I received a vision from a servant of Hedrada," he explained. "I was told that you were on a quest of some importance to Hedrada, and that my assistance would be needed."

Aria considered for a moment. She knew that he was the help Miridum had promised, but she had to know how much he knew, preferably without revealing the specifics of her quest. Eventually, she decided on the direct route. She turned to Linora and said, "I need to speak with Mr. Tarvinish in private. Could you give us a few minutes?"

Linora just looked at her for a second, then nodded and walked away.

Aria returned her attention to Jak Tarvinish. He looked younger than she was with short black hair and eyes the color of steel. He was a little over six feet and looked to be about two hundred and twenty five pounds. He wore dark studded leather armor, with a long sword at his side. He obviously hadn't shaved in the last week. She couldn't tell whether or not she could trust him, but she had to know.

She said, "How much due you know of our quest? How do you know it was truly a messenger of Hedrada? And, most importantly, why should I believe you?"

He smiled and replied, "I know only that your quest is somehow important to Hedrada. I believe that the messenger was indeed from Hedrada because I've dealt with it before. As far as trusting me, I am a vigilant in the servant of Vesh. I swear to you by all that I love that I will do everything I can to ensure the success of your quest, provided that it doesn't endanger Vesh, its allies, or help the titans or their brood. Anything more, I can not help you with."

Journey to the Past

When he finished, Aria nodded. "Do you travel alone? And how are you on provisions? Can you be ready to leave by high sun?"

"No. I have two companions waiting outside of town. They aren't usually well received in towns, but since I spend most of my time in the wilderness, we get along all right. As far as provisions and being ready, we're ready anytime you are."

She gave him a strange look, but he remained silent. She sighed, and could imagine how Shinara felt when she kept her secrets. "Meet us at the Soaring Falcon Inn at high sun. We'll be leaving then. And bring your two companions as well. We should all know each other by sight."

"Very well," he said. "I'll see you then."

As he walked away, Linora walked up and asked, "What was that all about?"

Aria just smiled and said, "It was the last thing I was waiting for. Find the others. Tell them to meet back at the inn about an hour before high sun. Tell them I'll be answering a lot of their questions then."

Linora raised an eyebrow at that, but went to inform the others. When she was gone, Aria leaned against the side of a building as waves of joy washed over her. If Hedrada believed her mistress to be Miridum, then surely it was so. Aria quickly gathered the last of their supplies and returned to the inn.

When she arrived, she saw that only Delmon had arrived before her. Their horses looked well fed and ready for the long journey ahead of them. She joined Delmon at their wagon, and they began loading the supplies. Soon, Shinara and Linora joined them. As soon as everything was stored properly, they sat around a table and enjoyed a light lunch.

Shinara, though, was unable to contain her curiosity. "So what was important enough to make us rush our schedule?"

Aria told them everything. She started with Jak Tarvinish and ended with Miridum. They were speechless. Finally, Shinara said, "You're dragging us across a continent, into the ruins of an ancient city, for the purpose of resurrecting a dead god?" When Aria nodded, Shinara just said, "And I'm the only bard who knows about it. This is going to make me famous."

Everyone started laughing and asking questions. Aria answered them as best she could, and soon the sun was directly overhead.

They noticed a crowd gathering toward the east gate, and getting closer. Soon they saw why, and Aria's heart almost sank. There was Jak Tarvinish with his two companions.

To his right, riding a chariot was an eight-foot tall assathi. He wore an intricately etched breastplate, and a gold cape. That was it. He wore two long spears diagonally across his back.

To Jak's left, a half-orc rode a huge warhorse. He wore a suit of scale mail with a white tabard over the armor. On the tabard was the holy symbol of Madriel. At his side was a large war hammer. He looked to be about six and a half feet tall, and at least five hundred pounds. He had short scraggly black hair, grayish skin, a sloping forehead and even had a couple of tusks sticking out of his mouth.

Journey to the Past

Both the assathi and the half-orc had red eyes. Both looked like very formidable challenges. And both were inciting a riot in the streets with their mere presence.

Aria could see why Jak had left them outside the city earlier. As the three newcomers made their way to the inn, several members of the town guard arrived to stop anything illegal from happening, though whom they were protecting wasn't too clear. Several held the growing mob back, but several more kept their weapons pointed at the two giants they were looking at.

Finally, they reached the inn's courtyard, and the guards took up positions around the gate and fence. Jak and his companions dismounted and approached Aria. Shinara said, "I suppose this is Jak Tarvinish."

Jak smiled. "Indeed, ma'am. And these are my companions. Tratzel of Yorek and Sessissin." He pointed to the half-orc first, and then the assathi.

Aria said, "I thought you didn't work with titan spawn. Assathi are known to be titan spawn."

Jak shook his head. "Sessissin isn't an assathi. He's an alligator warrior from far to the south. Both have my complete confidence."

Aria sighed. It was definitely going to be a long trip. The sooner begun, the sooner ended. "If everyone is ready, I'd suggest getting our new friends here out of town, before they decide to lynch us."

Everyone agreed, and soon they were making their way to the east gate. They reached the gate and left town without incident. Soon they were following the road east to Murmur's Pass. They traveled for two days, before seeing the Forsaken Forest, then another day going around it. They saw few others during this time, no one who wanted to stop and talk.

At the end of the third day, the Gascar Peaks were well within sight. Aria called Jak and Shinara together and asked, "What are we likely to be facing in there?"

Both responded at the same time, "Rockslides." Shinara fell silent while Jak continued, "Our best intelligence is that the slightest sound can cause horrendous rockslides in there."

Aria nodded and said, "I'll start reviewing my spell books for a powerful silence spell. How long are we likely to be in there?"

"The better part of a day, possibly two," he said. Shinara nodded her agreement.

Aria nodded, sighed, and began looking through her journal for a spell powerful enough to keep them safe for the next few days.

The next day, they reached the mouth of the pass. Aria could see why it would be a problem. The peaks stretched thousands of feet into the sky, and at places seemed almost to stretch together, forming an arch, but nothing she could see without magic looked very stable. Aria thought she'd discovered a way to keep them safe, but only if they hurried. She warned everyone not to tarry, and not to attack anything without extreme provocation.

She started casting her spell. It took almost five minutes to complete, but when she was finished, not a sound could be heard. They started into the pass.

Journey to the Past

Enkili seemed to favor them, for they only had to backtrack once, due to a previous rockslide.

They left the pass and continued north between the Fouled Forest and the Gascar Peaks. At the end of the fifth day, they could just make out what appeared to be a city on the horizon. Aria suggested they try to reach it, but was voted down.

Delmon explained it to her. "That is the city of Khirdet, a city dedicated to the worship of the titan, Mormo. They'd like to kill half of us just on general principle, and the rest just for traveling with us."

Aria considered and said, "Okay, we all shouldn't go. But how are we on supplies? Are there any other towns between here and the Kelder Mountains?"

Jak thought for a moment and said, "Our safest route would be to go around Khirdet, the Khet and the Stricken Forest, then head due east until we reach the Ganjus. However, we could save almost a week by cutting through the Stricken Forest, then straight to the Ganjus. We'd also be able to avoid the Khet and the Perforated Plains, as well as staying away from the Scrub Woods. Especially Khirdet, I've a price on my head there."

Aria considered the options as they rested that night. She knew a few of the legends regarding the Stricken Forest. She also knew that if she could bring Miridum back, sooner would be better. So she decided to risk it.

The following morning, they prepared to start, when they saw a strange man on the hillside. He watched them prepare for the day ahead, then disappeared.

It was midmorning before they saw him again, this time on horseback. He also had a dozen soldiers at his back. As they approached, he called out, "Halt, and present yourselves."

Aria brought her horse to the front of the group, and said, "I am Aria of Darakeene. Who are you to waylay peaceful travelers?"

The man smiled. "I am servant of Mormo, and representative of Her Most Radiant and Adumbratorial Majesty Sharliss Serpent-Kiss. We've observed an elf in your party, as well as a suspected vigil. I'm afraid you are all under arrest."

Aria just shook her head and said, "I'm afraid we don't have time to play your little games. Stand aside, let us pass and no one has to get hurt."

The stranger just smiled and started chanting a spell. Aria started casting a spell of her own. Aria finished just a bit earlier, and a small ball of light flew away from her towards the patrol. Everyone else started charging the patrol.

The patrol moved in front of the stranger, obviously one of the infamous druids of Khet. As Aria started preparing her next spell, the roots started growing around her. She was soon entangled, though she still had enough room to cast her spell.

Just before her friends got within range to engage the patrol, the small ball of light reached the druid, and exploded in a horrendous fireball. The druid flew to the ground, and the patrol fought to regain control of their panicked mounts.

The battle was quick and bloody. The patrol was in disorder and all but one was killed. He survived

Journey to the Past

only by fleeing. The druid was now blind and helpless. Delmon ran him through. Aria was disturbed by this, but realized that reinforcements could arrive at any time. With the druid's death, the roots and plants holding her fell away, and she led them away from the slaughter.

That night, though, she asked him why he'd killed the druid in cold blood. He just stared into the fire for a few minutes, and then said, "I remember Amalthea, and I remember when they tried to destroy us at Vera-Tre. I don't expect you to understand, but I'm unwilling to ever let them go unpunished for their crimes. The druids of Khet must be exterminated, if we can ever figure out how."

Aria was reminded then of just how old he really was, as she knew from research that Amalthea was a victim of the Druids' War decades ago. She let it go, but vowed never to get on his bad side.

There was perhaps another hour and a half of sunlight when they reached the Stricken Forest, but they decided to wait until morning before venturing in. They each took turns on watch duty, and the night passed without incident.

The morning brought a fresh patrol of warriors, and two druids. Jak and Delmon started getting ready to fight them, but Aria had had enough. She called everyone together, and led them into the Stricken Forest. She started to think they wouldn't follow, but they did.

She called a halt and started preparing a spell. Soon they were all invisible, and waiting for the patrol to pass. Aria started casting another spell, which

55

created a magical spear. She waited until the druids were in view then launched the spear. It took one of the druids square in the chest. The other druid suddenly sprouted an arrow in his forehead. Though the remaining patrol still outnumbered them by two to one, the companions once again took advantage of the confusion to attack. This time, surrounded, none escaped. Two, however, did surrender.

Jak and Delmon argued that they should be killed. Aria argued against it, saying she wouldn't be a party to murder. Finally, it was Tratzel who decided the issue, by tying them up and throwing them in the back of the wagon.

They continued on. The rest of the day was uneventful, for the most part. A small pack of wolves threatened the party, but fled when they realized they were outnumbered.

As darkness started to fall, though, everyone started getting tenser. They knew that at the point they entered, they should have spent less than a day in there, but darkness fell with them still inside the stricken forest. To the north, firelight could be seen.

Delmon and Jak went to investigate. Aria, knowing this forest to be the home of the Obsidian Pyre, decided to investigate herself. She cast an invisibility spell designed for battle, a silence spell and a flight spell. As she rose above the forest's tree line, she saw that it was indeed the Obsidian Pyre lighting the night.

She flew to the north to get a better view. She watched as four people in black robes danced slowly around the pyre. True to legend, the pyre didn't seem

Journey to the Past

to consume the black rock it covered. Aria cast a divination spell to see if she could determine whether the fire or rock was magical.

What she discovered was that both were magical, and of a type of magic she'd never seen or heard of. She concentrated on remembering everything she could. She could think of a couple archmages back at the Phylacteric Vault who would welcome the information she was collecting.

After a while though, things settled down. She saw Delmon and Jak leave the area, and knew she should leave too, before her magic ran out. So she flew back to camp, and prepared for the next day.

Shortly before dawn though, she noticed a disturbance at the edge of camp. She rose, walked over and found herself staring at the black robes she'd seen earlier. She turned to see who was on watch, but found everyone else asleep.

"We do not wish war with Darakeene or Vesh, child. Your friends are unharmed."

Aria returned her attention to the robed figures, trying to figure out who was speaking to her, yet was unable to tell, as the robes hid their faces.

"We do not appreciate being spied on, but will forgive you this once. But you will owe the Pyre. Do you agree to our terms?"

Aria knew she was outclassed in this situation, but couldn't commit herself without knowing what she was signing up for. "What will I owe you?"

"We've spared the lives of you and six others. One day, you will be called on to spare, or save, seven lives of the Obsidian Pyre."

"Very well, I agree," she said. Then she decided to try learning a little. "What kind of magic is it that keeps the fire burning?"

"In time child, in time." Then, as one, they turned and walked away to the north. As soon as they were out of sight, the others started waking up. They broke the nights fast with cold rations, and left as soon as they could.

When she told everyone about the visit, they agreed with her decision, though each was glad she'd been the one to see them.

They continued east, trying to discover an end to the Stricken Forest. Shortly before high sun, bodies dropped from the trees around them, startling everyone. Aria had just enough time to notice the pale skin and black leather, and then she too, was wrapped in a tether of some sort, and pulled from her mount. She tried to reach her components, but was caught up.

She looked around and saw that they'd been caught almost totally by surprise. Only Tratzel and Sessissin were still standing, and while she watched, Sessissin went down beneath a small horde of the tethers. Aria managed to gasp out a quick divination, which revealed the creatures attacking them to be a form of undead. She gathered as much air as she could, and yelled out, "They're undead."

Tratzel looked at her, and then brought his holy symbol around, calling on Madriel to destroy the abominations around him. Bright light burst from the symbol, and the creatures closest to it fell into true death, while those farther away fled for their unlives, or continued attacking.

There were five left when Aria got to her feet. She reached into her sash, uttered a quick incantation, and watched as three others dropped into true death. The remaining two were soon overcome by the rest of the party.

As they looked around, they noticed the corpses were only vaguely human. As they gathered their wits, they kept waiting for any sign of other dangers lurking in the trees.

Soon, they were on their horses, traveling east again. About two hours after high sun, they reached the edge of the forest. They rode out into direct sunlight, and everyone's spirits lifted. Shinara even broke out in song. They rode for another hour, trying to put the Stricken Forest behind them. They crossed the northernmost section of the Haggard Hills.

They could see the forest line of the Ganjus by nightfall. They also saw a small troupe come charging up the hill on foot. They looked like large apes with a row of small horns running down the center of their skulls, and coming off of their shoulders. Large multi-jointed legs, with fur even longer than the rest of their bodies, and cloven hooves. They each carried spears that they threw at the party. No one was hurt, but every one got ready for another fight. As the animals got within distance, they dropped the spears, and tried to claw at the companions.

Of the fifteen that had come up the hill, seven dropped in as many seconds. The other beasts seemed to relish it, some even seemed to grow stronger. The beasts started locking up with people, but everyone held their own as five more were cut down. The final three were noticeably bigger than when they'd arrived. These three looked at Aria, and started to go towards her. Aria launched another spell at one; it clutched its chest, and died.

The other two laughed at her, until Delmon, Sessissin and Tretzel took another one down. The last one roared and charged at Aria, knocking her down and hitting her in the head. The last thing she saw was an arrow going through the beast's head, and Jak running towards her. Then there was only the blackness.

When she awoke, she had trouble putting coherent thoughts together. The sky was dark, and everything was quiet. She looked over and saw Jak and Delmon on watch. "What time is it?" she asked.

They walked over to her smiling. Delmon smiled and said, "It's about an hour until sunrise. You gave us quite a scare earlier."

Aria smiled weakly. "It was no picnic for me either. What happened? After I fell, I mean."

Jak said, "Delmon and I killed it before it could kill you. And Shinara is pretty sure those things were feral, servants of Vangal." Jak made his face serious and asked, "Have you been bad mouthing the gods again?"

"I'm not sure why they targeted me, though it might have something to with the quest. I don't see why Vangal would object to Miridum's return."

Journey to the Past

"With the Ravager, you don't necessarily need a reason. He's never been accused of being the most rational of the gods," Jak said. They all laughed.

Aria relaxed and asked, "How close are we to the Ganjus?"

Delmon thought about it and replied, "A couple of hours, less if we ride hard."

Aria pulled the map out of her pack and asked, "If we can make it to this river, we might be able to catch a ship going upstream all the way to the Kelder Mountains."

Delmon considered it, then shook his head saying, "You'd never find a ship that could carry all of us, and our horses, that far north. I might be able to get us to the northern Ganjus, but that would be the best we could hope for."

Aria nodded. "Go ahead and ride ahead of us. Jak, start waking the others." Aria started getting to her feet, and almost blacked out again. Both Jak and Delmon caught her, and helped her stagger over to her horse.

Jak said, "You've got to take it slow. You took a bad shot to the head. Tratzel's been praying over you until Madriel got tired of listening to him. And he says you still need more help."

Aria nodded again. "We'll keep an easy pace today, but we need to keep moving. If Vangal is sending his minions after me, I'll be much safer on the move."

Jak and Delmon both nodded, and went about their business. Jak started waking the others, while Delmon mounted and rode down the hill. Tratzel argued with Jak for a few moments, then walked over to where Aria sat on her horse.

"I feel I must be honest, you're in no condition to travel, yet," he said. His deep voice had a degree of authority she'd never heard before.

Aria pointed to the Ganjus and said, "We'll have access to elven healers there. We'll also be much safer."

Tratzel sighed deeply, and nodded. He walked over to his horse and got ready to leave.

By high sun, they were deep in the Ganjus, with an elven honor guard no less. Delmon seemed slightly put out by them, but Aria knew that she and her companions would never be allowed to wander around the Ganjus at will. The elves spent way too much time maintaining their secrecy to allow that.

When they reached the river, they found nine boats lined along the shore. There were healers there who tended everyone's wounds. The commander of the honor guard approached Aria and said, "I'm afraid you'll have to be blindfolded from here on out. The blindfolds are enchanted so that you'll be able to speak with anyone else wearing one."

Aria smiled. "I understand. Tell whomever made the decision to help us that I appreciate it."

The elven commander smiled. A horse and its rider were put into each boat. The wagon was given its own boat, as did Sessissin and his chariot.

Aria still expected the trip to last several days. After several hours, the boats were taken to shore, and all of them unloaded. Aria walked over to the

Journey to the Past

elven commander and asked, "Isn't it a bit early to be unloading the ships."

"This is as far as we'll go, sorry"

Aria frowned and looked at Delmon, who was smiling. Delmon pointed to the north and said, "We're already there. That's the Lake of Mists. If we follow it east and north, we'll reach the Kelder Mountains within a few days."

Aria thanked the commander again, and everyone mounted up and prepared to start skirting the lake. The day passed uneventfully, and night found them well ahead of Aria's schedule.

That night a thick fog rolled in off the lake. Around midnight, a forlorn cry woke everyone in camp.

"Please help me." Aria watched as a woman stepped out of the fog.

At five and a half feet tall, and maybe a hundred pounds, the woman would have been attractive, if she'd been alive. But she was obviously a ghost. Aria could see right through her. Aria knew from experience that most ghosts would either attack, or leave them be.

"Please help me," the ghost wailed again.

Aria stepped forward. "What would you ask of us?" she inquired.

The ghost looked right at Aria and said, "I need my family, my husband, my son, and my daughter.

"How can we help you? We don't know where your family is. You'll have to tell us your name and where your family should be."

The spirit looked at Aria and then nodded. "My name is Dela Wistin. I lived here long ago. My family and I were tortured and killed here for some family heirlooms that we refused to surrender. An evil man placed a curse upon us, so that when we died, we'd wander the mists of this lake forever. Only by reuniting us, can we be freed."

Aria listened to the tale, nodding occasionally. Then asked, "What were your families names?"

"My husband was Karthon. My son was Tralok. My daughter was Rena. Can you really help us?"

Aria nodded. "I believe so." Aria directed everybody to stand back and removed her cloak. She started chanting, calling out the names of the family at seemingly random intervals. After an hour Aria gyrating and chanting, a man stepped out of the mist, followed shortly by two children. All four stood within ten feet of each other, but they had no reaction to each other.

Understanding filled Aria's eyes. She looked at each one and said, "If you can hear me raise your hand."

Each of the four raised their hands. Aria started chanting again, then flung her hands out. Bright light spread over the four ghosts and they turned and saw each other for the first time in centuries. Slowly, they faded from view, only to be replaced by another visitor from the mists.

This one practically radiated evil, and somehow, Aria knew he was the one who'd led the assault on the Wistin family. He was over six feet tall and very thin. His face was frozen in a maniacal grin and crazed

Journey to the Past

eyes. But even in death, he was a power to be reckoned with.

"You've freed them! Now you must either free me, or take their place."

Aria slowly walked around him and then started asking him the same questions she'd asked Dela's spirit. The wizard was named Dorthanius Devilkin, rumored to be the great grandson of a devil. He'd fulfilled everyone's expectations, by accumulating power, and wielding it ruthlessly. But one family had always defied him. They held on to the magic that their ancestors had used against his. He wouldn't have it.

The spirit bragged of the depredations it had inflicted on the Wistin family, by catching them in a purely physical attack when they least expected it.

Finally, Aria decided she'd heard enough. She started casting another spell. This one was obviously different from the one she'd used on the Wistins, though he had no way of knowing that. When she finished, she fell to her knees, exhausted. She had just enough energy left to point her hand at the spirit. It, too, was washed in light.

But unlike the Wistins, he began to scream, and fade from view.

Linora and Shinara helped Aria to her feet and the helped her get dressed. Shinara looked at her strangely. "How could you free him after what he did in life?"

Aria smiled weakly. "I didn't. In fact I cursed him in the worst way I could imagine. He will never again be able to use the mists to manifest. He'll never cast another spell. And he can never leave this world, until he gets Dela's forgiveness."

All three women smiled knowingly. If even half of what he'd bragged about was true, then that forgiveness would most likely never be given.

As they started settling in for the remainder of the night, they were roused once again by a spirit in the mist. Dela was back. "I can never repay you for your kindness. Please, take this book. I know that you will put my family's treasures to good use. We no longer need them."

Aria walked forward, picked up the book and began reading. She spent the entire night reading the book, committing it to memory. The next morning, they continued skirting the Lake of Mists. Then they followed another river to the northeast.

Two days later they arrived at the foothills of the Kelder Mountains. Aria cast her spell, and found herself alone in the dark, awaiting Miridum. After an indefinite period of time, the light appeared, and Aria was visited by the dead goddess.

'You have done well, young one. Prepare to receive your final instructions.'

"Yes, my lady."

A small fragment of light flew across the void, and Aria knew the intense joy of serving her goddess. The light started to withdraw, but Aria cried out, "Wait!"

The light returned. 'Yes?'

Aria swallowed. In more than ten years, she'd never asked more of her mistress than their deal. But

Journey to the Past

this problem Miridum needed to know about. "I believe the Reaver, Vangal, is trying to sabotage your return, my lady. What should I do?"

The light actually came closer. 'You're actually concerned about me, aren't you?'

"Yes, Miridum. I am."

The light took the form of a beautiful woman in a tunic and hose. Aria knew she was seeing Miridum as she looked before her death. Miridum floated up to Aria, and gently took Aria into her arms, kissing her once on the forehead. 'When the time is right, you'll know what to do.'

Aria bowed her head, and felt herself return to the world. Her friends looked at her. She looked back at them and said, "Tomorrow, we go into the Skykeep ruins."

The night was peaceful.

The next morning, everyone gathered to prepare for a few nights in the mountains. But Aria held her hands, and cast a spell. Then she led the way to the foot of the Skykeep Ruins.

As she stepped out of her dimensional door, Aria got the sense of immense power somewhere in the area. As the others stepped through, she signaled for quiet.

She realized that she was capable of seeing the magical emanations all around her. She signaled the others to follow her. She led them through the ruins to the courtyard of The Secret Ways, Miridum's oldest temple. In the courtyard was a small army of creatures. A few tents were pitched, but the majority of the residents simply lounged around.

As Aria and the others approached, many of the creatures rose. Others were prodded to their feet. The largest tent flap was opened, and a small giant stepped out.

Aria stepped forward and spoke in a language as old as the gods. "Greetings, Herald of Vangal."

The herald stood straight, showing the her full twelve foot frame. "Greetings, Herald of Miridum."

"Why do you assault my mistress' home?"

The Herald of Vangal stepped forward. After my fall at the Battle against Mormo, my blade was brought here. I would have it."

Aria was silent for a moment. She briefly considered trying to bargain with her, but decided against it. It was not a time for deals, but for alliances. "Have your minions leave my ladies home. I will take you in, and give you your blade."

The herald's eye narrowed. "What game are you playing?"

Aria stepped forward, casting a quick enchantment to increase her size. She stopped when she looked her counterpart eye-to-eye. "You are the Herald of Vangal. War is your specialty. In a fight, I would stand no chance against you. I am the Herald of Miridum. Lore and secrets are my specialty. There is a time coming soon when you and I will rely on each other. If we don't we will both be destroyed. If returning your blade to you will show you my sincerity, then so be it."

The Herald of Vangal's eyes widened. "Tell me, what have you seen?"

Journey to the Past

Aria shook her head. "I have not yet uncovered all that is needed, but now the search will begin in earnest."

The herald turned and ordered her minions out of the courtyard. Aria led the way into the temple. Down through the temple, to the ancient vault where the lore that Miridum herself had collected lay. Aria turned to the Herald of Vangal and said, "Before I open the way, I would have your word that you will destroy nothing, and take only your sword."

The Herald of Vangal nodded. "Granted."

Aria held out her hand and the doors opened. She led the way through the secrets of ages, past treasures far more powerful than the herald's blade. But she held to her word. In the back of the vault the great sword rested on an elaborate display case. The Herald of Vangal strode forward, took the blade down, and then stood as a portion of her power was returned to her.

Then she looked Aria and said, "You have helped me this day. That will not be forgotten." Then she left the vault. Aria knew that she'd done the right thing.

Aria walked back to the door, closed it and left. At the door to the temple, she watched as Vangal's minions left the valley. She turned to the temple, and began a long and complex incantation. When she was finished, she placed her hand on the door, and the building slowly faded from sight. She returned to her friends, and said, "Come on. It's time to go home."

Jak walked up to her. "Due you plan on staying that big?"

Aria realized she was still sized to speak to the Herald of Vangal. She made a mental note to find the herald's name. But that would come later. She released the enchantment and resumed her normal size.

Together they teleported back to where they'd been that morning.

Delmon looked at her and asked, "What, you can't take us all the way home?"

"I'm a herald Del, not a goddess."

As they all laughed she started planning her new home outside the Phylacteric Vault. She'd need somewhere private to do her research. She'd also need to take a brief trip down to Hollowfaust. If she intended to raise a dead god to life, she'd need to know something of the necromantic arts.

But all that would come later. Right now, she just wanted to go home.

Feast or Famine at Burok Torn

By Gherbod Fleming

For a fleeting moment, the great feast hall of Burok Torn was a vision of perfection. Dulan the Butler paused in the mouth of a narrow corridor, an unobtrusive passage leading to one of the numerous larders responsible for provisioning the dwarven defenders of the subterranean city. As he worked battle-scarred fingers through his beard of long, tightly curled ringlets and surveyed the hall, the retired warrior sensed the nearly impossible confluence of circumstances. Before him, every table was set: stout oak topped with plates and tankards of kiln-hardened clay, wooden spoons and tallow candles. Accoutrements noticeably more refined adorned the head table, elevated at the front of the hall. The king, unlike the masses, would not bring his own dining blade; utensils of mithril glimmered in the candlelight, as did a chalice of gold bespeckled with diamonds. Along the walls of the chamber, twelve fires roared in twelve hewn fireplaces, each thrice the height of the tallest dwarf. In the central well of the hall, a heaping mound of coal glowed red, rippling the air and spewing black plumes toward vent shafts in the stone-vaulted ceiling far above. Intruding upon those lofty shadows were sputtering torches in a score of wroughtiron chandeliers, each suspended by ancient chains forged by the first fathers of the city. Despite the crackling flames of torch, fire and candle, the chill of emptiness never relinquished the hall, not completely.

Observing the scene from above were the Worthies of Goran. Never, Dulan suspected, was a more stern and dour collection of carved busts

Feast or Famine at Burok Torn

assembled in all of Ghelspad. They consisted of Kelder the Companion, who fathered the clan and walked the land of Scarn beside Goran; Hroth the Judge, first to wield the mighty Scepter; Gimrut the Tall, who legend said stood well over five feet; Noraim Diamondfist; Ardell the Unforgiving; Draghnor, son of Dragh…and on and on. With their beards rendered in stone, they watched over the great hall, over the Impregnable Citadel of Burok Torn that was the seat of their power since time immemorial. Dulan, this night, did not notice their glowering displeasure that the stronghold itself was practically all that remained to the once mighty dwarves of the Kelder Mountains; the Butler's mind was momentarily free of the outrage and desire for vengeance that were his people's sustenance. Instead, as the footfalls of the last chamberlain retreated from the hall, and the fires crackled in harmony, he recognized that rare perfection. The fruits of his labor were complete, all of the preparations came together in that instant, unmarred; the feast hall beckoning the dwarven folk to come and, beneath the eyes of king present and Worthies past, draw strength to continue the struggle against darkness in all its many shapes.

Dulan breathed in satisfaction as naturally as he drew in air, as effortlessly as once he had drawn the ichorous blood of titanspawn. He sensed the coming together of disparate strands of past into a precarious, fleeting present much as years before he might have intuited the threat of lurking Drendali, ebony skin glimmering darkness and murderous blades poised in the deepest of sinister caverns. Reaching down to scratch his leg—an itch he could not possibly feel, habit, the tickle of a ghost limb—and his thick fingers feeling the harsh, incontrovertible grain of his wooden leg, still he knew victory and fulfillment— of a different degree and manner than that he had known as a warrior, granted, but victory nonetheless.

The perfection lasted for almost a heartbeat— suspended like a crow rising on the downbeat of its wings, or trapped like fractured light within the facets of a rotating diamond—and then it was gone. Gone, chased away as it must be by the footsteps of the hungry and the impatient, making their way to the feast hall; trampled beneath the boots of the scullions bearing loaves of freshly baked bread to the tables; smothered by the granite glares of the Worthies, demanding their legacy be upheld.

From deep within the subterranean city, the hour keeper struck the chimes, and a piercing vibrato tone, carried by acoustics and wizardry, summoned the dwarven folk to evedine. Dulan's transcendent moment slipped irretrievably into the past, scattered again by the vagaries of future.

They arrived at first in a trickle, those who happened to be nearby, those who tonight were not manning the aboveground battlements, nor patrolling the surrounding mountains in defiance of Calastian invaders and titanspawn alike, nor safeguarding the nether shafts of the Citadel from nefarious dark elves who, like stone ants, would gnaw at the city from its undermost edges. Then more assertively, inexorable as the tide of the great underground lake, did the inhabitants of Burok Torn appear: mail-clad warriors,

Feast or Famine at Burok Torn

loyal, grim, ever aware of the unflinching scrutiny of the Worthies; nimble-fingered artisans, fresh from their wheels and looms and gem-cutting; smiths still radiating the warmth of their forges, the workers of iron and tin, gold and mithril; miners, eddies of soot and mineral dust trailing in their wake. Man and woman they came, the women few in number but, in their quiet way, the lifeblood of the people. Fewer still were the children, each as valuable as the most precious gem; their number multiplied over many decades would scarcely offset the losses in battles, both disastrous and victorious, of the past years.

The brief perfection of the great feast hall having given way to bustle and clamor, the grand heart of the mountain now pulsed with the life and warmth that before it had lacked. Dulan the Butler bristled under the weight of command—though naturally, skillfully—directing his charges with the will and relentlessness that had served him so well in many years of battle. In his orders was nothing of bitterness or of wistful reminiscence, only the subsumptive force of duty, of necessity. His regiment of scullions and chamberlains scurried about in the rising din, each focused upon what was required of him or her, each intent upon seeing that none should go without. They brought around kettles of stew, ladling generous steaming portions into the hollowed crusts of bread already served. The distribution of beer and ale, as usual, required of Dulan the most direct supervision: left to themselves, the servers tended to quench their own thirst periodically, and by the end of the night, when time to clean was at hand, would otherwise be able to use a broom as nothing more than a crutch. In these early moments of the feast, Dulan paused only once, and that to offer a curt, respectful bow when he spied entering the great hall the Ruler of the Rock and Worthy of Goran, King Thain of Burok Torn.

As the king made his way among the tables, the sound of wooden benches scraping against stone filled the cavernous chamber, the dwarves of the Citadel dropping to their knees, bending like winter wheat before the north wind. A reverent hush descended. Then, when he gave them their leave to carry on, a hearty cheer arose, and fists brandished in salute, many grasping tankards of ale in honor of the king's health. Thain's beard, hanging below his belt as befit one of his station, was full and dark, streaked only slightly with gray despite the onset of his two hundredth winter. His chest was as thick as it was broad and strained against the weave of his woolen tunic; his legs strong as boulders; fists, blocks of granite. He wore neither helm nor weapon among them and the bosom of the mountain. He was not a gregarious dwarf, yet faced with the adoration of his folk, he could not repress his crooked smile, and the people loved him that much more for this, his one weakness; they cheered again until he acknowledged their affection with a slight bow.

***

As King Thain crossed the hall, he caught the eye of Dulan and nodded greeting—Dulan, worthy Dulan, worthy as any in spirit to have carried the Scepter of Goran, which currently lay in its place of

Feast or Famine at Burok Torn

reverence in the temple. Thain took his time achieving the head table, spending valued moments accepting the well wishes of his subjects and extending to them the same.

Behind him entered the Shield Arm, honor guard of kings, marching in step in their livery of royal blue trimmed in gold. Each warrior carried axe or hammer, and their cylindrical helms glinted in the firelight as they approached the dais and head table, taking up their customary positions. On too many occasions to count, the Arm had turned the tide of battle against titanspawn or Calastian regulars; for that reason, out of deference to the valiant contributions of these veterans and their forebears in times of need, Thain tolerated First Shield Garrit and his sergeants and their duty to watch over him.

Climbing the steps of the dais, the king felt a familiar sensation, one that had afflicted him each and every day for the years since his father had handed to him the Scepter of Goran: that of leaving his people behind, rising above them to stand in a place of prominence and loneliness, of destiny and subservience. For any pretender who might seek privilege without responsibility or imagine that such was possible, there were the stares of the granite Worthies. Taking his seat, Thain felt the weight of their collective gaze, honoring him, chastening him, taking his measure. In time, his likeness would join them; his mighty deeds were plentiful, and the troubadours sang of the many foes he had vanquished—yet during his reign the dwarves of Burok Torn had lost much, both in land and in blood.

Corean knew that Thain had strived against their enemies until his arms were weak and the Scepter dripped with blood, until it seemed his heart and lungs would explode, until his legs failed him and he could stand no longer. Yet the dwarven people died, and those who survived saw the borders of their territory pushed back and back again, at one point to the gates of the Citadel itself. On that day, Thain had stood strong and earned his place in history, yet he would that that battle had never been forced upon him. What failings of his had left his folk so vulnerable in the face of treachery? He looked for answers to the Worthies, finding instead condemnation or reassurance, whichever he chose to see. He looked to the visage of his father and remembered the words of Thune the Wise: *Turn over the golden coin of pride, and you will find the gypsum face of shame.*

Having mingled quite a while with his people, Thain found others seated at the high table by the time he took his place. There was Gislebert the Castellian, and Galbert, his cousin and Captain of the Watch; beyond those two, at the farthest end of the table sat hoary old Hrethulf, his Drendali-black crow perched upon his shoulder, as alert and loyal a sentry for which any rune wizard could hope. A separation existed between Hrethulf and the other dwarves, not so much of space as of perception, as if the secrets of Ukrudan lore into which he had delved had never fully released him, and now he lived partially in a world hidden from his kinsmen. While beneath the wizard's deeply furrowed brow his eyes were milky and as gray as his wiry bushes of eyebrows,

Feast or Famine at Burok Torn

the crow's black eyes glinted bright and knowingly in the firelight, taking on a devilish red hue when he turned his head. The seats to Thain's left, as he faced his people from the center-most chair, were empty, soon to be filled by guests to the Citadel.

***

When the trumpeters pursed their lips to the twisted zuglhorns, and the heralds stepped forward, Dulan, like all in the great hall, knew that outsiders were to be announced. Yet the heralds did not, except in the most formal of circumstances, ply their trade in honor of any king of Burok Torn, for to do so would imply that the king was not of his people and required introduction. The guests, both dwarves, were soon in evidence making their way across the hall. The residents of the Citadel, though generally lacking appreciation for the affectations of pomp and pageantry, nevertheless were a well-mannered people; pausing in their consumption of the great eyeless, white fish, which Dulan's legion of scullions had served after the stew, the assembly politely acknowledged the presence of the emissaries.

Freotheric of Ontenazu wore a beard as fiery red as the *pales gules* upon the arms of his lord Frem Artone. Beneath a supple leather vest, his tunic was fine Veshian linen, of the sort rarely procured any longer this far south, in the city under siege. The twin cities of Ontenazu, far to the north and warned of King Virduk of Calastia's aggression by the sudden attack on Burok Torn, had beaten back the boy-king and did not suffer such hardships. Freotheric's ensemble was far from ostentatious or garish—such was not the way of the Ontenazuans, human or dwarven—but merely made noticeable by the scarcity at hand. And by contrast with the second guest. Widsith of Durrover had not changed from his traveling clothes; spatters of clay dotted the hem of his cloak, and his beard was dusty from days and nights spent in relentless combat. Though an emissary, Widsith wore no arms of his lord, no double-headed eagle displayed, no crossed chevrons symbolizing the Kelder Mountains which, since the fall of Irontooth Pass to the Calastians, were as much prison to Durrover as fortress. Dulan, making his way to the side of the visitors, could not find it in himself to fault the Durroverite for this lack of decorum, for Widsith was obviously a dwarf of warfare—a temperament that Dulan understood better than most, but one with which any inhabitant of Burok Torn was intimately familiar. As dire a fate as the Citadel possessed, however, Durrover was worse than a city besieged; it was a city doomed.

***

The two dwarves reached the dais and bowed to King Thain, so low that their beards swept the reeds upon the floor, after which Dulan the Butler escorted them personally to their seats at the high table.

"Greetings, friends," spoke King Thain, "and welcome to the Citadel of Burok Torn. Eat, drink, fill your bodies, just as your presence fills with honor our feasthall."

"It is you who does us honor," said Freotheric the Red, lifting a tankard which Dulan promptly filled with ale before leaving the dais to attend other

Feast or Famine at Burok Torn

matters. "Salutations, and a toast to your health and prosperity, from Canyonmaster First Rank Frem Artone of Ontenazu." The table in unison lifted their ales with hearty hear hears.

"Greetings," echoed Widsith. "I bring regards from Lord High King Jeddard III of Durrover-between-the-Mountains...regards and a request."

Across the feast hall, the bustle of dwarven folk at their meals continued unabated, but at the high table a strained silence took hold. Freotheric, between the king and Wisdith, grew suddenly ill at ease. Galbert and Gislebert exchanged disgruntled glances. "This is hardly the place—" began Gislebert the Castellian, but a gesture from King Thain forestalled him.

"These are harsh times at hand," said Thain, "and perhaps harsher still to come. There may be nights before us when even in repast is not to be found the luxury of repose, times when the wolves do not howl in the distance but claw at the door, times like those which already have fallen upon Durrover."

Wisdith nodded solemnly, clearly aware of his offense against protocol but grateful for the king's recognition of the plight of the city between the mountains. "Jeddard III, king of the Lowlands, holds you and your people in the highest regard," Wisdith said. "As does Aeldhelm, Warfist of the dwarves of Durrover."

"As I do them," said Thain. "Jeddard has ever been a stalwart ally of our people, and Warfist Aeldhelm wielded his axe at my very side when we turned from the gates of Burok Torn itself the regiments of treacherous Virduk."

"It is in their names," Wisdith spoke, "Lord High King and Warfist, that I beseech you this night that you send more troops to Durrover to aid us in our struggle against Virduk, to help us drive the Calastians out of our valley and back through Irontooth Pass."

The earlier silence passed more quickly than a day lily in the deepest, darkest dwarven cavern. "Impossible," gruffed Galbert.

"Gall and wormwood," exclaimed Gislebert. Their outbursts ruffled old Hrethulf's crow (the wizard, for his part, was enjoying his cavefish, and took no notice); the bird squawked and took to wing from the wizard's shoulder, climbing quickly toward the vaulted ceiling and the granite Worthies, at last perching again atop the ample nose of Ardell the Unforgiving.

Again King Thain calmed them with a gesture—all save the crow, which continued its squawking from the distant, echoing heights, its cries all but lost among the constant buzz of the murmuring throng. "Are there not," Thain asked, "twenty-score of my ablest warriors in Durrover already, a squadron of the king's own Shield Arm among them?"

"It is as you say," Widsith admitted, "but Virduk of Calastia sends that many times ten every season, and we beat them back, and again he sends that many times ten." The emissary from Durrover could not keep the venom and the rising desperation from his voice. "The sands of the hourglass threaten to bury us, Your Lordship. Every day, more defenders fall.

Feast or Famine at Burok Torn

Every supply ship we send round Corean's Cleft is likely as not to be pulled to the bottom of the Blood Sea by a heinous serpent from the depths. If there is to be a savior for our city, you are he, Thain, son of Thune."

King Thain listened patiently. The request was nothing he hadn't weighed in his own mind hundreds upon hundreds of times. Durrover to the south, like Ontenazu to the north, was a kingdom primarily of humans but with a significant proportion of dwarven folk, primarily of Clan Kelder, as were Thain, most of the inhabitants of Burok Torn, and all of the Worthies who stared down from above. Again and again he had posited an all-out assault upon the Calastians laying siege to—sometimes entering only to be driven out of—the city of Durrover. But nothing that Widsith told him changed the facts of deliberation; no news the emissary brought tipped the scales the direction that Thain wished that they would fall. "We have sent the troops that we are able," said the king.

Widsith tensed at the refusal. His face turned nearly as fiery red as Freotheric's beard. "If you would but visit our city," urged the Durroverite, "if you just saw—"

"Ambassador," said Gislebert the Castellian tersely, "the king has spoken. We have sent the troops that we are able. You presume that we do not know how many warriors we require to defend our own city, that we are simply unwilling to aid you, our neighbor and staunchest ally."

"But every dwarf sent to Durrover is doing just that, *defending your own city*," Widsith insisted. "If Virduk captures Durrover, where do you believe those Calastian troops that have been oppressing us will go? I'll tell you where. Instead of south from Irontooth Pass, they will turn north—north along the Eastsnake River, and they will besiege Burok Torn from the rear, just as Virduk's other army besieges you from the front. What then? What then of your prudence, when you sit encircled and as devoid of hope as now you are of wisdom?"

***

Near the foot of the dais, Dulan sent one of his scullions hustling away. The unavoidable fact was that with practically every able-bodied dwarf pressed into military service, those remaining to service the kitchens and fill the Butler's retinue were necessarily not the strongest, not the swiftest, and often case not the brightest; this particular youngling, finding the west larder emptied of brown potatoes, left to his own might have required a fortnight to hit upon the idea of checking the *east* larder. But Dulan had sent him on his way, and there would be stew aplenty for all hungry dwarves. Scanning the hall for similar signs of trouble, Dulan couldn't help but overhear conversation from a nearby table:

"And so I go visit this Calastian bloke in the dungeons, you see," one grizzled veteran was saying. "He'd lost both of his legs, and one of his arms, and two fingers on the hand he had left, and one eye was gone, and one of our lads in the battle had sliced off

Feast or Famine at Burok Torn

part of his head, like this…." He made a hacking motion at his own temple.

"You went to visit him?" asked one of the listeners. "What in the Bloody Steppes for?"

"I had a nice basket of tart cherries for him," said the veteran.

"Tart cherries?" Another listener cried out, almost choking on his crust of bread. "Poisoned? Or maybe with needles inside?" A few chuckles arose from the table at that.

"No poison and no needles," said the veteran. "This was the juiciest, tartest basket of cherries you could ever hope to find."

"Well, I'll be a stone mason in Vera-Tre," said one listener. The others were equally incredulous, but the veteran of wars and stories held his peace until their scoffs had died away and one of his audience asked the question he knew would come: "Why in bloody Virduk's arse would you take a basket of cherries to a bloody Calastian?"

The veteran paused a moment longer, until the trickles of muttered agreement fell silent, then said: "Because he's the only bloody Calastian I've ever seen alive who was cut up enough to suit me."

A heartbeat of silence was followed by guffaws and backslapping, cheers and raised tankards. Dulan chuckled and remembered the rough, often ribald, talk among brothers in arms—talk from which, no matter how much honor he was accorded in the Citadel, he was now an outsider.

But suddenly a bellowed challenge rang out through the hall: "Enough!" thundered King Thain, rising from his chair and slamming his tankard against the table. His cry echoed to the heights, upsetting Hrethulf's crow enough that the bird alighted from Ardell and flitted nervously to Thune the Wise, whose features were noticeably replicated in Thain's angry visage. On the heels of that one word, silence rippled through the great chamber, drowning all sound except the crackling of fires and the clearing of nervous throats; all eyes shifted toward the front table. For a gut-wrenching moment, Dulan, as well as the veteran and his listeners alike, assumed the outburst was directed at them. Then they saw that the king, eyes burning, faced one of the emissaries at his table. Dulan intercepted a chamberlain and commandeered the lad's tray of sweetmeat pies bound for the head table.

***

King Thain resumed his seat. Gradually, nervous and curious mutterings crept to fill the silence of the feast hall, and soon the normal sounds of evedine resumed—hundreds upon hundreds of voices, shifting benches, clanking pottery—if slightly less robust at first.

Thain's displeasure, however, was far from dissipated. "You do your king and your warfist a disservice by slighting their steadfast friends," he said. "You say that you speak in their names, but I cannot believe that they sent you to say such things. They did *not* send you on this embassy, did they, Widsith of Durrover?"

Feast or Famine at Burok Torn

Widsith, absorbing the full measure of the king's anger, could not meet Thain's eyes. The emissary was caught in his deception.

"I thought not," said Thain. "I am not blind to the urgency of the Durroverites. Jeddard and Aeldhelm both know this. You may claim to speak in their names, but not by their authority, not with their consent. They would not make such unreasonable demands, because they are men of honor and know that my first duty is to my people."

"Shall I remove this false ambassador?" asked Galbert, rising from his seat.

"He is not false," said Thain, fighting to control his temper, "just overwrought, and his only crime is that he loves his city too much." The king pushed away his plate with the cavefish hardly touched, his appetite victim to the dangers ever lurking beyond his city's gates, drawing closer and more compelling. Seeking distraction, he picked at the sweetmeat pie that Dulan placed before him, but had no stomach for the pastry either. "And what say you, Freotheric of Ontenazu?" Thain asked at last. "Now that we have ruined the mood of the feast with talk of Virduk, you might as well tell me the purpose of your visit."

Freotheric the Red glanced at Widsith, who was cowed to sullen silence, and then tried to put on a more cheerful face. "At the very least," he said, "I do not come to make demands, but rather to extend an offer."

"Aye, that is welcome news," said the king, making a show of his forced smile and raising ale to his lips.

"Rumor has reached Frem Artone," Freotheric continued, "that the dark ones are threatening your city...." Here he hesitated briefly, aware that he presented conversation unfit for the dinner table, but the king had commanded.... "The Dier Drendal."

From behind his upturned tankard, Thain's eyebrow arched in displeased surprise. He lowered his ale and turned and spat ceremoniously over his shoulder. Echoing above the dwarves were the cries of Hrethulf's crow, which seemed to say, "*Dier Drendal, Dier Drendal.*"

"Titans be cursed," Thain growled. "To think that I would be accused of cowardice and foolhardiness *and* then be lectured about the dark ones at the same meal...at my own table! No, no, continue, dwarf. You might as well now."

"Frem Artone has sent me," Freotheric said, overcoming his own sheepishness in the face of Thain's ire, "to offer aid, Your Worthiness. You see, Master Isep Ganstreng has long studied Drendali lore, though little enough of the dark ones is known...." The emissary's words trailed away as he noticed the dark storm rising on the king's face. "Your...Your Majesty..." he sputtered. "Have I offended...?"

"Master Ganstreng," Thain said evenly. He glanced at Hrethulf (who was too busy with his sweetmeat pie to converse), then returned his steely gaze to Freotheric. "Ganstreng. A human wizard."

"Yes," Freotheric nodded, relived that the king knew of the master. "That is correct. He has long served Ontenazu with distinction and—"

Feast or Famine at Burok Torn

"You and your canyonmaster believe," Thain interrupted, "that the rune wizards of Burok Torn are incapable of dealing with this menace?"

"*Ganstreng, Ganstreng,*" cried Hrethulf's crow, far above, and then as if to register it's opinion, shat from the heights, much to the ire of the dwarves seated beneath its perch.

Freotheric's relief rapidly turned back to worry. "No, Your Majesty, that is not what I meant at all...not what Frem Artone meant. We merely thought that to best—"

"You have been among the humans too long," Thain accused him. Galbert and Gislebert indignantly agreed. "The Drendali are a dwarven problem, and will be dealt with in a dwarven way," the king announced. "We need no human wizard telling us how to protect Burok Torn."

"Your Majesty, we meant no disrespect in this matter," Freotheric insisted. "Please, sir, recognize our good intentions, your humble allies, and be assured that to offend was most certainly not our intent."

Thain considered this a moment, mulled what he knew of the Canyonmaster Frem Artone and his unassuming ways, but could the ruler of Ontenazu not see the implications of this proposal? And if not, surely this emissary, this *dwarf*, must understand! The king attempted to master his anger; he could tell that his cheeks above his beard were ruddy and warm to the touch.

"It's your damnable pride!" Widsith burst out suddenly. "You would rather doom all your people than accept help—even help offered with the best of intentions from proven friends!"

Color rushed more profusely to the king's face, and any feelings of compassion he had harbored for these two emissaries washed from his being. He rose to his feet once more. Realizing he held his mithril bread knife clutched in his fist like a weapon, he threw the utensil onto the table. The other dwarves all leapt to their feet as well. Dulan, slowed not at all by his wooden leg, lurched forward and caught a crystal chalice that Freotheric, in his haste to stand, had knocked toward the edge of the table.

"I will hear no more of this," Thain said through clenched teeth. "For the sake of the love I bear your lords, perhaps I shall speak with you again, but you'd both best consider carefully anything you might have to say to me."

"You would damn your own people and mine as well," Widsith snarled. "I'll not allow it. I'll not allow it!" And as quick as he pulled back the sleeve of his robe and revealed a small spring-loaded contraption, two diamond-tipped bolts were in the air.

***

Under the pretext of saving a crystal chalice that Freotheric had knocked over, Dulan stepped between the king and the emissaries. Though the rudeness displayed by these visitors was not unheard of, especially in these desperate times when vile enemies threatened the decent people of Ghelspad from every direction, the Durroverite's agitation was beyond unseemly—so much so that Dulan did not care to wait for the Shield Arm to climb the dais steps. An

Feast or Famine at Burok Torn

instant later, when his intuition proved all too correct, the Butler had time for only one thought: to see if Freotheric too was party to this attack. The bolt that slammed into and through the Ontenazuan's throat answered that question. Dulan saw only the blur of the second bolt.

***

The first bolt was lodged squarely in the throat of the emissary from Ontenazu; a spray of blood arched into the air, unmoving, frozen in time. The second bolt was suspended in air, inches from Dulan the Butler's breast. The castellian and captain of the watch rushed forward—or would have if they were in motion, much as Garrit's upraised foot was poised above the third step up the dais. King Thain saw all of these things, but the commotion of the feast hall was replaced by stark, unsettling silence: no murmur of conversation emanating from the hundreds of dwarves present, no cries alarm at the assassin in their midst, no grunts and curses of the deadly struggle at hand. The odors, too, were noticeably absent: eyeless fish grown cold, ale, sweetmeat pie, fearsweat. All gone.

"You may venture forth," said a familiar voice.

Thain turned to Hrethulf. The rune wizard stood duplicated, a vague spectral image beside his solid, unmoving, normal self. Somehow his crow, the actual bird, flew down from the Worthies and perched upon the shoulder of the ghostly wizard.

Slowly, Thain stepped forward, *into* the midst of the table. He did not feel the wood that bisected the shimmering image of his body, nor was he surprised to turn and see the actual, grimacing form of himself. He turned almost at once to those about to die.

"Both of these stepped in front of deathblows meant for me," Thain said. His mind was surprisingly clear; anger was muted here in this hazy world, as was sorrow, pain, regret. He looked to the Freotheric. "See how he leans," the king said to Hrethulf. "This was no unintended stumble, not an attempt to flee gone awry. He threw himself before me, though I am not his king."

"Perhaps he didn't have time to think better of it," Hrethulf said wryly.

Thain shook his head. "That is not the way of it. And this after you and I taking umbrage at his offer of succor."

"I...?" said the wizard.

"Do not play innocent, Hrethulf, and leave me to accept all the blame. I know you better than that, and though you might hide your feelings, there is always the bird to give you away."

"*Ganstreng*," said the crow. "*Ganstreng*." And then made a choking sound in its throat. Hrethulf shooed his familiar away.

"I must reconsider," Thain said. "I must give more thought to this offer from Ontenazu." He reached an incorporeal hand toward the blood that, by all accounts, should have been his own, passed through the spray without touching it, and remembered again the words of his father: *Turn over the golden coin of pride, and you will find the gypsum face of shame.*

Feast or Famine at Burok Torn

"I must give more thought..." he said again absently, as he turned toward the keeper of the feasthall, his loyal subject, his fellow warrior, and friend. "Dulan," Thain said softly, already feeling the loss. He tried to take hold of the bolt, to pull it from its chosen path. "He has sacrificed all for this city, for his people. Better that I had taken this arrow."

"He has sacrificed all for his *king*," Hrethulf said. "Were you to be struck down this way, Burok Torn would never recover. But Dulan, with this sacrifice, has earned himself a place in legend. He has made the city stronger. Having given his leg, still, when need arose, he gave his life. Others will follow his example. They will persevere; they will lay down their lives in your name."

"Not in my name," Thain said. "In the name of Burok Torn.

"They are one in the same," said the wizard.

King Thain stood there a moment longer, in the feast hall as silent as death. He looked to the would-be assassin, not a killer for hire but a warrior driven by his passions to despair. In two swift steps, Garrit would put his hammer to use; the Shield Arm would be careful to take the king's assailant alive, so that they might ferret out any wider plot, but Thain could see already the futility of that endeavor. Reluctantly he looked again to Dulan, worthy Dulan, he who had lost his leg defending the gates of Burok Torn and his life saving his king.

"It is time," said the wizard.

"*Time,*" said his crow. "*Time.*"

And the king returned to himself.

***

Time returned—as did anger and voices and fearsweat—with the slice of a diamond-tipped bolt through flesh. As the Shield Arm pummeled the assassin to submission, King Thain cradled the crumpling body of his friend, one of so many to die. The swirl of chaos erupted around them, with shouts and screams and shoving. Thain felt himself still a ghost amidst it all, and he wished that he could return to Hrethulf's spectral realm—for a moment, for an hour, for a lifetime—in hopes that there the heartache would not rend him so. But the granite Worthies were looking down upon him, and they made no allowance for weakness; each of them had suffered enough in his own turn. All that remained was to go on. Far above, in the shadowy heights of the vaulted ceiling, the crow cawed over and over, witness to death and to hope.

Three Dreams of Belsameth

By James Stewart

James Stewart

Ezra

A feud between the titanic and the divine has stricken forests and toppled empires older than gods, but the city of Shelzar doesn't mind. Shelzar is a dream dreamt in the middle of a battlefield. A dream of booze and women, a dream of circuses and plays and buildings that aren't rubble. The Old Veneer aristocracy, bored and exiled, sips nepenthe with Little Virduks from Rahoch and Calastia, washed-up nobility ready to sell the family jewels for a blow job and exotic liquor from the other side of the Blossoming Sea. The Pleasure City takes any currency, any customer. It's a good place to take your mind off things. The sea is red, the land is scarred, but don't worry—look at the gladiators and all the strange beasts! The Jack of Tears of the whole show, the lord of the carnival, His Most Gracious Host Minister Fratreli will make sure you have a good time. Especially if you're rich. And why not? The rest of Ghelspad's backward and broke. So see a show. Get a whore. Drink. Smoke. Gamble. Stab. Money!

I love this place.

But some places in Shelzar aren't meant for princes on holiday. This tavern, for instance. It's called Knight's Crossing, not that any knight would ever cross here. I love this dive—it's just a few blocks away from one of my flophouses, so I can always come here and work up a truly sideways drunk. But Lilly hates this place. She sucks on her beer and stares straight ahead at me. Not into my eyes, but at the two-handed hammer emblazoned on my tunic. I snap at her. "Hey." She looks up. "Hedrada don't like it when you stare."

Lilly gives me a look like she did before the Hollowfaust job and heads for the bar. She returns with a beer three times bigger than her last. She stares at me with those glassy little slits that pass for eyes when she's in one of her moods. Her tail twitches like it's covered with flies.

Three Dreams of Belsameth

"Don't be like that Lilly. Why complain every time work comes around?"

"He's called the Titanslayer, Ezra. You think you can kill someone called the Titanslayer?"

"He's a catatonic lunatic waiting to be snuffed. Let's put him out of his misery and collect." Lilly downs her beer, never taking her eyes off me. "We go to this temple," I say, pointing to the sketch at the bottom of the contract, "and collect five large."

Lilly slams her stein down. The pennies I've been compulsively stacking spill across the table. Foam flies from her drink and splatters all over the contract. I snatch it up and dab it with my sleeve.

"Good work, Lilly. I'm sure it will reassure King Virduk that we're the right bastards for the job when we return his contract covered in beer."

"You think Virduk will ever see that thing? You've got a lot to learn, 'priest.'"

"Why don't you puke on it too? Show him we're serious."

Lilly pulls her ice pick and grabs my collar, yanking me over the table without a hint of strain, though she's a woman and almost a foot shorter than I am. She pulls my face up to hers. She doesn't have eyes anymore, just two little black lines. Sweat runs down past her horns.

"We're not good enough for this job," she says, spitting in my face. "Let's stick to ambassadors who can't pay their bookies."

"No, Lilly, this is a good job, and we should take it. The goddess of shadow told me so."

James Stewart

Vladawen

Even after 150 years sitting in the darkness of his ruined temple, I cannot remember the name of my dead god. It used to slip gladly from my lips each morning as the first rays of the sun shone in through the east windows and woke me. Now my people call him That Which Abides because we cannot remember calling him anything else. His destruction is so complete that even his divine name has been erased. Not even his most loyal priests can resurrect a memory of what we called him. But it feels like my own fault, like I have lost the name of my father. I awake each morning and feel like I've left something undone. Then I despair. It's a sorry thing to forget the name of your own god.

"Vladawen? Are you still in here, Vladawen?"

Someone calls to me from the darkness. The voice seems familiar. One of my own kind, elvish. A female voice. And a female shape, a red heat in the darkness.

I think it's my wife. "Avlana?"

"Will you be leaving the ruins of your mighty temple today, great Titanslayer? Isn't 150 years long enough to sulk in the dark?"

"The temple is as splendid as it ever was."

"It's an illusion, Vladawen. Your temple's blasted and ruined like everything else in Termana."

"I'd forgotten."

Avlana throws a rude heat gesture. Even in the dark, the exaggerated motion of her hand is plain to me. She threw it the last time she was here, or the time before. She seems upset.

"Have you also forgotten that we're forsaken? There's no time for this misery, Vladawen. You won't live forever."

I don't want to live forever.

Three Dreams of Belsameth

"Your mother could have sewn two coats in the time you've spent here."

"Mother's dead."

Avlana throws the heat gesture for surrender. She turns toward the door of the temple, takes a few steps, then stops. With my darkvision, I see her reach toward something near her belt. In her hands are two cold blue spheres. She drops them on the floor. As they fall, they leave cerulean tracers in the darkness.

"Here's your food."

Looking to the door and back to the altar on which I sit, Avlana waits, like she expects me to say something. Like I have anything left to say to her or anyone else.

"By the way, Vladawen, I've been sleeping with Arimel for the last sixty years. We're getting married."

"Really. How many of those deformed wretches have you squeezed out for him? Do you steal away to human towns and swap them with human babies?"

"At least I'm doing something to preserve our people. What are you doing, Titanslayer? You're waiting to die."

"Haven't I done enough?"

"Destroyed a titan, lost a god. I realize now that what my father said is true: You're far better at destroying things than revering them."

I bolt off the altar onto my feet. I see Avlana's body explode with heat, turning from a dull red to the bright orange of fear as I streak toward her in the blackness. My knuckles meet her brow and she falls to the ground. She curls into a ball. A scream catches in Avlana's throat, a stifled choking sound in the dark. Cool blue rivulets wash down her face.

"No matter how hard you hit me, Vladawen, what I say is true. You've destroyed everything, including yourself."

Avlana's fingers splay across the floor. She lifts herself up into a sitting position. She cradles her head. She regains her voice. No scream, just a jagged sobbing. I kneel down and extend a hand toward her face. She bats it away.

"I should kill you for saying such a thing to me. But you're right," I whisper. She looks up at me. "I've been here too long. I've lost too many years. It is time for me to redeem myself. Get up now. Bring me my weapons and my boots."

Avlana stands and walks toward the entrance to the temple. She opens the inner doors. She walks to the outer door, turns the key and throws it wide. I see the sun for the first time in 150 years. Now it's my turn to cry.

"You want your weapons, Vladawen? Come out of the darkness and get them."

The sun floats low and orange at the edge of dusk. The light blinds me and I almost let slip the name of god but I stammer with uncertainty. Termana was once his land. I blink and, as though the last 150 years never passed, the land of That Which Abides lies before me.

Termana looks just like I remember it. Just like the days before the Divine War. The temple of That Which Abides—the home temple of my order, the host of our people's rituals for a thousand years—has lost none of its majesty. Around the steeple, lines of silver swirl in intricate spirals finer than fingerprints. The windows, thirty feet tall and three feet thick, depict the history of my people. That Which Abides, first among the gods, selecting the elves from all of the races to be his champion and the keeper of his ways. Jillian, the First King, returning from the hunt with the hide of Tanil's Fox. Hezra the Eunuch feeding Denev the Fruit of Winter. The league of elvenkind emerging triumphant from the war with the Saints of Black. Jillian's ghost returning the Amphitheater to sing the Song

Three Dreams of Belsameth

one last time, in the presence of Belsameth, goddess of the darkness, and her daughter Drendari, goddess of... I forget.

But the temple lacks one window in particular, and this omission makes the rest of the story nothing more than a lie. There is no depiction of the titan Chern laying waste to That Which Abides. There is no depiction of the moment our race was forsaken; of the moment god's name was lost.

The glory of Termana is nothing more than an elaborate illusion; a closed coffin at the funeral to make us forget that what lies beneath is rotten and will soon be dust. Fake opulence conceals crumbling ruins. To see the windows of the temple as they truly are is to see a zigzagging mess of boards covering the holes where my kind's greatest art once stood. Half of the structures in Termana, intricate in their detail and sturdy beyond the limits of their stylish construction, are unfit for habitation. Even those buildings that survived the Divine War mostly intact still show hints of their ruin—a draft noticed in the night or a rain of shingles and rafters when a storm blows through. All of Termana's lies have such inconsistencies.

As I walk through the streets, my forsaken brothers and sisters stare at me as though I'm the most majestic of all of Termana's illusions. They look at me like some legend that just stepped out of its stain-glassed world. I avoid their gazes and walk with a solemn purpose, aloof, my posture telling the lie that I am the Vladawen they once knew.

My former home offers no false faces to the world. Even before I left for my mourning, I refused the wizards' illusions. Most of the second floor lies in charred tatters. Only a few support beams, splintered and burned, remain of my parent's chambers. The first floor remains inhabitable, but the inscriptions that my great-grandfather and great-great-grandfather spent 3,000 years carving into the rock are worn and unreadable. What remains of my house would seem dull and unadorned even in a human settlement.

When I enter my ancestral home, Armiel—who I have known since birth and expected to know until That Which Abides called the last dance—sits at my table. He is not my ancestor. Armiel looks like he doesn't know whether to hug me or dash my brains out with a rock. He takes three steps over to the doorway from the foyer to the dinner hall. He gives a false smile.

"Vladawen. You're back."

"Get me a drink."

Neither of us says another word until long after the sun has set. Armiel backs away from me toward the kitchen, never taking his eyes off my hands. He busies himself preparing me a mixture of ale and ganjus tincture. He finds other jobs to distract him while I drink. He takes hurried steps to the other side of my table and picks up a book, closes it, and puts it on a shelf. He stokes the fire. He takes his plates and flagon to the kitchen. He disappears up the stairs. I hear him arguing with Avlana. He returns a few minutes later, his false smile a little worn at the edges.

"Avlana's not feeling well, Vlad. She needs to sleep a little…"

"I don't care Armiel. I really don't. Let's talk about That Which Abides."

"He's gone. Dead. Broken."

"I can fix that."

"No, you can't. He's gone, Vladawen. No one observes the old rituals. Even I can no longer bear to honor him. I feel almost embarrassed after… after we failed him. The favor of That Which Abides is useless. All but the simplest of his blessings fail me. Yesterday I rebuked the ghost of a pit bull that haunted the mill, but my wounds were so

Three Dreams of Belsameth

severe that I had to see the physician afterward. When was the last time you invoked his aid?"

"Not since that day. Not one little spell. Not one."

"Nothing? Are even the first lessons of the temple lost to you? It must feel…"

"Numb."

"That Which Abides used to be so generous with us. There used to be so many temples in Termana…."

"And there will be again."

"Vladawen, the darkness has driven you mad."

Armiel grabs my glass and finishes the rest of my drink. Though the night is cool and dark, he sweats like a field hand. He turns away from me and stares into the fire. "How could you possibly do it, Vlad?"

"Begin in Ghelspad. Talk to our kin on Uria or Vera-Tre. I'll need my weapons."

"Some of the years during your sequester were hard years, Vlad. Most of them. We sold both weapons."

"To whom?"

"A black-haired stranger. A human woman. Pretty sure she was human. But that was fifty years ago."

"What about my boots?"

"Sold those too."

Armiel resumes his nervous fidget, as though I would allow him to steal my wife but not my boots.

"Be calm, Armiel. I will reclaim them later. It's more important that I leave tonight, immediately, before I decide to lock myself in the temple once more."

"Take me with you."

"No. But I'll take your boat."

James Stewart

Virduk's agent unrolls a scroll with his dirty little hands, twist-by-twist revealing Virduk's Black Dragon emblem. "Looks like you, Lilly." The agent is a filthy thing, one of Virduk's halflings from the Heteronomy. An ambassador for the Satrap, as he explained. Then, as if his scroll were proof of his allegiance or credentials, he releases the scroll with his left hand and lets it roll back into shape. He shoots me a dirty, little halfling smile. I have dreams of chasing little beasties just like this one, smashing their dirty little heads with a bloody big mallet.

"So you'll take it."

"We'll take it," I say. Lilly spits.

The creature nods and promises that he will meet us back in Shelzar once we return with proof that the job is complete. A black pool opens up under the vile midget, a pool of shadow with a hint of starlight. The waters begin to bubble under his feet. He plummets into the pool, not with a splash but with a sound like a delicious slurp.

"What the hell was that?" Lilly asks. "This is too big."

"Don't start again. We've got a contract, we've got an immobile victim, we've got a big payday coming."

"What kind of king hires an assassin in writing? Why a contract?"

"Virduk's stupid. Everyone knows that," I say. "Now, how will we get there?"

"Ride me, I guess."

Vladawen

I awaken to rain on my face. Armiel's boat rises and falls and rocks in the storm. Ceruleans wrestle in the sky. I sit up and try to hold a sail barely taller than the windows of my temple. The growing storm conceals the stars, but Termana—whatever direction it lies—is invisible in the

Three Dreams of Belsameth

distance. The waters that bear my ship rise and fall in great cascades of white foam. When the lightning flashes, I see the silent beasts of the Blossoming Sea flailing for prey. My stomach revolts at the violent sloshing.

When I set sail, the skies were clear. Thin white clouds stretched on for miles. Now, a storm bigger than Liar's Sound has coalesced from nowhere. Even with the gods in charge, no one's paying attention to the weather, and the sea has always been a fickle thing.

After tying off the sail, I take to the rudder. The Blossoming Sea spits up crimson foam. Red splotches dapple the white cloth of the sail. This storm blew in from the east, from the Blood Sea. The blood of a fallen titan fills the little ship faster than I can bail it. I cup my hands and return the watery ichor rapidly filling my boat back to the sea. A pathetic gesture. In this downpour, there can be no hope. I have never taken to the sea, but now it seems that it will be my grave. After offering a brief prayer of apology to my dead god, I try one last time to hold my course through the storm.

For my prayer and my effort, I'm rewarded with a great red swell. I see it approaching the boat and cease my labors. It rises over a white foam, pushing away the waters of the Blossoming Sea in its path. The wave submerges with a great crashing sound. Then it resurfaces. Under my boat.

The force of the wave launches me from my tiny ship. I watch it capsize and roll under the wave. I hit the water, but do not sink at first because the sea is so thick with the titan's blood. For a moment, I'm the highest thing on the Blossoming Sea, surveying the storm for miles around me as the tide carries me along. Then everything comes crashing down as the force of the wave pulls me under. Blood and water course into my nose and mouth, drowning my lungs. My last regret is that I have tasted titans' blood only twice.

Ezra

I sit astride a black dragon as big as a Karrian warship. Its wings rise and fall in broad, patient arcs. The smell almost overwhelms me, but the air—charged with electricity—counteracts the stench. Beneath us, a sheet of clouds punishes the Blossoming Sea. Things look weird when you're flying this far above the ground—though it is the dead of night, the clouds look like the clouds at sunset over a burning village —fat and pink from the ash in the air.

I pound my fist against one of the scales on the back of my mount and say, "Lilly. Hey, Lilly."

"Stop that or fall." The voice that answers still sounds like Lilly's, but the voice comes from deep in her belly. When she speaks, she rumbles. I feel it in my hips.

"Lilly, I have a question I've wanted to ask you for years."

"So ask."

Personally, I find Lilly much more pleasant when she's got wings and scales. Her dragon-form isn't conducive to talking. She complains a lot less when she can breathe fire and crush opponents in her teeth—armor, horse and all. Nice in a brawl too, if you've got the room.

"Lilly. What the fuck are you?" The dragon seethes. I feel her take in a great breath and blow it out flaming from her nostrils. "I can't figure it out, Lilly. First, your name—Lillatu. Obvious noble name. I'm thinking Old Venir or Dunahnae. No farmer's got the balls to name his kid Lillatu. And you can turn into a dragon. And, when you're not a dragon, you have those horns and that spastic tail. So, that makes you a... what?"

A low whining sound passes through Lilly's nostrils before she answers. "Daddy was a king or should have been, mommy was a dragon, and princess has bad luck with enchanted folk. Always with the curses, those forest people."

"Well, you got a tail and horns out of it. You terrify me, and I'm your partner."

"Pixies. Elves. I hate them all."

Vladawen

The dark side of the moon is a cold and barren place. The horizon, no doubt as far from me as Termana is from the Plains of Lede, is nothing more than an arc of light. In front of me is a statue of That Which Abides, missing an arm and half the head. The thing perched atop the statue has many smiles on its face. The moon is cold, especially in wet clothes. I try to maintain my stoic pose with the blood of Kadum dripping off me into pink puddles.

"Titanslayer. Welcome."

"This is a dream."

"Yes."

"And you are Belsameth."

"Yes."

"Then I am dead."

"Soon, soon."

With a groan that an old woman might make if she had sat a few centuries too long in an uncomfortable chair, Belsameth stretches her vulture wings and harpy legs. The statue of That Which Abides becomes a basalt throne. The goddess lowers her wings and sits in repose, the talons of her feet clutching at the corners of her seat.

"You wallowed in darkness for 150 years. You show great promise."

"I'd like to wake up now."

"For your kind, that's a record."

"Now."

"The record for doing so voluntarily, at any rate."

Her movements are too fast for me to see, but Belsameth pivots in her seat, throwing her legs over the right armrest, and brings a talon to one of her many lips. "You are a rude one. I am Belsameth, the Slayer and the Assassin. How do the mortals say it? The goddess of darkness and deception. They are among my talents, I admit."

"I mean no disrespect. I'm busy."

"First you are rude and now you are too formal. We are, after all, old friends… and I know you're not busy doing anything but drowning in the Blossoming Sea. Not as much fun as dying in your temple, I suppose?"

I blink and miss the change, but now Belsameth and I stand in the temple of That Which Abides in Termana. The brightness of the moon's horizon slips away and leaves us in a darkness all too familiar to me. Belsameth lies flat on her vulture wings in a lurid position atop the altar I once sat upon. In the dark, she is an icy blue. She is the coldest thing I have ever seen.

"More comfortable, Titanslayer? Let's sit awhile, you and I, in the dark. We can whisper our secrets to one another and the years will pass as nothing. Perhaps at the height of some lurid rapture, you'll shout the name of your god and it will return to the world." Her cackle makes my stomach long for the gentle tidal sloshing of the Blossoming Sea.

"Have you summoned me to throw taunts?"

Belsameth leans up on her side as her fingers play between her legs. "Not at all, Vladawen. Not at all. I've called you here to praise you. Few understand the darkness better than you. A Titanslayer sitting in the darkness for

Three Dreams of Belsameth

150 years, thinking dark thoughts! A tempting morsel, yes?"

"What has become of That Which Abides? Where is your fallen brother?"

Belsameth cackles again. "That Which Abides! Oh, what euphemisms men and elves concoct! Perhaps you should consider a new name for my brother? Since, in retrospect, he clearly did *not* abide."

"Wake me."

"Perhaps you should call him 'That Which Almost Abided?' 'That Which Temporarily Abides?'"

"What was the name of my god?"

"His doom was so utter that not even the gods remember."

"Belsameth, I have no time. I know why I'm here. Make your offer."

Now we're back on the dark side of the moon. Milky oceans roil in great round lakes. Belsameth sits upside down in her basalt throne, her head leaned back over the edge of the seat, her legs in the air.

"Now Vladawen. You need a patron. Let me help you restore my brother. I miss him so, and your life embodies my every ideal."

"What do you get?"

"Each time I help you—like plucking your water-soaked carcass out of the Blossoming Sea—I get to bestow a blessing upon you. You will call it a curse, but it is really a blessing."

"Such as?"

"Anything I choose."

I consider her offer. A few centuries ago, I would not have given her bargain a thought. Every child knows what happens to those who truck with Belsameth. And the very suggestion of a priest in the service of That Which Abides also serving the Queen of Nightmares would have been an insult to my faith. The little part of me that still remembers those sunlit days revolts at the mercenary path I'm considering. My good sense returns to me.

"No, Belsameth. I'd rather drown."

"If you drown, forsaken one, your god drowns with you. No one else reveres him. Without you, he is lost. Will your pride still lead you to reject my patronage? Are you willing to destroy yourself and your lord just to prove a point? Be smart, elfling."

I felt, at that moment, a black flower bloom in my heart. With it, a realization that Belsameth, though she is the Mother of Deceit, speaks the truth. I knew then why she had chosen me for her "blessing." I realize it just at that moment: In the end, I will go to any length to restore That Which Abides. Whatever pain or curse or misery I have to endure to see this pilgrimage through, I will endure it.

"Tell me, Belsameth—if I were to accept your offer, what would my first blessing be?"

"You will fall in love with a thing that is more evil than good. She can bear the darkness better than you because she lacks the kernel of decency that makes your darkness so much blacker. She will cause you more grief than you have ever experienced in your 800 years."

"Impossible. I accept your bargain."

I awaken in a bed of warm wool sheets and pillows of the softest down. The room drifts slowly left to right with the gentle rocking of a ship in calm water. Moonlight streams down on me through circular windows of flawless glass. Outside, pink clouds still hover near the horizon, but the storm has broken. The winds no longer roar. The water has settled.

I get up out of the bed and find that my soggy clothes have been replaced with a silk bedgown of Urian purple. I am dry and feel as though I have just eaten a feast. Shaking my head free of sleep, I exit through a small door in the rear of the cabin. I am on a raft with nothing more than a single cabin atop it, but it is a raft built of the darkest obsidian, a gentle ride though it should not float. In the water behind the ship, I hear a wet slithering sound of something batting its way through the water. The raft moves across the Blossoming Sea with the speed of eagles. Jutting out of the water, I see two pairs of black hands clutching—no, pushing—the raft.

"Go back to sleep, elf. You are in Drendari's protection."

I turn to see a creature as beautiful as Belsameth was revolting. Her raven hair and her midnight gown seem almost indistinguishable from the starry sky above us, jet-black with twinkles in its depths. Her expression, her pupil-less eyes and the sharp corners of her mouth give the impression of supreme confidence, supreme power.

Drendari. Goddess of what?

Ezra

I scream as Lilly swoops down through the clouds and plants her claws deep into the soil of Termana. I launch off her back, roll across the ground, clutch my stomach and vomit. If a dragon can smile, Lilly does.

"Too fast, Ezra? I'm so sorry."

Lilly folds her wings around her massive belly and begins to shrink. Her legs straighten out and return to an upright human configuration. Her tree trunk of a tail diminishes to one small enough for a cat. Her wings melt away like shadow under a lantern to reveal my horned, tailed, disgruntled Lilly once again. I hand my partner her weapons and her satchel. We set out for the temple in which a mad elf awaits our redemptive touch.

We travel for an hour through wilderness. This is not a traipse through some enchanted wood full of magical beasts and hidden treasures—much to Lilly's relief, I'm sure. The trees here are broken and splintered, and those that still endure appear small and sickly. Soon enough, a blurry light to the south eclipses even the stars. We emerge from the woods and set eyes on the most elaborate, ornate, tall, impossible civilization I have ever seen. Then I blink, and what was seemingly glorious looks like nothing but ruins.

Lilly can barely speak. "I've never seen anything so…"

"Such illusions cannot fool a priest of Hedrada. All lies disperse as a dust storm before him. Now, let's find that temple."

"Priest of Hedrada my ass."

A few hours before morning, the streets of Termana await us, barren of life. This elven home has a sad quality of a dilapidated fortification no longer worth defending. We make our way across broad streets unquestioned and unmolested. Lilly believes the streets are paved with silver and inscribed with the wisdom of a thousand hands. I see them for what they are—long muddy stains.

Lilly and I follow the roads for an hour more, looking for the temple drawn on the contract. Finally, Lilly puts her hand on my shoulder, and, for the first time since we took this job, she speaks to me without a hint of her foul mood.

"Look at the windows, Ezra. How beautiful."

"For someone who hates elves, you love the tricks they play on you. This is the place. Be ready."

The outer doors are locked, but Lilly slams her shoulder against them and they open with ease. No explosions erupt, no magical alarms, no holy servants to stop the intruders who have breached the temple. We walk into the darkness of the place unopposed.

Three Dreams of Belsameth

"What do you see, Lilly?"

"Nothing. No one's here."

"This is the wrong place. The Titanslayer must be in another temple."

"No, this is the place. Virduk screwed us."

Then comes a voice from the darkness. A woman's voice. "Virduk didn't screw you. He didn't even hire you. I did."

Vladawen

We sleep out the day moving across the Blossoming Sea at coursing speeds. I wake up in Drendari's bed just after sunset. A hint of daylight lingers in the air. Soon the moon will emerge over the bloody clouds in the east. Drendari's arm rests across my chest. I lift its cold mass off me and slide out from under the sheets.

I walk out to the deck. In the twilight, I can see the two things propelling the ship. Their bodies are long and black, and look as if they are shadows with ambitions toward becoming flesh. Their obsidian arms are muscled and strained. Their featureless faces barely clear the surface of the water. Behind them, great black tails lash about, pushing the raft toward Ghelspad.

"Who are you?" I ask the creatures.

"We are the beloved of Drendari."

"And you push the boat for the love of the goddess."

"We do. You will too."

Untying the sash around my gown, I say, "And I've got a prophecy for you." I piss in the water between them. The creatures increase the pace of their swimming and begin to emit an unpleasant shriek. I head to the front of the raft.

I see the continent of Ghelspad in the distance. To the west are the island chains that the rising waters freed from the Swamp of Kan Thet during the Divine War. Far to the east is the coast of Zathiske. Dead ahead, on a peninsula south of the Sweltering Plains, rises a city that could compare with Termana in its heyday. Great spires of jade and ivory, of stone cut and carried from the halls of Burok Torn. Banners and flags proclaiming the presence of royalty from all over Ghelspad wave in the air.

We're heading toward the Pleasure City of Shelzar.

I feel the presence of someone behind me. Not a dangerous presence, but an unmistakable gravitas. I turn to find Drendari behind me. She smiles gently and approaches, leaning against the railing at the front of the raft before she speaks.

"My mother tells me you wish to restore your god to his former glory. How?"

"I don't know. Consult holy men, look for books from before the Divine War."

Drendari laughs at me. I feel the ire within me rising, like when Avlana mocked my name. The black flower inside me spreads its petals a little more. "Elf," she says, "that is not the way to go about resurrecting gods. Take it from a goddess. You won't find the salvation of… what was his name?… in an old book or in the words of a cloistered old man."

"Where will I find it?"

"In the belief of the multitudes. You need rituals performed on a regular basis. You need sacrifices and worship. You need followers. These are the things that give gods form."

"This sounds like one of Belsameth's lies."

Drendari slaps me, her demure arrogance transforming in an instant into a child's rage. "I am not my mother,

Three Dreams of Belsameth

Titanslayer. And I will not suffer your insouciance like her. Do not accuse me of mortal sins like dishonesty."

"So, you are telling me truthfully, goddess, that if my people never despaired, never abandoned the worship of That Which Abides, he'd have recovered from his wounding by Chern?"

"Eventually."

I wrap my hands around the railing and suppress the urge to scream out to the sea. "Faithless cowards. All of them."

"Not everyone is a Titanslayer, Vladawen. Look, Shelzar is near."

The things in the back of the boat slow their flailing tails. The raft turns slightly to the west, heading to the docks that line the coast at the edge of the Pleasure City. Further along the coast to the east, hundreds of workers load and unload heavy merchant galleons and warships. A train of armed soldiers escorts a cage of gibbering charfiends off a Toe Island corsair. The western docks, where men and stranger things in robes of white linen await visiting dignitaries, high-rollers and vacationing nobility, I see only pleasure barges and royal vessels. Passenger ships, cruise ships—expensive ships.

"Won't there be an outcry when they see your lovers in the back?"

Drendari smiles at me. Not the gentle smile from her awakening. "I come here all the time. There are docks for mortals, and docks for those like me. Shelzar is a splendid city, but it sees only the least splendid half of itself. Not even His Most Gracious Host Minister Fratreli knows what storied visitors his city attracts."

When our vessel pulls up alongside a pier, a legion of the attendants, some composed of the same shadow-stuff as Drendari's boatmen and some with the features of beast, ties off the raft. Guards with the heads of rats position

James Stewart

themselves on either side of a ramp and slide it over the water to our deck. A few yards away, traders and sailors move about the docks of Shelzar, oblivious to the divine reception taking place in their midst.

When Drendari disembarks, one of the attendants takes her hand and steadies her. "Mistress. You have returned to us once again. Shall we escort you to your temple?"

Drendari kisses her attendant on the cheek. "Not this time, Carmen. I feel like slumming it for a while. If I require anything more, I will return to make use of your able attentions."

The attendant—Carmen—rubs his paws together in a frantic scratching motion. His ears twitch. "You are... too kind to me, demigoddess."

Drendari and I leave the docks and make our way through the city. Human women—a breed I have always found to be too fat and disgusting for my tastes—leer at me with promises of pleasure in their eyes. In the doorway of a casino, a child puffs on a hollow stem of ganjas root longer than his arm. Inside, the crowd roars. Someone is either winning money or losing a fight.

"What to do first, elf? I notice that your fabled weapons did not accompany you on your voyage. Perhaps they are lost forever on the floor of the Blossoming Sea? Perhaps you should equip yourself, find a reliable mount?"

"No money."

Drendari greets my admission with outrageous laughter. She doubles over and makes quite a show of holding her stomach as if it would otherwise erupt. Barely able to speak, she squeaks out, "You mean... you mean... you have embarked penniless on your quest to restore your god? I'm surprised you lost him the first time, as attentive as you clerics of That Which Abides seem to be."

Three Dreams of Belsameth

"I appreciate your assistance, Drendari, but I will not be mocked by a mere demigoddess. A goddess, Belsameth or Tanil, I'll abide their jabs. Not yours."

"Look! Money!" As if to change the subject, Drendari reaches out toward the belt of a drunk stumbling out of the casino. She reaches for his purse, and, too quick for me to perceive, her fingers untie the strings and free the bag from the belt. She pours a tidy pile of silver and gold coins into her hand. "Not much, but enough for you to eat and sleep on for a few nights."

"Why not stay at your temple? Why not whisk us away to someplace safe and comfortable?"

"It's more fun to steal. Survive by your own effort, Vladawen. Besides, my temple in Shelzar is neither as convenient nor as safe as you might expect. Come, I have business to attend to in the city. Let's find you a shelter for the evening where you can get sloppy drunk and commiserate with all the other poor souls who have mislaid their gods. That one looks good."

"Knight's Crossing? I see no knights."

Ezra

"Who's speaking, Lilly?"

"I don't see anyone."

But I feel someone here with us in the darkness. A dangerous presence. A familiar one. I step forward and try to sound bold, though my instincts tell me to run and not stop until I reach Albadia. "What do you mean King Virduk didn't hire us?"

"My agent might have misrepresented himself. Virduk's a fool, but do you really think he hands out contracts to prospective assassins? Certain courts in this world and the next might construe such a contract as tangible evidence."

I feel Lilly tugging at the back of my collar. "Shit, Ezra. We've put it in writing. The gods are fucking with us."

The melody of laughter spirals through the darkness. "Yes, we are. And you've signed my contract, which, if you could read more than 20 words between the two of you, you'd note specifies quite clearly that you have undertaken this job for *me*, Drendari. Surely you understand the intractability of your obligation now?"

I spit on the tiles of the ruined temple. "Well, I have never heard of a goddess named Drendari, but I can read numbers. And the contract specifies 5,000 Shelzar-minted gold pieces upon completion."

"And you'll have it. Every last coin. I'm compelled to fulfill my end of the bargain, as you are compelled to fulfill yours."

I hear Lilly suck in a great breath. I feel something leathery brush me aside. Lilly roars, then, suddenly, begins to scream. "Don't bother," the invisible goddess says. "Whatever form you take, you are no match for me." I hear Lilly gasping for breath on the floor beside me.

"Listen," the goddess continues. "Vladawen is now in Shelzar."

"Shelzar!" I say indignantly. "We were just there."

"He's at Knight's Crossing."

"We could've been drinking this whole time?"

"The Titanslayer was roused from his stupor by insults from his wife," The goddess says. I was once married myself, and I nod knowingly. "He would have destroyed you both like a boot stomping on roaches. The only way you'll get him now is in his sleep or in his confidence. So, back to Shelzar with the both of you."

"I told you this job was twisted," Lilly says.

Three Dreams of Belsameth

In a flash, the ruined temple comes aglow with a thousand burning candles. The tiles beneath our feet lie cracked and broken, as do the boarded-up windows looming over our heads. Before us is an altar with a slight indentation in its surface, as if it had been polished too hard for several decades. A woman with a gown and hair like a starlit night sits before us at the end of the only pew still in one piece. She holds an egg of a gem in her hands. It emits a slow, deep pulse through the room that I can feel in the place where my jaw hinges to my skull.

"Vladawen is with me in Shelzar, and he is very much asleep."

"So why not kill him yourself?" Lilly asks. "It'll take us hours to fly back to Ghelspad."

"That's against the rules where Titanslayers are concerned. And it won't take you hours to fly back. You'll walk through this door." Drendari stands and holds her gem out at arm's length. She raises it slightly above her head, and, with all the pomp of a wizard reciting the final words of an ancient incantation, speaks the words.

"Whoring's done!"

A black portal rises out of the tiles. I now feel the hum of the gem in my shoulders and knees. Lilly's tail spasms.

"I stole this gemgate from Lord Gasslander. A stupid, stupid king. Usually, its sister gem would take you to a broom closet in his summer keep in Shelzar. But manipulations of gemstones are not as seriously policed as manipulations of Titanslayers. This once, the portal will take you straight to the room in which Vladawen sleeps. I suggest you do the job quickly. Finding another opportunity will be difficult." Drendari hands Lilly the gemgate and winks.

Before we enter the portal, I turn to Drendari. "You're the goddess of shadow, aren't you. I had a dream about you."

"Everyone has a dream about me. Now go."

We step through the portal, emerging in a small room overlooking the road to the Shelzar docks. Sleeping on his back, his hands behind his head, is an elf with an almost morbidly square jaw and long black hair. The room reeks of smoke. If we are lucky, he has smoked himself unconscious and will not stir.

"He's so beautiful," Lilly says as she hands me her ice pick. "Do it quick."

Vladawen

Tonight the dark side of the moon is cold and windy. I find myself wiping dust out of my eyes every few minutes. Belsameth has her middle finger in her nose up to the knuckle, digging.

"You need my help again, Titanslayer."

"Do I?"

Belsameth nods. "It seems that my daughter, who I have sent to help you, has decided to kill you. She is jealous of everything I have. The goddess of shadow seems unwilling to spend eternity in the shadow of her mother. Even now, her assassins advance on your quarters."

"Then let me wake up and I will deal with them."

The Queen of Lies pulls her finger from her nose. Stretching from her fingertip to her nostril is a flesh-colored mucous with a vaguely humanoid shape. Its incomprehensible pipsqueaks sting my ears. "Patience, Vladawen. For my warning, I must grant you another blessing. In your task to restore your god, you will enter into a bargain so mercenary and so callous that That Which Abides, if he is restored, will be most displeased to learn of it."

"It seems that I've already entered such a bargain."

Three Dreams of Belsameth

"Not at all. I'm your patron now and will see that you come to no harm. Your success is my success. So I will awaken you. By the way, you have another problem to deal with aside from your assassins."

"What?"

"Knight's Crossing is on fire."

Ezra

I whisper to Lilly in the dark. "This place stinks. What's he been smoking?" Lilly's barbed tail twitches like crazy. I turn her ice pick around in my hand and advance on the bed. Lilly grabs my shoulder.

"Wait, something's not—"

Behind us, we hear gibbering and the sound of rushing wind. Vladawen opens his eyes just as the wall to our backs falls in, coming loose from its supports in the ceiling. Lilly rolls over her shoulder and escapes the blast. I'm not so lucky. The wall collapses on top of me. It is a cheap, thin plaster—painless, really, except for the beam that falls across my knee.

And the wall's on fire. It falls away to reveal an inferno in the next room. Hot air rushes over us. Then comes the stench. Not just the stench of a burning building, but the stench of burning flesh. Burning flesh, sizzling fat and something else. Something awful.

A dozen speeding forms run through the smoke. They stand no taller than my chest, but they look wiry and fast. They course through the room, filthy goblins that stink of scorched meat and ash. Some move to surround Vladawen and Lilly. Others come tossing fire, throwing burning chunks of wood and broken plaster.

"Charfiends," Lilly says.

James Stewart

Vladawen's bed ignites when a lamp lands on his blanket and shatters, but he is already up. He grabs the fiend nearest the bed by the back of the neck. He smashes it against the wall, and a few of its jagged canines go flying. The creature writhes and hollers, but Vladawen keeps ramming its face into the wall until it stops kicking. Then he moves on to the next one and throws a punch right into its mouth. The charfiend barely has time to bite down before it begins to shriek. Vladawen pulls his arm out with the creature's tongue and the better part of its throat in his fist. He grabs a chair, breaks off the two front legs and goes to work on the rest of them, undeterred though the fire will soon consume his room.

Lilly, with blood in her mouth and under her nails, unwraps her tail from around a charfiend's throat. Its carcass falls to the floor. One of the things latches on to my neck. I don't react in time because the stench of the creature overwhelms me. I vomit in my mouth and then beat the creature away with my mace.

"You've got to get out of here," Lilly yells to Vladawen. "They're all over the inn." At first I think Lilly's turned, but quickly I realize what she might be up to. In his sleep or in his confidence, Drendari said.

Vladawen nods, stabs one of the chair legs through a charfiend's abdomen and grabs the arm of another, chair leg still in hand. He hefts the creature over his back, its arm snapping as it whips over Vladawen's head. He hurls the beast forward, smashing through the flaming door. He points past the threshold and runs. Even through the fire, I hear the creatures' death-shrieks.

Lilly drags me through the door as I try to wipe my face clean. The hallway is a vision of hell. Flames seem to engulf everything, burning straw drifts down from the ceiling in a shower of cinders. Charfiends scurry through the hall, some dragging immolated corpses from their beds.

Three Dreams of Belsameth

Others squeeze in around the bodies, fighting their fellows for a taste of well-done flesh.

Vladawen looks at Lilly as if he is about to say something, but he stops. They lock eyes. For a moment, Lilly's tail relaxes. Two of the charfiends bowl Vladawen over. The threesome rolls on the ground, Vladawen's bedclothes catching fire when he brushes the wall. Lilly snaps out of her reverie and, like a fisherman with a spear, plucks up one the creatures with her ice pick. Vladawen throws his other attacker out the window. He looks down at the ground and shakes his head. "Too far." While he pulls his flaming shirt off over his head, he yells at me. "Clear a path to the stairs. Go!"

My fantasy of whacking halflings with a mallet almost comes true. I advance down the hall, batting away charfiends as I go. Lilly and Vladawen follow. A section of the wall falls where we stood moments before. More of the creatures stream out of the rooms into the hall. A charfiend drops down on Lilly and breaks its teeth when it tries to bite into one of her horns. I hear the screams of a few surviving guests in other rooms.

Vladawen runs room to room as I clear the hall. From most, he returns empty-handed, but he emerges at last with a man who looks old enough to have seen the Divine War firsthand. Immediately the charfiends scurry to surround them. Vladawen hands a chair leg to his charge and thrashes his way through the mob. He grabs one by the face, buries his index and ring fingers in the creature's eyes, and sticks his thumb in the creature's mouth. The charfiend bites down on his thumb, so Vladawen shouts what I assume to be an elvish profanity and rips the creature's lower jaw off with his free hand. Then he slams the creature's skull into the skulls of its brothers, using the convulsing creature as a shield to keep them away from the old man.

James Stewart

I feel it like a hammer to the gut when I realize that I'll never, ever fight well enough to kill this guy.

We make it to the stairs. On the landing that divides the two sections of steps, a single charfiend has a completely naked man trapped against the corner, afraid to advance through the fire. The creature takes taunting nips at the man's arms as he swings at it. Lilly rips a circular lamp mount off the wall. Her hand sizzles a bit and she clinches her teeth. She hurls the iron mount at the charfiend. It connects with the back of his head. There's a wet cracking sound and the beast falls. The naked guy gives her an ornate bow that seems ridiculous under the circumstances, yells something none of us can hear, then runs down the stairs.

We're about to follow, but we turn toward a howling from the other end of the hall. A charfiend, as big as a man, climbs in through the window and charges us at full speed. I raise my mace over my head and match his cry with my own. When he's close enough, I slam the ball of the mace onto the top of his head. Like a retreating turtle, his head sinks down into his shoulders.

Perhaps absorbing too much force from my blow, the floor collapses underneath us.

We land in a huge pile of hay in the stables beneath. A nice landing, except the hay's on fire. Lilly picks desperately at her tail, trying to snuff the flame. Vladawen bats at his burning hair with both hands. Burning elf hair stinks. My Hedrada robe is completely gone, lost in the conflagration, but my chain mail has kept me safe for the moment. It hurts like hell to fall in armor, but by the time the mail gets hot enough to melt, you've got more serious problems.

I dash to the doors of the stable and try to open them. Won't budge. "They've blocked the door from the outside!" I yell. Lilly bashes at the doors with her shoulder with the same result. She bangs on the door for a few seconds more

Three Dreams of Belsameth

before she falls to her knees coughing. I look to Vladawen for help. His hair's extinguished, but now he has two charfiends hanging on his back, their arms wrapped around his neck and their jaws close to his face.

I look around for another exit. I can't see anything through the flames except for the blocked doors that open to the street. I head toward the only wall that isn't completely ablaze and hop a short gate that holds back the visitor's mounts. Most have them have succumbed to the smoke. Half a dozen are fallen and still, one is dead standing up, and one lies on the ground panting out short, wheezing breaths. But one big bastard of horse, a spooked look in his eyes, still seems alert.

I kick open the gate and jump-mount the steed. I dig my heels into his sides. "Go! Go, fucker!" Nothing. The horse doesn't budge. I dig my heels in a bit deeper. Nothing. I raise my legs and slam them down, kicking the horse's chest from both sides. It snorts, but otherwise nothing. I dismount and move to the front of the horse. "Go!" I shout as I punch it in the face. "Go!" "Go!" Blood runs down its nose. "Go!" The horse bolts. I wrap my arms around its neck and manage to get one leg up over its body.

I try to steer the horse into the doors to no avail. The bastard runs dead ahead into the opposite side of the stable and crashes into a vertical support. In one blazing piece, the entire wall falls in on the Knight's Crossing tavern. Vladawen runs past me, the old man over one shoulder and Lilly over the other. I kick a half-dead charfiend in the back and follow him.

No one's in the tavern, no one alive anyway. Except for Drendari. She sits at a table, sipping from a tiny glass as the flames lick the air around her. She points to the ceiling. "You should get out here. This roof's about to collapse." Vladawen and I run past her. Vladawen lumbers out into the night with his heavy burden. I'm almost out, but Drendari stops me by yelling my name. I turn and she points to a man collapsed on the floor—the naked guy from the stairwell. "Take him. You'll need him." I drag him from Knight's Crossing and take gluttonous breaths of fresh air.

We sit outside on the ground, Vladawen and I gasping. Lilly regains consciousness and sits up. The naked man begins to cough and come to his senses. The old man that Vladawen rescued upstairs barely stirs.

In a few minutes, everyone but the old-timer is back on his or her feet. We help place the old man in a stretcher as Shelzar militiamen stream into the area, tending to the wounded, extinguishing the fire, killing those charfiends who escaped our swath of destruction. One squad works to pull a huge wagon with a missing wheel away from the doors of the stable. Pockets of strangers huddle together in the street, as does a small legion on onlookers. We watch the fire, thankful for having escaped it.

Vladawen

As the Shelzar militia rushes in to finish off the last of the charfiends, Knight's Crossing burns. The entire building, engulfed in flame, sends waves of heat over the circle of survivors I stand within. Drendari is here, as is a man with the holy standard of Hedrada inscribed in the breast of his armor—though I've never before seen a servant of Hedrada beat a horse. Also with us is the man from the staircase. Though he wears not a stitch, he holds himself with the most regal bearing—chin up, nose in the air, shoulders square, puffed chest. The last stranger is a woman with short, spiral horns that curl around her temples, and a frantic little tail. Something about her captivates me, though she is a hideous combination of human and beast. We lock eyes again. I try to conjure a

Three Dreams of Belsameth

picture of Avlana in my mind, but I can no longer remember what she looks like. To distract myself, I begin the introductions.

"I am Vladawen, Titanslayer and the last priest of That Which Abides."

"I am Lillatu, errant daughter of House Estlemeer."

"I'm Ezra, servant of Hedrada."

"I am Drendari, demigoddess of shadow."

"And I am Lord Gasslander of the Wexland Province in Darakeene. Never before has a man worn so little before company so distinguished." Lord Gasslander bows before each of us, taking an especially ostentatious bow before Drendari. "I know that you are who you say you are, for surely Lady Drendari would suffer no imitators. My wife is a devout disciple, my goddess."

"And you, my lord?"

Lord Gasslander shrugs and says, "All gods are worthy of reverence. To choose… well, I am not too picky in my piousness. No offense to the particular faiths so well represented in our midst." It takes me a second to realize that he's talking about Ezra and me; I can't stop looking at Lillatu. She gives me a little smile that lingers until the heads of everyone in the circle turn in the direction of Knight's Crossing as it finally collapses in a ball of fire.

Silhouetted by the flames, someone approaches in haste. Bare feet slap against the cobblestones. A sooty woman with charred hair, a gaudy silver necklace and nothing else approaches. She pokes Lord Gasslander in the chest.

"Where's my money?"

Drendari looks at Lord Gasslander and asks, "Your devout wife?"

"Sadly, no."

127

James Stewart

The naked woman shouts at the naked king, shoving her finger in his face, saliva flying as she screams. He offers a thousand apologies and promises remuneration. "I would reward you handsomely for your diligent attention, woman, but through fiery mishap my purse and I are forever separated. If you insist on being paid tonight, perhaps we can recover your wages once the flames diminish and the departed have been respectfully removed." The prostitute spits in his face and stomps off into the night. Lord Gasslander wipes her spittle from his face, never allowing his regal composure to drop.

Lillatu whispers to me. The sensation of her breath on my ear inspires thoughts I would not dare think were my all-seeing god awake and aware. "If he's spending the night with whores like that one, he is a cheap king indeed."

Lord Gasslander raises his finger into the air. "I have heard your slanderous whisperings, Lady Estlemeer, and I must plead now a worthy defense. It is true that, in Shelzar, one need never compromise on the quality of one's evening companions. Still, if you spent but a minute in the presence of my most beloved queen, you would understand that... gods save me! My gemgate!"

Lord Gasslander bolts toward the burning ruins of Knight's Crossing. Lillatu and I look at each other, then charge after him. I grab his left arm, Lillatu grabs his right, but still he struggles to run into the fire. Finally, he ceases his flailing and falls to his knees, weeping. "The stone, the stone, my precious gem! I am undone! Oh, the ways in which I am undone!" He stares into Lillatu's eyes with a pleading look. "Kind stranger, would you ram your pick through my ear?"

In the distance, Drendari and Ezra look as though they are arguing. Lillatu looks them, then at Lord Gasslander, then at me, shrugging. I pull the king to his feet. "Recover your composure, Lord Gasslander. End your theatrics and explain yourself."

Three Dreams of Belsameth

"My wife... Listen, my wife is a vile creature, a practitioner of the most loathsome necromancy. I assure you, this is not the hyperbolic complaint of a man who has endured too many years of nagging. I mean, quite literally, that she spends all of her time copying lines from books bound in human skin, in her chantry conjuring demons, neglecting entirely her wedded duties. She has become a pale, wicked thing. I thought that a summer in Shelzar would return the color to her cheeks, or at least allow me a worthwhile dalliance or two. I lost all hope of the former when she damned the souls of our attending staff with the curse of undeath, and now I have lost all chance of surviving the latter."

"What the hell are you talking about?" Lillatu says.

"Do you know of gemgates? Do you understand their operation?"

"I've seen one before."

"A gift to me from Minister Fratreli. With one gem anchored in a closet near my chambers—my queen and I have not shared quarters for years—I could slip out before the gates of our summer keep were locked. Then, the other gem in hand, I could open a portal that would return me to the confines of my keep before dawn, my wife none the wiser. The skeletons who watch the front gate seem impervious to bribes and will no doubt tell her of my passage, if I were I enter at this late hour. I suppose now that I am an exile. My beautiful queen is a woman of extremes; I fear I would join the legions of the undead in her service for this affront to our vows."

It's then that I feel Belsameth's second curse fall over me like a heavy blanket. I succumb to it gladly, a temptation I cannot resist. Everything I have been taught, everything I believe, I toss aside willfully for the sake of opportunity. Belsameth's mercenary blessing is upon me, and even as I realize that it is horrible and cruel I cannot let slip this chance to restore my god. "Lord Gasslander, you are king of the Wexland Province, yes?"

"Until my queen awakens, at least."

"And as ruler of the province you are also high priest of all its temples and churches?"

"Such has it always been in Darakeene. Now that Emperor Klum has united the provinces, the nine kings retain only nominal taxation rights and the duty to uphold the piousness of their subjects."

"But you are not 'picky' in your 'piousness.'"

"In Darakeene, all worships are officially respected. Why incite religious strife?"

"Darakeene's about to change. Wexland, anyway. I'll kill your wife for you, and you'll mandate that every temple in Wexland honor That Which Abides above all other gods."

Lord Gasslander immediately moves from his pathetic crouch back to his regal bearing. No longer covering himself, he points at me and declares me mad. "To be rid of my wife only to instigate a holy war? Offend the gods for the favor of one that can't hear my entreaties? This is not a good bargain, elf."

I stare into the king's eyes and move toward him until our noses touch. "I know something about deals like this. You have no choice. Risk a holy war, or join the unliving ranks of your queen's servants."

Lord Gasslander turns toward Drendari. "Lady in Shadow, have you heard this madness? Surely, the gods would be displeased?"

Drendari breaks off her argument and approaches the king with a vicious look. Now this little king, barely a king, a king in name only, has a Titanslayer and demigoddess in his face. Right in his face.

Three Dreams of Belsameth

"I have heard this madness, and I'll tell you what displeases the gods. Spinelessness. Irrationality. Mortals turning down their last chances at happiness. Take the elf's bargain. That Which Abides is much missed by his brothers and sisters. Bring him back to us, and your province will know our favor."

"And you'll be rid of your wife," Lillatu adds. "Vladawen, your cause arouses me to righteous fervor. Let me stand at your side and destroy this wicked queen."

"Me too," Ezra says. "I share Lilly's appreciation for all things elvish. And Hedrada compels me to repair that which has been sundered."

Ezra and Lillatu lead us to a small tenement on the outskirts of Shelzar's port district. We decide to rest for a few hours and make our assault in the hour before dawn. Ezra and Lillatu retire to their separate quarters. Lord Gasslander, after borrowing a shirt and britches, sits with me and describes the layout of his summer keep and complains some more about his wife, leaving no gruesome specific unmentioned. After our talk, he curls up by the fire and falls asleep instantly. Finally, Drendari and I can speak privately.

"It's time for me to leave you now, Vladawen. Your ambitions are on their way to realization. I wish you luck in restoring my brother to his former self. Do not trust my mother."

"I trust neither your mother nor her daughter. I know who unleashed those charfiends on me in my slumber. Interfere with me again, Drendari, and I shall add Godslayer to my list of titles."

Drendari kisses me on the forehead and gives me a look that I can't quite decipher. Perhaps among the gods it is an expression of nostalgia, longing even. She steps into shadow and is gone. I make my way to Lillatu's room and find her waiting for me, a red heat in the darkness.

James Stewart

Ezra

We wake an hour before dawn. While Lord Gasslander sleeps by the embers of the fire, Lilly, Vladawen and I prepare to kill his queen. I gather what implements still remain in my tenement—Lilly and I use it for a flophouse but don't keep it supplied beyond booze and a few preserves. I give Vladawen a change of clothes and a dented flail that served me well in my younger days.

Something about this job irks me. After all, I don't make money doing free hits. But it's in the execution of another hit. I might be conflicted, if the other hit wasn't five large and divinely bound with a contract from a goddess.

The three of us huddle in the alley behind my building. Lilly slips the gemgate out of her sleeve. She holds it aloft and speaks the command phrase. I feel the magnifying hum of the gem as she says the words.

"Whoring's done."

A portal rises from the dusty street without a sound. The portal is completely black. We cannot see what's on the other side. Vladawen steps through first. I follow, then Lilly.

We emerge in a dark closet barely large enough for the three of us. I can't see what's going on, but Lilly and Vladawen can see heat in the darkness. I hear Vladawen tell Lilly to listen through the door. "Nothing," she whispers.

Vladawen turns the handle and peaks into a hall. At the next door, 20 feet away, a corpse leans against the wall. I think someone's beaten us to the kill until its eyes open and it turns its head. It lowers a spear and advances upon us, silent but steady.

"Rebuke it," Vladawen says.

"You're the priest, you do it."

Three Dreams of Belsameth

"My god is dead. Do you even have a god?"

"Yes and no."

"I thought so."

Vladawen grabs the thing's spear and pulls, smashing the zombie against the wall. He moves down the spear as if he were climbing a rope, never releasing his hold. Then he grabs the creature's head on both sides and twists. He doesn't stop twisting until the head comes off. The corpse falls, truly dead.

No sooner does the decapitated corpse hit the ground than a horrible scream begins to echo through the hall. A choked wail, like a tornado passing through a small trumpet, bounces through the stone hall, echoing as whatever is screaming takes a breath before screaming again.

"What the hell is that?" Lilly asks.

Vladawen answers. "That's his wife."

Vladawen

I lead Ezra and Lillatu through the keep, following the directions that Lord Gasslander gave me. We make our way toward the north tower, Ezra decapitating zombies with his mace, me with my flail. We ascend the spiraling staircase, the wailing in the keep growing louder with every step. We stop at a round wooden door. On the other side is Queen Gasslander.

I'm about the wreck the door when Lillatu stops me. "They call you the Titanslayer for a reason, right?"

"Have you ever heard of the titan Chern?"

"Yes."

"I swam in through his eye, gouged my way down his throat and took a bite out of his black heart."

"Then let's go."

Lilly reaches out to the brass handle in the center of the door and pushes. As soon as we open the door, the unearthly keening ends. On the other side of the door is a library. Books line the walls. Shelves reach up into the darkness above. At a table, in the light of a single burning candle, sits an ashen lady. Even with the yellow candlelight cloaking her face, Queen Gasslander resembles an immaculate corpse. A bit pale, no decay and definitely dead.

She looks into my eyes and I cannot move. Ezra and Lillatu freeze beside me. She places a bookmark in the volume before her. She rises from her seat and approaches Ezra. She looks him up and down, then moves on with disappointed eyes to Lillatu. After studying her for a moment, the languid corpse approaches me. She does not frown at me. She doesn't smile either, but her eyebrows relax and, from her expression, she seems almost at peace.

"Everything perfect desires death. My goddess sent me a dream, promising a destruction worthy of me. Thank you, Titanslayer."

Ezra

As soon as Queen Gasslander falls, I raise my mace and charge at Vladawen. I don't even give him time to take a breath. He turns, grabs the shaft of my mace, and stares in my eyes. For the first time since I met him, I see Vladawen smile. I remember Drendari's words from the temple in Termana: a boot stomping on roaches.

"You're no priest," he says.

I don't know how to react, but it turns out that I don't have to. I feel a prick between my shoulder blades. I feel the weakness first in my knees, then in my arms. My hands loosen. My mace clatters to the ground. I've seen Lilly kill a hundred times, and I always imagined that her pick was more painful. All along, it was just a little prick.

I try to say something. Nothing comes out but a bubble of blood. I fall to the ground. I'm dying, and my eyes are open. Lilly steps over me, my blood dripping off the tip of her ice pick. She reaches her arms around Vladawen and embraces him, hugging her face to his chest. I can't quite hear what they say to one another as they rock together in the near-darkness. I see Lilly's lips moving. I see the tears as she closes her eyes. She nods with her cheek against his chest, leaning against him for support.

But when I close my eyes for the last time I can hear their every word perfectly. Lilly says, "I'm so sorry, Vladawen. I have a contract."

I hear a thump, a thump of dead weight falling to the ground. With the contract fulfilled, I die.

Vladawen

"Dying again, Titanslayer? You're becoming predictable."

Since leaving my temple, the dark side of the moon has become my most constant landscape. An arc of light at the horizon, Belsameth on her basalt throne. The difference this time is that Drendari is here. She sits on sharp rocks at the left hand of the Queen of Lies; she looks very much like a little girl who has just been scolded by her mother. At her right hand sits the ghost of Ezra, who looks very much like a little boy who just wagered his last marble and lost.

Belsameth smiles at me with many mouths. "How could I have known that my daughter was so jealous of your love for that cow from Estlemeer? It really is quite unbreakable. A love to be sung by bards until the titans rise again. How could I know that she'd be so jealous that she'd put out a contract on you? It is understandable for a goddess of shadow—excuse me, a demigoddess—to be jealous of the goddess of darkness itself, but for her to mix up my new elvish champion in her designs? Perhaps if she had won you, Titanslayer, she would have been a little less 'demi.' Still, an awful business."

"How could she be jealous? I never met Lillatu before you sent her to kill me."

"I have many lovers across the Scarred Lands," Drendari says. "Do you think there are no fortune tellers or prognosticators among them?"

Belsameth reaches down with her taloned foot and caresses her daughter's hair. "It must have been an oversight on my part, like when I sent that storm screaming out of the Blood Sea. Or when I unlocked the cages of those charfiends. Dreadful."

I hold my tongue just for a moment. I'm ready to lunge at her, to pull at her filthy carapace until I hit bone. But I won't give her the satisfaction. In death, perhaps I have found some restraint. "If you keep this up, Mother of Deceit, I might have to find myself a new patron."

Belsameth's cackle echoes across the surface of the moon. "There's no new patrons to be found in my domain, I'm afraid. Don't forget, you're dead."

"Am I to spend eternity with the three of you? Surely I have lived a better life than that."

"No, you'll go back to Scarn, with another of my blessings in your pocket."

"I don't want any more of your blessings. I've given That Which Abides new temples in Darakeene. Now let me die."

Ezra stands up. "Fuck him if he doesn't want a second chance. I'll go back."

Three Dreams of Belsameth

Drendari gives Ezra a look of disgust. "Silence, you ghost of a false priest." Ezra sits back down and mutters to himself in a most pathetic and off-putting way.

"Can you chance that Lord Gasslander will keep his word? Even if he does, can the temples of That Which Abides—ah, I tire of euphemisms, find a name for him, will you?—withstand the reprisals against them that are sure to follow Gasslander's forced conversion? Your new faith is so small, Vladawen. Who will champion it?"

"Wait." Ezra stands up, gesticulating wildly. "Just wait. He said he doesn't want to go back. Send me back. I'll take a blessing!"

"Take a vow of silence, false priest," I say.

"Can I have this ghost, mother?" asks Drendari.

"Absolutely. So what's it to be, Vladawen? Death or my blessing?"

"Let's hear the blessing."

Belsameth brings her finger to one of her mouths. She leans her head back on her throne and begins to mull over the question. "This one is simple. You will find one of your weapons, but not the other."

"No more games, Belsameth. If I agree to this, you must play fair. You can't keep putting me in mortal danger only to rescue me and behave as though it is a favor." For once, Belsameth loses her lascivious expression. The corners of her mouth drop, and she takes on a somber countenance. It really is an ugly look.

"Do not try to manipulate me, Titanslayer. This is the dark side of the moon. You're not the one in charge here."

"What do you mean? You're the most gullible, malleable creature I've ever encountered. You can kill me now, but you'll have no more entertainment from me. You'll have the wait for another Titanslayer to spend 150 years brooding in the darkness. Even if you let me die, I'll still have accomplished something. You think you've caused me any pain that I haven't felt before, a thousand times worse? Goddess, you're nothing. You've accomplished nothing. Now resurrect me and be quick about it."

"Yes, if the conversion of Wexland takes, you'll have accomplished something. But one grain of sand does not make a beach. You have such a long way to go. Vladawen, such a long, long way to go. A shame that elves no longer live forever, is it not?"

"I'll live long enough. By the way, I'll find both my weapons. You can keep the boots, Drendari. I'll talk to you soon about the rest."

"How bold this mortal elf!" In a few breaths, Belsameth has gone from wicked to serious to pissed. "You may be a Titanslayer, but the army that helped you earn that title is nowhere to be seen. And there are many gods that can claim to be Titanslayers themselves, me among them. Don't threaten my daughter as if you're actually dangerous."

"One way to find out, Belsameth."

I open my eyes somewhere else. My ribs feel pulverized and there's a hole in my back, but I'm alive. The first thing I see is Lillatu with her ice pick poised at her throat, her face red and wet as she considers which is the better of the two paths she can take.

An image of Avlana flashes through my mind. I see her in a long-gone autumn before the Divine War, walking with me through the silver streets of Termana. A spot in my back stings with pain as I sit up and place a hand on Lillatu's shoulder.

"Don't."

Merrin's Tale
By Keith Sloan

Keith Sloan

The gray-hooded figure stole furtively up the empty street of the town. It was that vague part of the night, after those with legitimate business had gone to their homes for the evening, but before the drunken revelers had left the taverns or been thrown out into the street. It was a thief's hour.

Moving amongst dim shadows cast by the occasional torch or fire, the small shape moved like a cat and passed unseen alongside a ramshackle building across the street from a gray stone tower. The figure peered about the place, then faded silently into the darkness along the wall. A sound of shuffling feet nearby caused the figure to instantly produce a dagger and assume a defensive crouch.

"Jumpy tonight, aren't you?" whispered a new figure emerging from the deep shadows mere feet from the first figure.

"No, not at all," whispered the first unconvincingly.

The two short figures faced one another in the darkness. The first removed her hood, revealing a young woman with long brown hair tied back with a leather thong and an attractive, perhaps even beautiful, face with slight Elven features. "I merely did not see you, Haldir."

The second figure chuckled quietly as he removed his own black hood. Haldir was a Halfling, though tall for his race, with curly brown hair and a ruddy complexion when seen in the light. "That bodes well for our business this night, Merrin. Did you bring the rope?"

"Of course!" she replied quietly but with a flicker of annoyance from having been startled. She paused and looked at the Halfling, a mere foot beneath her own five-foot height. "I told you to wear gray, not black. You'll stand out terribly against the gray stone!"

"You did not see me, girl!" he chided in a low whisper. "And besides, black is much more in keeping with our profession."

Merrin's Tale

Merrin relaxed. "Mayhap, but there are so many famous people called 'the Black' already; Korlax the Black, the Black Shadow. You know. Gray would be unique. The Gray Cat would suit me fine. The Gray Cat—the most dread thief in all Venir, or even all Ghelspad!" She stared past the Halfling, becoming lost in a daydream.

Haldir motioned her to lower her voice. "More like the Gray Prisoner if you keep making so much noise. Sometimes I think you are more interested in fame, or infamy, than loot. What's wrong with you?" He grabbed her arm to bring her out of the reverie she had slipped into. "Come, Gray Dustheap, we have a tower to pillage."

Merrin nodded, her fantasy over. The two quietly prepared a rope and grappling hook, carefully wrapping the hook with cloth to minimize noise. Nodding to Merrin, Haldir crossed the street quickly, the hook already swinging from the rope in his hand. As he neared the tower, he let fly the hook and rope. It sailed easily over a balcony rail some thirty feet above and landed with a dull thud. He tugged hard once and the hook held.

Haldir looked over his shoulder and winked, though Merrin could not see it. The Halfling began shimmying up the rope along the wall. Merrin shook her head. *I told the fool his black cloak would stick out badly against the gray stone.* As he neared the top, she ran across the road and followed him up the rope.

She easily reached the balcony in seconds. There was a stout wooden door with iron bindings leading into the tower, though no windows except for a few dark slits further above them, all too narrow even for the small thieves. They had carefully cased this tower for days, and she knew every detail of the outside of this place better than her own hovel at that nameless inn she called home for the moment.

Haldir had already produced a narrow wire tool and was working at the door's simple latch. Within seconds, there was a dull scrape and the Halfling pushed the door slowly open. This time, Merrin was able to see the Halfling's wink and ridiculous grin.

Merrin followed him into the tower's third of what they believed to be five levels. From their observations, the only inhabitants were a few servants and the owner, an old man. The locals whispered he was Magi, but nobody they had spoken with had ever seen him cast the smallest spell. Everyone did agree, however, that he was undoubtedly wealthy and quite reclusive.

The two thieves moved into a well-furnished hallway, only dimly visible. Despite the darkness, Merrin's nose twitched at the dust they both kicked up. Obviously they were in a disused corridor.

Haldir was moving ahead into the tower now, already grabbing small objects and stuffing them into a sack at his belt. Merrin followed suit, though in the darkness she was not at all sure what she was taking. She had lied to Haldir about her experience in thievery, telling him she was a skilled burglar. In truth, she was little more than a pickpocket and a snatch-thief, albeit a very good one, with dreams of becoming a legend like Mallian the Cutpurse, or Kurlak the Invisible.

As Merrin was considering a particularly heavy statuette she had just picked up, she bumped into Haldir's back. "Sorry..." she started to whisper, but was cut off by a slight hiss from the Halfling. In an instant, she saw his concern—a dim, flickering light growing ahead of them out of the darkness. Someone with a candle was coming up the staircase.

Merrin could now see Haldir's silhouette clearly in the growing light. The Halfling motioned her back into an alcove they had passed with a statue in it. For an instant, Merrin considered running back to the balcony and escaping, but Haldir put his hand on her arm and shoved

Merrin's Tale

her quickly into the alcove. Torn by indecision and fear, she hesitated, and then the figure carrying the candle was at the top of the stairs.

It was definitely the tower's owner, though she had seen the old man only once during her surveillance of the place, and that but briefly. He was walking towards the balcony door, which Haldir had wisely shut after they entered. A few seconds seemed like a lifetime for Merrin, who tried to become invisible beside Haldir and behind the statue of a figure in armor. A hundred evil thoughts passed through Merrin's mind, and she wondered if life as a Mage's toad would suit her.

But as the old man passed, she saw that he was intently watching the floor and did not even peer into the alcove. She nearly sighed with relief until she saw what had his attention—their confused footprints in the dust. He was attempting to track them. She saw Haldir's look of fear. He had realized their plight as well. The Halfling gestured down the stairs and back to the balcony, then shrugged his shoulders, seeking for her ideas on what to do. She responded with a shrug of her own.

"Ahem," came a deep voice from very close by. Both thieves turned at once to the old man who had quietly appeared before the alcove, his candle placed on a nearby dusty table. "What have we here?"

Haldir drew his dagger and gave the old man his most defiant glare. Merrin drew her own blade more slowly. She had dreams of becoming a great thief, not an assassin or murderer. The old man did not move, but began to chant in a strange voice. Suddenly, a great heat erupted from him, forcing the thieves as far back into the alcove as they could go. *The old man is Magi*, thought Merrin.

Haldir cocked his hand back to throw his dagger, but froze in mid-throw, his dagger falling helplessly to the floor. Merrin felt her own muscles go tight, and she found herself paralyzed. The wizard, still radiating an intense heat, plucked Merrin's dagger from her hand and tossed it into the corridor.

"Thieves? How convenient. Come with me." The mage abruptly turned and walked away towards the stairs he had ascended. Compelled by the spell he had cast upon them, Merrin and Haldir were forced to follow, though both fought their captivity and moved along jerkily.

The mage led them down several stairs and corridors to a small study. Books lined shelves along the walls, more than either thief had ever seen. To the rear of the study, an opening led into a dimly lit chamber that appeared to be a laboratory of some sort. The mage sat in a leather chair behind a desk, the heat from his body having largely dissipated. He looked them over for a few moments, and spoke. "Your appearance here is most fortuitous, though perhaps not for you two." He chuckled slightly.

"I have need of a thief, and had been contemplating how to locate one I could persuade to perform a task for me. One of you will now do this for me. The other I shall keep as hostage pending a successful quest."

"Some miles north of Gelion, in the Haggard Hills, there is a cave inhabited by a Cavern Hag, one of those most dread she-beasts of the wastes. Secreted in this Hag's lair is said to be a mithril-bound box containing three vials of Titan's Blood, that wondrous relic of the defeated ones. I desire you to steal for me those vials; I have need of them for my work. In return, I shall set you both free and even reward you with some coin." He paused. "Alternatively, I can have you both flogged to death by the town guardsmen." The mage looked them both over carefully, considering each of them. He then waved his hand and muttered indecipherable words. Suddenly, Merrin felt herself released from the spell. She did not even consider fleeing.

Merrin's Tale

"You, girl, shall go. Mayhap you would do better if the Hag were to catch you, though in truth it might be even worse. Heed me. If you do not return in three nights, I shall have your partner put to death, and you as well if you have merely fled and not already been slain or taken by the Hag."

The mage handed her a small slip of parchment. "Here is a map to the Hag's lair. Can you read?" Merrin nodded. "Good. I have not been there personally and have no desire to do so. Whatever happens, do not speak with the Hag. Her words will be designed to confuse and trap you. Go now, and do not tarry."

Merrin was too much in shock to even ask questions. She glanced at Haldir, who despite the spell, looked to her with imploring eyes. She felt like she would cry, but refused to do so in front of the mage. The old man escorted her to the front door, leaving Haldir behind, and let her out the front door. "Three days. No more," he said simply as he shut the door on her, leaving her back in the night outside the tower.

She considered her plight for a few minutes, whether to flee and abandon Haldir, or climb back into the tower and rescue him. The first she could not do and the second seemed impossible. She started to sob, and began walking down the street. As she often did under stress, she began talking to herself. "Madriel's Mercy! How could this have happened? How can I steal something from a Hag's lair when I can't even rob an old man in town? I could run, but Haldir would be killed. This is my fault!" The fact that Haldir had recruited *her* was forgotten.

She was quite scared, nearly as afraid as the night she saw her family massacred, the night she had hidden and done nothing. That event had been the genesis of her vow to Drendari of the Shadows to never be weak and helpless again, no matter the cost. She felt her resolve crumbling, her vow slipping away.

As she continued to mumble to herself, she made her way to the tavern where she had a small, flea-infested room. Still sobbing, she climbed into bed and, miraculously, fell asleep.

The next morning Merrin awoke with many of her doubts gone. She had dreamed of a successful quest and the release of a grateful Haldir. Her exploits had become the stuff of legend, and she was known as the Silent Slayer for defeating the Hag in combat. Heartened by this vision, she dressed in her traveling gear and made her way downstairs to the tavern's common room. She purchased a few days food and a wineskin with most of her remaining coins from the sour-faced woman who ran the place.

Armed only with her spare dagger, she left the tavern into the bustling streets of Gelion. Intent on her quest, she barely noticed her surroundings, where normally she would be eyeing potential targets. The occasional greeting of someone she had met during her few weeks here, or the cries of hawkers, went unheeded.

She walked out of the open gates of the town and immediately turned north towards the hills. One soldier standing watch looked at her for a few moments then glanced at a comrade, who merely shrugged. There was nothing north of the town except dangerous wilderness; nobody ever went that way.

Merrin spent the better part of the day following the wizard's map into the Haggard Hills. The terrain quickly grew rough as she proceeded. There were no trails and only occasional game paths here. These hills were the haunt of fell creatures, even this close to Gelion, but she saw none that day. Fortunately for the young thief, the map had her follow a small brook, so she found it quite easy to avoid

Merrin's Tale

becoming lost. A born town-dweller, she had little practical wilderness survival skill.

As the sun set after a long day of climbing, Merrin realized she could not reach the Hag's lair by sunset. She continued onwards a short way with an eye towards a campsite, and eventually settled for a small hollow somewhat removed from the brook. After a brief, cold meal she settled down to sleep. The silence and openness of the outdoors was beginning to wear on her, and she missed the noise and closed streets of the town.

Her dreams were deeply troubling. Gone were the pleasant dreams of success. Instead, Merrin found her dream-self being stalked in a strange wilderness. A voice continually whispered words of comfort, but she knew these to be lies meant to trap her. She continued to flee, but felt pursuit closing in. She was nearly caught.

She awoke with a start. It was at least an hour before sunrise and Merrin shivered in the pre-dawn chill. The lingering fear of the dream remained with her, but she drew several deep breaths and steeled herself to continue. She rose, ate half of her remaining rations and drank not a little of her wine. Then, as the sky began to lighten, she began the final part of her journey.

As dawn broke, she came upon a large standing stone. Strange runes covered the twenty-foot high menhir, and her map indicated this was some sort of ancient Slarecian marker stone. More importantly, it marked the proximity to the Cavern Hag's lair. In stories she heard in her youth, such creatures lived in dank caverns and were often defeated by wily children. In reality, other stories told of how they ate humans and were nearly invincible sorceresses that hated all living things, especially humanity, from which they sprang.

Merrin began to search the area carefully. Within minutes, she spotted a cave a hundred yards or so to the east at the base of a steep, rocky hill. Above the hill she could see a dull haze and smoke rising from fissures in the rocks above the cave. Merrin spent over two hours circling the hill and climbing up the backside of it, periodically watching the cave for activity and looking for alternate entrances. All she found were numerous old bones scattered about and a foul reek emitting from the cave. The rock fissures apparently used as chimneys were far too small for someone of even her size to climb down.

She saw no alternative to the front entrance. Despairing, Merrin said a short prayer to Drendari, Mistress of Shadows, asking for aid. This comforted her greatly, as did remembering how Haldir had befriended her shortly after arriving in Gelion. Though many despised Halflings, she did not, probably because she identified with their under-dog status. With a deep breath, she began moving as stealthily as she could from rock to rock towards the cavern mouth.

From twenty feet away she could see some slight distance into the cave. It was quite tall, possibly fifteen feet or more. Though unlit, it was obviously natural and not hewn by hand. Further, it sloped downwards as far as Merrin could see.

"Madriel show mercy," she whispered. Quickly, she ran the open distance to the rock face adjacent to the entrance at a crouch to avoid being seen by any watching eyes in the darkness. Once alongside the entrance, she slipped into the cave and hugged the right wall, careful not to silhouette herself against the entrance. She kept her right hand touching the rough stone at all times.

Strangely, she felt more comfortable now that she was in the darkness of the cave and out of the sunlight, despite the foul odor that nearly made her gag. The cave ran roughly straight for a time and always downwards at a moderate slope. It quickly grew very dark, but she did not

Merrin's Tale

risk a light as she trusted her eyes and other senses to adjust to the darkness. The sandy floor of the cave was a great boon to her, as it allowed her to move silently. She came to an opening along the right wall and decided to take it. She knew that if one hand never left a wall, she could always backtrack out of even the most confusing maze.

The new passage was level and smelled slightly of smoke, an improvement over the foul reek of the other passageway. Soon she saw the ruddy glow of a fire ahead. With the greatest care, Merrin continued ahead. The passage opened into a very large cavern, at the center of which was a large fire pit ringed with rough stones, a huge cauldron suspended over it. Apparently a kitchen, the cavern was at least thirty feet tall at its apex but was somewhat dome-shaped. At least two other entrances were visible, as was a fissure above that acted as a chimney. All manner of items were hanging about—plants, dead animals, even something that could have once been a goblin, though Merrin could not be sure. Other items littered the floor, primarily bones, but Merrin was grateful that the fire's deep shadows made identifying most impossible. The sight sickened her, but since the place seemed unoccupied at the moment, she began searching through the cave for the mithril-bound box.

Merrin had not been searching for more than a minute when she froze—dull footsteps were approaching. She quickly ducked behind a large pile of rotting vegetables and wormed her way beneath some of them. She barely dared to breath. In her fear-choked mind came unbidden the thought, *Merrin the Gray does not hide in rubbish.*

Buried in the filth, Merrin was still able to see the Hag as she entered the cavern. The creature was immense, a full ten feet tall, though much like an ancient crone in appearance. Her skin had an odd hue to it, much like old, dried leather or weathered stone, and hung loosely upon a gaunt frame. Her claw-like hands picked fitfully at the tattered skins she wore as a crude sort of clothes. Her teeth were long and sharp, though yellow and rotten. Merrin also noted that the Hag's eyes had grown shut—she was undoubtedly blind. For a moment, Merrin felt that she might finally have some good luck. Then, the Hag starting sniffing around the cavern.

Suddenly, the Hag turned and faced Merrin's general vicinity and cackled with a shrill, booming voice. "I can smell your air, girl child. I know you are here. Don't be afraid of Grandmother, little one. I won't harm you." Merrin remained motionless with terror as the Hag began to sniff again and move in her direction.

Without warning, something brushed Merrin's arm. She shrieked, jumping free of the rotting vegetables. A rat as large as a dog was at her side, nudging her with its hideous head. The Hag cackled hysterically at Merrin's distress. "Did my pet frighten you, girl? He won't harm you unless I let him." The Hag now stood a few feet from Merrin, who was convinced the Hag knew exactly where she stood despite the creature's obvious blindness. Merrin remained as silent and motionless as she could, her dagger in her hand, while the giant rat snuffled around her feet.

"I smell your steel and your fear, dearie. And, I dreamed of you last night. Don't fret. Grandmother will not harm you unless you disobey her. Now come, what is your name and how did you find your way to your Grandmother?" The Hag's fetid breath almost caused Merrin to faint, but she managed to keep from panicking.

"I am Merrin the Gray, and I was lost and hungry. I did not mean to intrude... Grandmother." She said the last reluctantly.

"Eh? Lost? Not so, child. Mother Mormo sent you to me. I can smell your ambition, your desires. Your visit is no accident. I am to be your guide in Mother Mormo's

Merrin's Tale

ways. She has blessed me for my deeds with a companion for my delight. I have much to teach you."

Merrin did not like this talk, though it made little sense to her. The Hag was obviously insane. The Titan Mormo had been literally cut to pieces in the great war and her parts scattered widely so that she might never be reborn. Still, the Hag seemed more interested in adopting a "granddaughter" than in harming the thief. In this, Merrin saw the seeds of opportunity.

The Hag started to mutter to herself, while the giant rat tried to nuzzle Merrin's leg. She suppressed her revulsion and concentrated on the Hag.

"I sense your fear waning somewhat, my granddaughter. That is good. Fear is for our enemies, those that seek to harm or reject us." The Hag paused a moment. "But yes, you said you were hungry. That is very good. Your Grandmother has a special stew for you, yes, very special indeed." She cackled again and shuffled back up the passage she had first come from.

Merrin, as if released from another holding spell, looked towards the way she had come in and considered fleeing. However, the giant rat nipping at her tunic dissuaded her from this. She swatted it away gently with her dagger, but this seemed to make the creature more insistent on gnawing on her clothing. She kicked it with increasing force as it grew more aggressive and made to run when the Hag returned, mumbling softly. In her hands was a small box grimed with unidentifiable material.

"I see Little Gaurak wants to play." She cackled again. "Fret not, granddaughter, he obeys my will. Now, to break your fast—your Grandmother's special stew."

The Hag set the box down across the cavern from Merrin on a flat stone that served as a table. She took a crude wooden bowl from a pile on the same table and ladled some broth from the great cauldron over the fire. She mumbled incessantly, apparently used to talking only to herself, or her "Little Gaurak." The Hag picked seemingly random bits of material - animal, vegetable, and unidentifiable - and mixed these into the broth.

After several minutes of watching the Hag prepare her stew, Merrin almost forgot the creature was blind. She moved without err and Merrin supposed the Hag would be a fearsome opponent in total darkness. She continued to watch without moving, as the giant rat now had lost interest in her and shifted to rooting through the pile of rotting vegetables.

"Almost, almost, granddaughter," the Hag said. "Grandmother just has to add her special ingredient. Yes, most special. Indeed, yes," she said, trailing off incoherently. Merrin saw her set the bowl on the stone table and pick up the small box she had carried out earlier. Opening it, the thief saw the Hag withdraw a vial of dark liquid—the Titan's Blood!

"Just a bit, dearie. Yes, very little for you, for now. More later, maybe. Yes, more later. Our Mother Mormo's very own. For you, indeed, yes," she babbled, pouring a single drop of the liquid into the bowl of stew. She replaced the vial in the box and shut it, leaving it on the table.

Turning to Merrin, the Hag walked across the cavern and handed her the bowl. Merrin shook slightly at the proximity of the Hag, almost dropping her dagger as she saw the Hag's stone-like skin and deadly demeanor. The stew smelled oddly unpleasant, though not rancid. It steamed heavily, obviously still quite hot. The fumes made her light-headed and dreamy.

"Drink, granddaughter. This will make you strong. Make you tall, like your Grandmother. Yes, it will make you powerful!" She said the last word with great emphasis, startling Merrin with her intensity. "Those that have harmed you, that laughed at you, that turned their backs

Merrin's Tale

on you. They will be crushed under your heel. Your Grandmother will show you how. Yes. She will teach you great magicks. She will make them fear you. They will not hate you anymore. Only fear. And then you will kill them all!"

The Hag's sudden and fierce intensity was unnerving Merrin. Raving about killing and destruction, the creature moved about the cavern, though Merrin was unsure at whom the Hag's furious outburst was directed. Strange thoughts filled her mind from the soup-fumes, thoughts of power and the security it would bring her. She looked again into the bowl, and froze—some sort of eyeball was floating in it. Her revulsion nearly caused her drop the bowl, but also served to clear her mind and settle her on a course of action.

"Grandmother? May I have another bowl, please?" asked Merrin in her most innocent voice.

"Eh, what's that?" The ravings stopped. "You want more you say, dearie? Done so soon? I did not hear you drink your first bowl down. More already? That is quite good, dearie, quite good indeed. Yes, another bowl." The Hag took another bowl from the table and moved to fill it from the cauldron once more. She seemed almost jovial, despite the madness of a few moments before.

Without pause to consider, Merrin threw her stew into the nearby rat's face while she launched herself at the Hag, dagger extended. She impacted the Hag just as the creature stiffened at the piercing wail of the scalded rat. Though only half the height of the Hag and of far less weight, the momentum of her desperate leap managed to nudge the Hag into the edge of the fire, and her arm into the pot of stew. Merrin's dagger merely skittered harmlessly off the Hag's stone-like skin and did nothing.

The Hag howled in pain and rage from the boiling stew as her tattered clothing caught fire. Merrin did not hesitate, but ran around the fire to grab the box and headed for the passage from which she had entered. As she exited the Hag's kitchen, Merrin thought the Hag's screaming and the giant rat's wailing would deafen her. She ran up the corridor, her left hand brushing the wall to guide her as she left the dim firelight behind.

Suddenly, the light of the fire was eclipsed, but Merrin did not pause to look at the Hag she knew was in pursuit. "Vile traitor! I shall consume you for a year and a day and not let you die," wailed the Hag as she sought to catch Merrin. Despite her large size relative to the cave, the Hag moved much faster than the small thief.

But Merrin made it to the main passage a dozen yards in front of the Hag and turned towards the dim light and open air above. Merrin fled upwards, but could hear the Hag now very close behind. She risked a quick look back and saw the Hag mere feet behind her. She would be caught in moments.

Merrin, eyes wide with fear, suddenly dropped to a sideways crouch on the passage floor. The Hag, intent on chasing her prey, did not react quickly enough and ran into Merrin, tripping over her. Merrin flew sideways from the impact, her side in agony from the Hag's stony foot. The Hag fell forward, her face impacting on the irregular stone side of the passageway.

Despite her pain, Merrin leapt to her feet and began to run again. The Hag reached for her leg, but only came away with a bit of gray fabric. Merrin did not look back again, but continued to run into the daylight, not stopping even then.

She ran for several minutes in the beautifully fresh air, and smiled despite the pain from what were probably several broken ribs. A booming voice brought her up short. "Spawn of filth. Know you that I will find you, and I will take you. But I will not kill you. Oh, no. I will prepare for

Merrin's Tale

you such anguish as our Mother Mormo endures. You cannot escape me forever, gods-lackey! I curse you in the Mother's name!" The intense hatred in the Hag's voice sent a chill down Merrin's spine, and would often haunt her normal dreams of fame and glory in months and years to come. Merrin shuddered, and continued south towards Gelion.

Merrin swallowed once as she rapped upon the tower door. Within moments, it swung silently open. The mage was there before her.

"Master wizard, your vials'" she said simply.

The mage betrayed the slightest hint of surprise in his eyes, but otherwise was all business. "I'll take those," he said. Merrin gave him the box and he quickly opened it. Gently, he took out each vial and held it up to the light from his doorway, slowly considering each one. After replacing the last vial, he gently shut the case and looked back at Merrin.

"It seems you were more resourceful, or lucky, than I expected of you. Well done." He cracked a broad smile. "You and the Halfling are free to go. In fact, the Halfling has been making a mess of my study, looking at my books and never replacing them on their shelves..."

"Merrin!" came Haldir's shout. The Halfling had just rounded a corner and spied his friend. He seemed in good health and in good spirits—he had spilled some of the latter on his tunic. "It is good to see you," he said, hugging her fiercely. "Pelenore is a decent host and free with his wine, but you are a sight for sore eyes."

"And you are a sight for sore ribs," she said wincing in pain. "I am glad you have not been flogged to death, either."

"Please, enter and be welcome," sail the wizard Pelenore. "But don't take anything!"

"We won't," said both thieves in unison.

"You would not really have had us put to death, would you?" asked Haldir.

"I sent your friend on a suicidal quest, did I not?" the old man said simply.

"Mayhap we had better leave..." said Haldir, his smile fading.

"Fear not, I promised coin for success, and this young girl could use a healing draught." The wizard motioned to the hastily rigged bandage about her side. He led them into his tower and shut the door.

"Could you not stay on in Gelion?" asked Haldir. The two thieves stood at the town gates.

Merrin smiled. "I can not, Haldir. Gelion has been good enough to me," she said, petting her fat purse, "but I feel the need to move on." Merrin had told Pelenore and Haldir the story of her adventure, but had left out the Hag's final curses. For some reason she could not fathom, she was ashamed and afraid of what had been said, and wanted to move on. Most disturbingly, she did not tell them that, for the briefest moment as the soup-fumes overcame her, she considered drinking the Hag's potion and becoming truly powerful, even at the cost of her humanity.

"Well, I for one will miss you, girl. May the gods speed you safely on your way and bring you back to visit me someday."

"Mayhap they will," she said dreamily. With a final hug, she set out to the south and did not look back, not wanting Haldir to see her tears. Merrin the Gray did not cry.

A Game of Silk and Mirrors

By Eric Griffin

"Harder!" Meerlah gasped past clenched teeth. She took a stumbling half step forward, nearly falling. It was only the cords binding her that kept her upright. Her back arched beneath the weight of the foot firmly planted at the base of her spine. That pain was nothing, however, next to the excruciating constriction across her breasts and ribs.

"Mistress, I..." the young woman fumbled and blushed. Anise had heard the whisperings, of course. Of the fate that had befallen each of Meerlah's long line of "confidentes." But she could hardly have credited those wild tales before tonight. Before she herself had been singled out for initiation into the mysteries of the lady's boudoir.

That offer had filled Anise with an ill-defined trepidation—a feeling that was a mixture of two parts cold panic, one part the allure of the forbidden, one part scandalized curiosity. There was never any real question whether or not she would accept the lady's invitation to her chamber. What the mistress wanted, the mistress got.

Anise's grip on the silken cords slackened.

"Damn you for a wilting flower, I said 'Tighter!'" Meerlah barked. "Now one more time. Ready, set..."

Anise paled, her hands trembling on the cords. She closed her eyes, muttering a silent prayer, and heaved as if her very life depended upon it.

Meerlah drew in a sharp breath, a grimace of pain contorting her face. At the sight, Anise nearly lost her hastily-marshaled courage. "I'm sorry, my lady. I..."

Her mistress cut her off abruptly with a flat slash of one bejeweled hand. "Now lash it off—and quickly!"

Anise was close to tears as her usually deft fingers fumbled with the hooks and eyes. There. She stepped quickly back, bowing her head nearly to the floor as the lady wheeled upon her.

Meerlah seemed a good half-foot taller. Her back was as straight and severe as a razor. Her shoulders were drawn back regally. Anise half expected dark wings to unfurl from them.

The lady fixed Anise with a piercing glare that pinned her wriggling to the floor. She tugged with both fists at the waist of the tight-fitting whalebone *corsetti*. The constricting undergarment seemed more snug than her own skin. It did not so much as budge under her determined tugging and stretching.

"This will have to do, I suppose," Meerlah scolded. "I trust you will be quicker about it the next time. Now fetch me the turquoise promenade gown. With any luck we might complete my hair before midnight."

"The next time?" Anise mumbled wretchedly, fighting back tears. She winced realizing that she had voiced the though aloud. She tensed for a blow.

Meerlah saw the girl flinch and stopped abruptly as if she herself had been struck. The avenging angel seemed to recede a pace. The threat of storm in her eyes was replaced by a look of concern.

"I'm sorry," Meerlah said in a quieter voice. "I guess I'm a bit on edge tonight. My first night back at court," she said, as if that explained everything. She shrugged apologetically. "And this damned *corsetti!* I've worn boiled leather breastplates that were more comfortable than this."

Anise managed an uncomfortable smile, uncertain whether she was being mocked. "Armor, my lady? Surely you are having some small jest at my expense. No one would dare raise a hand to a Lady of the Mirror Court of Vashon. It is unthinkable. It is..."

"If you had seen the battle leathers that I arrived in you might think differently." Meerlah smiled and wrinkled her nose at the thought of them. "They were so trail-worn and blade-scored that I had to commit them directly to the pyre."

Anise only shook her head. "The things you hear if only you live long enough..." she muttered.

"You don't believe me." Hands on hips, she stared down at the bold young servant girl, who squirmed under the scrutiny. "Turn down the bed, then. Go ahead, do it."

The girl feared she had gone too far and began apologizing all over again, but the lady's command was unequivocal. Anise hung her head and slunk across the chamber to the bed. She turned down the rich brocade coverings.

There, atop the precisely folded linen sheets, lay a naked blade.

The *etoille* was long and straight as a needle—after the fashion favored by the *gracci*, the brotherhood of professional duelists that only the decadent Guild Elders could afford to employ in the

A Game of Silk and Mirrors

settling of their obscure and labyrinthine points of honor.

Even Anise could see that this weapon was no courtly affectation. The sword's hilt was wrapped in a blistered and sweat-stained leather that spoke of years of loving use.

"My lady," Anise hissed. "You should not have such a thing here! What would my lord the Duk say? Why someone could be…"

"Hurt?" Meerlah interrupted. Lightning fast, she snatched at the nearest corner of the bedsheet and yanked it taut. The blade sprang into the air. Anise shrieked and covered her eyes. This altogether spoiled the intended effect as the whirling steel slapped down unerringly but unwitnessed, in the palm of Meerlah's outstretched hand.

She lowered the blade in disgust. "You can come out now, Anise." Without turning, Meerlah tossed the blade hilt-first into the pile of pillows and stalked back towards the dressing table.

Anise peeked out and, seeing that the danger had passed, took a hesitant step forward. "I… I won't say nothing. To your uncle, I mean. About the sword.. You can rely upon me, my lady."

Meerlah gave her a wry smile. "Well that is a relief. I trust that the discovery of the war bow won't weaken your new resolve. It's hung behind the looking glass, by the way."

Anise's had already turned apprehensively towards the looking glass before she realized that this too might be some sort of joke at her expense. Her face reddened but she held her ground.

"You don't believe that either," Meerlah realized, shaking her head in undisguised wonder. "You are quite the skeptic, Anise. My dear uncle should find a place for you at the *lyceum*, among the *philosophes*. You talents are wasted here. Ah well, I am afraid that you will have to discover the truth about *Fancy's Flight* on your own time. We still have much to do tonight. And now if you will would be so kind as to fetch the turquoise promenade gown…

"Right away, my lady." Anise bobbed her head in leave-taking and ducked out of the chamber. She ran half-stumbling down the hall.

Alone inside her chamber, Meerlah found her thoughts straying to the ordeal that lay ahead. She could feel her irritation rising. How she hated all this—the posturings of the court, the affectation. The elaborate gowns and hairstyles. Most of all, she hated being an outsider in their midst—being dependent upon the generosity of relatives, patrons, lovers.

For all the wonders and amenities to be found in the *palais* of her dear Uncle Gervais—Duk of Padua and Wing-Marshall of the Dragonsmarch (retired)—a competent lady's body-maid was obviously not among them.

Gervais was not her real uncle, of course—not her blood uncle. But he was a doting old chevalier of a more genteel era. He had always been kind to Meerlah, even before she had carved out her own place in the Mirror Court of Vashon. Back when she was simply a traveling *ululator*—one of the dwindling

A Game of Silk and Mirrors

handful of voice-sculptors, trained from youth in the nearly-forgotten Venir tradition.

She would never dream of coming all the way to the capital without staying with dear Uncle Gervais. And in the cosmopolitan (some would say, risqué) Mirror Court of Vashon, such an arrangement did not even raise an eyebrow.

Meerlah began to comb out her waist-length hair. In hue, it was precisely the warm brown of the cinnamons that were so prized in the Rahoch market bazaars. By the time Anise returned, Meerlah's hair cascaded all about her, shimmering like firelight. "Sit here," Meerlah said, patting the space on the bed beside her. "Watch. *Carefully*."

Until the bell for Nadir struck, she painstakingly separated, braided and coiled her hair. As Anise stared, open-mouthed, a graceful, elaborate and improbable construction rose above the lady's head. The operation took no less than one sheer silk net, thirteen silver pins and one honeycomb—the core around which the entire edifice wound. Anise intently studied her mistress's every movement, but by the end of the operation, her best guess as to how the feat was accomplished still involved conjuration.

Meerlah caught the befuddled look on the girl's face and sighed deeply. "Again," she said, with patience. She unbound the entire coiffure with one graceful twist of her wrist and started over from the beginning, combing out each tangle in the long cascade of hair.

After three attempts to emulate Meerlah's efforts—each of them only slightly less disastrous than the last—Anise finally summoned up enough courage to squeak out, "Begging pardon, my lady, but do you think, just this once, that we might try something a bit... simpler. It is after, all, my first go at it."

Gently, Meerlah took the girl by both hands. If nothing else, this had the effect of putting an end to the nervous flutter of pins about the lady's eyes. "Now Anise dear, I am going to be honest with you. This hairstyle *is* a simple one. And it's probably months out of date by now. But if we do manage to finally pull this then it's just possible I might not get myself immediately laughed out of court. Now if you had something else in mind..."

"We'll try again, my lady," Anise mumbled, squinting to pick out the dropped pins from the pattern of mosaic tiles on the floor.

"It is enough," Meerlah said. Gently she guided the maid's shaking hands through the elaborate dance of curls and pins. "I'm sure you will do better the next time. In the meanwhile, I would like you to scurry down to the library and fetch me a book for this evening."

"Begging the lady's pardon again," Anise said, looking even more wretched than before. She could barely concentrate on Meerlah's words. She kept hearing that one phrase repeated over and over again in her head, *the next time*. "But I'm afraid I haven't my letters, ma'am."

"It's all right, Anise. I don't need you to read it to me." For a brief, but painful moment, she pictured the girl sitting on a stool at her bedside stumbling interminably over the unfamiliar characters. "Just

A Game of Silk and Mirrors

pick me out something lightweight, but attractive. Something in a sea-green, I should think."

"In a sea-green?" Anise repeated uncomprehendingly.

"Yes, something between a light blue and a dark green. You've been to the sea, haven't you Anise?"

"Where I grew up, my lady, the sea weren't any kind of blue nor green," Anise said, a look of doubt playing across her features.

"Oh, the Blood Sea," Meerlah muttered, comprehension dawning. "Well you can take some small comfort in the fact that those waters are the exception. I've traveled quite a bit myself, so I should know. Most seas are a pleasant sort of blue or green. Like the water in the ewer, or my gown. Yes, just get me something to match my gown and you'll do fine."

"Yes, my lady." Anise again backed out of the room and flew in a rout through the empty corridors. By the time she returned, not only was Meerlah's hair redone, but she was dressed as well. She was radiant in long flowing turquoise. The bodice of the gown was rimmed with a line of perfect Albadian pearls. Each of these rare and much sought-after gems curled slightly along one edge, giving them the shape of a delicate fang. The pearls gleamed ice-blue in the lamplight. Meerlah's other jewelry, as well as the intricate embroidery on the gown, was all done in a fine silver tracery.

"My lady," Anise gasped, "I've never seen anything so beautiful in all my days. Why, you'll put the Queen herself to shame."

"Thank you, Anise. Let's hope it doesn't come to that. Now what you have brought me? It is my first night back at court and already I am anxious to get this over with."

Anise shuffled forward. She extended her arms, presenting not one, but a stack of five books, ranging in color from a royal Corean-blue to a Vera-Tre green. Meerlah smiled.

"It seems that there is hope for you yet, dear," she said, relieving Anise of her burden. She regarded the top book and then tossed it casually onto the vanity. "Too bulky. I won't have the Dulcet whispering that I've run off and become a sorceress. This next one is about the right heft. Looks like something delicate that might grace a lady's bedside." She absently flipped through the first few pages and then held the book out at arm's length by one corner. "Oh my. A bit too bedside... Ah, but this one looks promising." She let the second book fall forgotten to the floor and turned to the third with enthusiasm. "Now this is precisely what I mean by sea-green, Anise. And look, its delicate little clasp is of silver. Better and better. I think it's a diary! I will say that I had withdrawn from court to record my confidential memoir. That ought to stir the pot a bit. Well done, my dear. You have outdone yourself."

Anise blushed to the collar. "Thank you, my lady. Pleased to be of service, my lady."

"And now, if you would inform dear Uncle Gervais that I will be engaged in the Receiving Room for the remainder of the evening—and that he need not wait up for me—you are free for the night. You

A Game of Silk and Mirrors

may avail yourself of the heated baths in the annex. No, do not thank me. You have earned it. But I will see you one hour before sunup and no later. If I must be up and around at that dreadful hour, I certainly do not expect to be kept waiting…"

"I understand. Thank you, my lady." Anise bowed low as Meerlah swept from the room in a whisper of long skirts gliding across the tiled floor.

***

The Receiving Room was little bigger than a closet. It was empty of all ostentation—containing not one single furnishing nor even a lone decorative piece to break its monotony. Yet the bare room was worth more than any half dozen summer villas—including their attached acreage and vinyards thrown into the bargain.

There were, Meerlah guessed, perhaps a dozen residences in all of Vashon—and certainly no more than a score in all the Empire!—that could boast such a salon. The room was hexagonal. High arched mirrors covered five of its walls, each taller again by half than the height of a man. The final wall contained the door. Where the mirrors met at the corners, the seams were caulked with mithril and engraved with a spidery arcane script that put Meerlah in mind of gliding desert caravans, wrinkled *kher* fruits and sun-warmed boys with eyes like almonds.

Meerlah scrutinized herself in the mirror one last time, brushing a wayward strand of hair back behind one ear, arranging the pleats of her gown, affecting a pose of studied nonchalance with her book cradled in the crook of her arm. She wrestled down the impulse to return to her chambers to retrieve her *etoille*.

No matter how many times she had done this, it took an effort of will to voluntarily put herself at the mercy of the Mirror Court of Vashon. And if there was anything worse than being lowered head-first into a serpent pit, it was making the descent unarmed.

She took a deep breath to steady herself, not unpleased with the effect this wrought upon the bodice of her gown, and counted slowly to ten. There was no turning back now.

Tamping once sharply with her foot in the very center of the plain marble floor, she triggered the mechanism. Meerlah felt the familiar tremor of the room thrumming to life. She closed her eyes against the sudden play of lights, pinpricks of brilliance mirrored back and forth between the facing reflective planes, winking brighter at each rebounding.

And then the fanfare of lights vanished as suddenly as it had begun. And Meerlah opened her eyes upon the Ballustraded Gallery of the Mirror Court of Vashon.

The view was breathtaking. The Gallery itself was a raised promenade that wound its way above the military splendor of the Serpentine Ballroom and extended out over the Queen's renowned Garden of Moon Petals. The night air was filled with that curious mingling of jasmine and brass polish that always recalled Meerlah to the trepidation of her very first appearance at court.

A Game of Silk and Mirrors

It was a daunting prospect. Meerlah could almost see the younger version of herself standing before her now—naïve, terrified and grim at the prospect of being called to appear before their Imperial Majesties. She had not so much as managed to acquire a proper Presentation Gown for the occasion. She wore only the loose-fitting ash-grey robes of her profession. The ensemble bore the unmistakable marks of having spent the better part of the previous weeks wadded up in the bottom of a backpack. Her only adornment was the delicate choker—the band of purest amber— that identified her as an *ard-rhea*, a journeyman of the Ancient and Revered Brotherhood of *Ululators*.

If she had been aware at the time of the scathing insults, the devastating mockery that greeted her appearance, she would have fled the court never to return. But the secret discourse of the Mirror Court was closed to her. It was a subtle and devious code— a covert language whose syllables were the flutter of a lady's fan, the depth of a gentleman's bow, the precise angle a glove lay upon the lap.

Years later, after Meerlah had painstakingly mastered each nuance of the shadow-talk, she had often tried to recall the precise details of that first introduction to the casual cruelties of the court. She tried to call to mind exactly who had been present that evening to titter at each of her gaffes. She scoured her memories for evidence of the distracted gestures that had cut her younger self to pieces. And all with an eye to exacting very personal and private revenges.

But it was no use. She had simply not known what to look for at the time. The same gestures that today would bring her instantly *en garde* simply did not register at all on her younger self. Not enough to make the slightest lasting impression.

So as Meerlah surveyed the Mirror Court tonight, as on so many other nights, she found herself staring out over a sea of smiling faces, any of which might be cherishing and gloating over an unavenged slight.

She hated them, this clutch of politely nodding serpents. Hated them for what they had done to her. Hated them even more for letting her curtsey and gush and thank them profusely for their kindness and generosity—even as they were tearing her to pieces. Most of all she hated them for the power they held over her—for the fact that she could not keep from returning here, time and time again.

It was impossible to keep still. Her low roiling resentment spurred her forward. Meerlah briskly crossed the promenade, her shoes making not the slightest sound upon the sumptuous carpets. She leaned over the carved ivory railing and gazed down over the ballroom below. Her pose was one of affected indifference, but her angry grip was as white-knuckled as the ivory itself.

The Serpentine Ballroom was packed with the *elegentia*—the titled aristocracies of the six kingdoms, the dashing military commanders, the profanely wealthy guild elders, the constellations of diplomats, dignitaries, legates, supplicants, tributary lordlings. Meerlah recognized at least one flamboyant pirate prince who was, she was quite certain, under penalty of death from this very court. Around one arm, he wore a young lady who Meerlah vaguely recalled had

A Game of Silk and Mirrors

achieved some local repute in the theatrics. He was deep in heated concourse with the Queen's Confessor.

Just as Meerlah was warming to her people-watching, her musings were interrupted by a veritable shriek of delight from directly behind her.

"Meerlah, darling! You did not tell me you would be here this evening. I would have arranged something special to welcome you home." A black lacquerwood fan tapped her scoldingly on the forearm. Meerlah caught the motion, saw the patterned wood rap against one turquoise sleeve, but she did not feel the contact. They were aloof from such intimacies here, shielded by the very nature of the Mirror Court itself.

Meerlah winced, but not in reaction to the voice, not the abortive touch. To her trained ear, the voice sounded gratingly high-pitched, almost shrill, and (she could not help thinking) more than a bit nasally. It was also precisely the voice that she had been dreading most. She turned, forcing her most painfully formal smile onto her pursed lips.

"My dearest Dulcet, you know I would not dream of so taxing your generosity. You look absolutely radiant tonight. That gown has always been a particular favorite of mine."

"It's new dear," the Dulcet replied curtly. The two embraced stiffly. If they had been standing in the ballroom below, the arch of that embrace would have left room for a column of dancers to pass between them. "You're wearing your birthmark on the other cheek this season, I see. Always keeping the gentlemen guessing." Her fan snapped open and waved once crisply. To the trained eye, the gesture was as elaborate as the flourish of a bull-fighter's cape when he has driven his point home.

Even amidst the viscous serpent-pit of the Mirror Court of Vashon, Her Dulcet Ladyship, Patrizia della Cordossa was always accorded the place of honor—usually basking on a high sunlit bough, peering down upon the wriggling masses of her lessers. And handing out apples of dubious repute.

"The same cheek, Dulcet dear," Meerlah countered. "Surely the authentic is not out of style this season? I find that the gentlemen are so very discerning on that point. You should give them a bit more credit. Is that not so, *Capitan*?"

Addressed directly, a gentleman in the crisp red, black and bronze of His Majesty's Dragoons detached himself from the Dulcet's shadow and stepped forward. "I am sorry, my lady. I did not wish to eavesdrop and so my thoughts were elsewhere. Is what not so?"

"I was just telling the Dulcet that gentlemen are of a more studious bent than we are. Don't you agree? I have found that, at close quarters, gentlemen have little difficulty discerning nature from artifice." Meerlah absently twisted a strand of peerless cinnamon hair between thumb and forefinger. She avoided looking directly at the Dulcet's own golden tresses—which were justifiably famous among the gentlemen of the court for their beauty, and among the ladies of the court for their staggering expense.

A Game of Silk and Mirrors

Meerlah crowned her little dig by shifting her book to the other hand—a movement which, performed with a closed fan, amounted to a cry of *touche*!

The Dulcet recovered quickly, cutting off her escort before he could answer. "But look! You have left your fan behind, my dear. Here, you will take mine. No, I insist. I would sooner let you walk away with a torn hem in your gown where you have walked all over it."

"But I am not carrying a fan this evening," Meerlah said. She raised the corner of her little book to her chin in imitation of the fan-gesture that meant that one was overlooking the obvious.

"Of course you're not dear. I will have words with that uncle of yours when we dine together next week. To think of allowing a lady of such... *promise* to go to court without the barest necessities. No, better not to think on it. Have no fear, I will see to the matter presently. In the meantime, you will take my fan."

"But that will leave you unarmed," Meerlah protested.

"I will make do. And I have the *Capitan* here to protect me. But I should not like for you to feel that you are in my debt. Here, I will make you an exchange. You will take my fan, and you will give me, in return, your little book. Surely, you can have no objection to such an equitable exchange."

Meerlah looked skeptical. "I would not have expected so much at your hands, Dulcet dear. But if you are certain that there is no other way for you to save face…"

"I have said as much. Here." The Dulcet hastily pressed the fan upon her.

Meerlah tapped twice sharply on the floor with her right foot, again triggering the mechanism in the Receiving Room. She felt a moment of vertigo as she became suddenly and jarringly aware of the tiny hexagonal room around her with its five mirrored walls, each showing a slightly different aspect of the peerless view from the Ballustraded Gallery, overlooking the Serpentine Ballroom, in the Palais of King Virduk, half a city away.

In the same instant, she felt the wood of the fan where it pressed against her palm. She blinked to clear the strange juxtaposition of light, perspective and sorcery from her eyes as she handed over her little book in return. She felt the slight resistance as it sank slowly through the reflective surface of the Dulcet's own protective field.

The Mirror Court was the product of an earlier, more volatile age—a time when open violence, duels and even assassination attempts were commonplace perils of court life. The elaborate and arcane solution to the problem allowed the members of Vashon's leading families to appear in court in relative safety. If there were a few small sacrifices to be made—being relegated to haunting the elevated shadow-galleries, being unable to feel the brush of a covert caress—well, that was certainly small price to pay. Besides, it was always possible to voluntarily suspend the silver-backed barrier between the two mirror worlds for a short time—to hastily exchange a note, a kiss, perhaps even a fan.

Meerlah bowed slightly to the Dulcet and excused herself on the pretense of sighting the Marquis of Dalomir, a particular favorite of hers—all the more so for the fact that she had veritably snatched him from the threshold of the Dulcet's boudoir.

The Dulcet smiled in return, a warm, genuine smile. If the truth were known, she was more than slightly relieved to be finally rid of their little low-born songbird, if only for the evening. Meerlah was a mere curiosity to her, a keepsake, a bauble. The goose with a golden voice. She enjoyed some small, seasonal favor at court and then was quickly forgotten again.

This little sea-green book, however, was of more lasting interest. The Dulcet had recognized it at once, or at least guessed at its import. It was a lady's personal diary, of that there was could be no doubt. The Dulcet was openly skeptical as to whether Meerlah could even read, much less write. No, the diary must belong to another. And unless she dramatically missed her guess, that other had to be the Lady Shanna Gervais, the deceased wife of Meerlah's benefactor, these ten years in the grave. The contents of this little volume might prove extremely illuminating…

The Dulcet retired early that evening, despite her *Capitan's* none-too-subtle counterproposals. She could not have known that she had made quite a sensation among the more impressionable young ladies of the court with her bold substitution of a book, in place of the traditional fan, as the accessory of choice. By the next evening, the fashion had been widely adopted among a certain class of girls who had not been properly taught, from an early age, that a book was far too frivolous a thing to ever communicate anything.

By daybreak, the Dulcet had nothing more to show for her flawlessly executed scheme than a matched set of sour bags under her eyes from a late night's reading and a single disconcerting—and potentially embarrassing, should word get out—revelation regarding the paternity of her dearest cousin on the distaff side. That and an unshakable conviction that Lady Gervais had been a sickeningly upright and unimaginative old bird and was no great lost to anyone concerned. Scant fruit, indeed, to show for the Dulcet's labors.

She opted not to appear at the Queen's Formal Processional the next evening, owing to a rather haunted cast to her eyes that, despite the determined beating of her body-maid, neither of them could quite manage to conceal.

Her absence proved fortuitous. The talk of the court that evening was all of scandal and indiscretion. Apparently, only the night before, a notorious enemy of the state had made so bold as to appear in the Serpentine Court, under the very nose of his Imperial Majesty. In the morning, when the agents of the crown knocked down the door of the house where this rogue was reportedly hiding, they found that he had already escaped back to his ship. That would probably have been the end of the matter, were it not for a curious side-note—the fan of a certain prominent court lady that was discovered at his bedside.

Love Incarnate
By Stewart Wieck

And so it came to pass that relatively soon after his initiation into the ways of druidism—and the consequent discovery that he would throughout his life recall the memories of lives he'd lived before as an Incarnate—that Andelais found himself traveling without companions. This was unusual for the half-elf, for he greatly enjoyed companionship even though he sometimes felt a quiet solitude even when surrounded by friends.

For someone who deserved it and earned it and could be trusted as only the truest friend or lover can be, Andelias could be a lifelong companion. With love especially, Andelais found he was freer than most. Most men (and for that matter elves too) were free with their lust, but rarely looked beyond this simple emotion, this single facet of love. Since childhood, Andelais had sought to explore every strand of life—a characteristic he now associated with his Incarnate nature—for the more experiences he could weave together to form the web of his life, then the more enmeshed in it he would be. And he could be quick and seemingly frivolous with his offers, for he truly believed that noble and kind souls abounded, even in these dark and desperate years that followed the Divine War, and he felt even the smallest portion of love or compassion or friendship sown at first often reaped a far greater companionship with such friends.

Perhaps it was his first recollection of a past life—that of a falcon—that opened Andelais's soul and mind to the solitude of the sky and the consequent willingness to be completely alone and so allowed this state of mind that may have led him to find

Love Incarnate

himself without companions at this time. But it was not as a half-blooded elf or even as a falcon that he this time sought self-discovery and peace.

He traveled in possession of an odd item that was his only material reward for thwarting an undead assaathi shaman who had been in hiding since the end of the War and who had recently been exposed. And with the help of Andelais: defeated.

A crudely-lashed, wooden framework of six long sticks and a dozen or so shorter ones formed a sort of primitive dog. Despite the lack of craftsmanship, the idol possessed a charm that Andelais found fascinating, perhaps even a bit dangerous and threatening. Either way, Andelias felt it revealed something more of itself to him than merely the handiwork of an unskilled sculptor. He imagined it to be a fox, and it stared at him lifelessly—but not without emotion—through two eyes made of fired-charcoal or perhaps onyx.

The wise-woman of the village most proximate to the undead shaman's latest (and last) horrors confirmed the half-elf's suspicions of his fox when she explained to the Incarnate that the construct was one to conduct the soul of a being into the form fashioned by the sculpture. This could be done once only, but the duration was potentially limitless. This magic could be activated by any number of means, at least one of which the Incaranate knew was at his disposal: the mere fact that he could transform himself into other shapes without the use of the construct.

Transformation back, the wise-woman promised, was at the conscious will of the transformed. Yet she cautioned that animals could well forget that they were men. Andelais thought back on his time spent soaring and knew that this was true. And dangerous.

Not quite sure what it was he specifically needed to escape, Andelais sensed the dark and threatening clouds of destiny that seemed to always pursue him. He decided he Andelais felt he could put this fox statue to use to ease his soul and mind. So, Andelais traveled east of the Ganjus toward the foothills of the great Kelder Mountains to a secluded and supposedly still virgin forest known only to elves and druids though seldom visited by either in order to preserve it as an untouched splendor. After some brief reconnaissance of the valley in the form of a falcon, Andelais settled on a spot: a hidden grove so well choked off by a frenzy of vines and brambles that even the nearby squirrels missed the yearly harvest of nuts that fell within it. This became base camp for Andelais.

He placed the framework fox outside the grove (for it would not do to be trapped within it in his new form). Again he returned to falcon form, fluttered into the treetops and picked his way down through the branches to the barely discernable grove beneath. Standing on the ground within the thicket, Andelais felt as if he was at the bottom of the well of the world—some place where a titan might be bound—and for an instant, the barest fluttering of a partial second, he felt the great weight of loneliness, which is the insidious side of the solitude he sought. Though that split second could afford a decade of contemplation, Andelais resumed his half-elven form

Love Incarnate

and proceeded, hoping for an experience more heartening and hopeful, for though he feared his life (for indeed as much was prophesied in many quarters) would be full of such instants, he hoped he might fill the minutes to greater fulfillment.

He activated the medallion he wore—an item that he could use once per year to enter a deep and safe state of hibernation that could last for as many as three months, which is as long as Andelais believed it would be safe to remain as a fox anyway.

Then, he began to imagine himself a fox. The cautious cunning. The nervous stealth. The timid curiosity.

All this he wrapped around his thoughts and then cast his senses into the wooden fox outside the grove. Then, quickly—much sooner than he expected—he began to see through its eyes and hear through its ears. Almost instantly, he felt not released but bound, bound within the sculpture and not made twin to it, and the memory of that first moment in the grove blossomed again in his mind. Was this then a trap? And he now bound not within vigorous sinew but instead unyielding stick and stone? But as quickly as before, the sensation passed, for the determined walls of himself were suddenly supple and the construct that was now Andelais was transformed into a marvelous, young red fox—a young male in the flush of life.

And so, desiring to find himself and perhaps better understand his Incarnate nature, Andelais began a three month-long existence as a fox and first ran on four legs. It was as a fox that Andelais first knew the trials of surviving without tools or fire. It was as a fox that Andelais first knew the dangers of predators larger than he. And it was as a fox that Andelais first knew a love that made him wonder if his past loves were not in fact lust.

It is a love that haunts Andelais still.

The fox he spied was a gorgeous animal. Her fur was shiny and sleek. Her body trim and well-fed. Her eyes bright and watchful. The gorgeous red of her fur so rich it was nearly gold. This was the companionship Andelais sought: a friend with whom he could share his delight in this natural world.

She was at first wary, but instincts worked in Andelais's favor, for mating season was near. So the two became fast friends, and she who knew the woods so much better (though she did not ever venture near the grove where Andelais's current form was hidden) feasted Andelais's senses with dew on honeysuckle at first light, the sweet and pungent mushrooms at a boulder's base that made the mind become playful, the freshest wind ever smelled that gusted across a field of wildflowers before channeling through a narrow gorge of stone... all that and more, much more.

The friendship grew and grew as mating season drew near and then swept into the present. So dear was this fox to him that Andelais would at night, with her warm body bundled so near his, realize that he'd spent the day without an educated thought, without recalling that he was anything other than a perfectly contented fox. The wild promise of what was before him swept any other needs away. Which is as he wanted it.

Love Incarnate

No more loving mates could be found among all the animals of the forest that Spring. When the actual mating took place, though, Andelais found that he could not think only as an animal might: with only the thought of fulfilling a biological destiny, but that did not surprise him for he was in love and he was more than just an animal of the forest. What did surprise him is that their gorgeous coupling seemed just as dramatic and awesome to his companion. Something immense and magical was passing between them, the result of which was a deeper friendship than before…and a litter of fox pups.

And every moment Andelais wondered when the magic that made all this possible would end, for after three months end it would. Not only because of the magic of his half-elven form's medallion, but because of promises and oaths to himself that he must not forever run from his destiny—or worse continue to pretend to contemplate his destiny, as if his thoughts by a dribbling stream would froth revelation in his mind. Little did he know, though, that magic other than his is what would disrupt the harmony of this life.

Andelais was hunting small game for himself and his lovely but nearly earthbound companion to share when he scented that the birth had taken place. How he could have missed the signs earlier he remains to this day unclear, but now he knows enough to blame this misfortune on fate and not merely on his insensitivity. These last events could have unfolded in no other way.

Hot in the pursuit of a rabbit when he scented the revelation, Andelais immediately broke off the chase and rushed back to the hollow the foxes shared. A confusion of scents and signs awaited his return. Second most important to Andelais was the litter of the most spectacular fox pups he could imagine. He saw at once that they shared all the best traits of himself and their mother, and he loved them dearly.

But the one he loved most of all was gone. And without a trace. The only sign was the tracks of a barefooted human departing (and departing only— there was no approach) the hollow the foxes shared. In a glance Andelais saw that his children were safe, so he covered the entrance to the hollow so they would not wander out in their close-eyed staggering, and he dashed after the trail.

The scent of his mate was on the trail, but he could not fathom why a barefooted human would scoop a new mother fox from her home. If it was a predatory action, then surely the pups would have been sacrificed as well. This thought that his love might be dead spurred him to greater effort and his red-furred legs were crimson blurs as he shot along the trail.

Only when he achieved the edge of the forest was his pursuit successful. For some reason hesitant of bolting from the cover of the forest, Andelais slowed as he neared the edge. This bit of patience was rewarded with one of the most spectacular sights he has ever beheld—the kind of sweet vision one holds jealously guarded in his soul for a time of great

Love Incarnate

trial or need to lend strength and confidence to a sagging will.

He beheld a human woman who was as lovely a creature as he'd ever known. Naked and trembling from the ragged breathing of the hard run through the forest, this woman stretched herself in the rays of the sun descending from a cloudless and pure blue sky. Her hair was long, luscious and luxurious. The rays turned its nearly waist-length cascade into a fiery red glow akin to the brilliance of sunlight shining bronzed through a field of strong wheat grown by a sure and loving hand. So red it was almost gold.

He knew instantly that this was the fox with whom he'd spent the past months. And he knew just the same that she was an Incarnate. Only later would he learn her name—Helena Goldsmeadow—and the story of how she'd been trapped in her fox form for nearly two years and how she could only be freed by… well, as Andelais freed her.

So awed was Andelais by the sight of this beauty, and too so shocked by this discovery, that he drifted from the edge of the forest and into the clearing. He made himself plainly visible and in a flutter of hair, Helena turned round to face the fox that had been her lover and who was the father of her children.

When first their eyes met, Helena's face illuminated with a smile that caused Andelais to flush and thank the power of Nature that granted him enough lives to finally find such joy. But then her lovely face sank, and her tender lips trembled, and her expression went blank. She gazed at Andelais with some unfathomable mixture of confusion, fear, regret and foreboding for she must have suddenly recalled her own plight, her curse and how the fox before her both freed her and trapped himself. Andelais's flush turned cold and became a shiver that jangled his nerves and bones.

And as all passion fled his frame, the magic that caused Andelais to bring flesh to the crude fox framework reversed. Andelais found himself being pulled backward down a long, dark tunnel, the terminus of which was the ever-receding vantage of the his fox eyes. And as he was drawn away, Helena, with an unnameable expression still ruling her face, approached. Her expression changed to surprise as she regarded the wooden fox that had moved the other direction and now stood in the clearing where Andelais had been. The last sight Andelais had of Helena was her soulful blue eye looking into the charcoal eye of the fox puzzled and searching for some sign of life.

Andelais thought it eight days later before the shock of the magic wore off and his hibernation ended. He emerged from his hidden grove on the wings of his falcon form once more, unable then as now to explain how the magic was reversed except to surmise that it was something to do with the curse placed upon Helena. With mighty strokes of his wings, he flew quickly to the site of the den he'd shared with his the woman, his fox lover. The pups were gone, and Andelais was relieved to find no sign of violence.

Of Helena there remains no sign at all.

Tie Your
Own Rope

By Brian Williams

"The interaction of disease between various races and species is truly quite fascinating, though not my particular field of interest." The albino's voice was smooth and his words methodically pronounced. He spoke to the bound woman without the hisses and chittering stutters most of the ratmen known as Slitheren suffered from when attempting the Common tongue. In fact his accent seemed almost Veshian, or else from another of the lands nearer the Blood Sea. The sophisticated tones sounded almost surreal coming from the mangy, pockmarked Slitheren. "Take for instance the gray mantid, several specimens of which you can observe in the shallow pool below you."

Bisseth's human captive dangled above a small slick-sloped pit, hanging by the rope which bound her wrists from a wooden gantry that looked to have been hastily constructed solely for this purpose. She glanced down and saw that, as the albino rat-priest had said, a number of gray insects with slender bodies almost as long as her forearm and bulbous triangular heads swam in the few feet of water at the bottom of the pit. In the sparse torchlight of the grotto, the water seemed to boil from the amphibious mantids at the surface, scampering over one another and attempting to climb the slippery rocks at the edges of the pool.

"Tussilx, in addition to being Chern's Chosen Leader of this promising young warren and our host, is most knowledgeable about gray mantids," continued Bisseth. He quickly scanned the cavern for the other albino, but Tussilx had gone off to

Tie Your Own Rope

another chamber to tend to the warren's defenses. "He tells me that after a female mantid has mated her eggs will rise through her midsection and come to rest in a pouch behind her mouth, which causes a noticeable swelling at the back of the head. Then she'll acquire a taste not for the tiny fish and lizards that are a gray mantid's usual prey, but for larger, farther-wandering game."

The young woman shut her eyes. She didn't have to look into the watery hole to know that the heads of all the insects beneath her had distinct bulges. She let a whispered "Why?" pass her lips.

"Because when she bites into the flesh of a larger victim she'll vomit the eggs into its blood," said the pale Slitheren. "From there they will distribute themselves throughout the body as they grow into larva. Before the eggs hatch their host provides safety, warmth and carriage away from the previous generation's territory. And after the eggs become larva, it provides the young gray mantids their first meal."

Bisseth was quite certain from the girl's face that she'd understood what happed to the eggs before he'd described it and had meant her feeble question as "Why me?" But the ratman enjoyed the distress that his vivid description seemed to cause her, and there was plenty of time to address the other question. After all, they were only a few hours into Fleasbirth Night and he was sure that her would-be savior would show himself well before dawn. Then he and Tussilx could give the gray mantids a host worthy of the greatest pox.

Brian Williams

"Ah, but the versatility of disease!" said Bisseth. "That was my point in discussing Tussilx's little gray pets. For you see, it is the jelly surrounding the eggs, and the mother's saliva which prove that this rare insect may turn out to be the mighty Unclean Chern's most wondrous gift yet. There are, of course, agents of disease in the fluids that are injected along with the eggs. That's quite common among biting insects, but what makes the gray mantid unique is that it doesn't merely carry existing contagions. It actually creates new ones!"

The human was no longer paying sufficient attention, in Bisseth's opinion. She'd opened her eyes around the time he'd mentioned the larva and had been looking around the cavern the Slitheren had dragged her to. Not that there was much to see. Tussilx had only brought his small pack here less than two months ago and hadn't done much digging or construction to make it a proper warren. The human village near the mouths of these natural caves, called Wagonflow by the surface dwellers, was little more than a trading post with a few farms clustered around it. But if tonight's experiment went well the caves themselves would soon become a bustling city of ratmen. There was much work to be done raising and studying an entirely original plague, after all.

Now the female seemed to be studying Chykri and Tailless, his two bodyguards. These dark-furred rats were Shields of Chern assigned personally to protect Bisseth with their strength, their towering shields and their lives. Though as fanatically loyal as any Slitheren outside the albino priesthood, the pair

Tie Your Own Rope

of zealots hated Bisseth's methods with a passion. Tailless in particular chafed at the presence of a living, uninfected human. His clawed fingers clenched the handle of his four-headed flail and he wished he could rake its spiked balls across the woman's absurdly hairless flesh.

"If we can't kill the pitiful godcreature," he muttered to Chykri, "He should at least let me free her blood to the night air so Chern may taint it." Chykri nodded approval, but the Shields of Chern knew their place. Their priest had said the human was to be saved for deeds that would please the Titans far more than her mere death, so Tailless stayed his hand.

"Are you imagining your noble Girtnu Shav defeating my vicious guards here on his way to spirit you from my grasp?" whispered Bisseth, leaning over the edge of the pit so close that she could feel his stiff whiskers brush her shoulder when he spoke. The woman jerked her eyes away from Chykri's stubby fur braids and stared at the albino ratman in open-mouthed shock. Bisseth leaned back and a contented grin spread across his snout.

"Yes, I know of your heroes," Bisseth snarled. "Why does that surprise you so? You god worshippers have too much faith and too little fear! Did it never occur to you that a man who slays gorgons, fights off hordes of spider-eye goblins and scatters a coven of red witches would gain a reputation among his enemies as well as allies? If all we'd wanted to take from Wagonsflow were the simple peasants who now rot in our caves we could have done so swiftly, without ever being seen by eyes accustomed to daylight. The villagers had faith that the champion they begged to come would save them from us, but lacked any fear that the tracks we'd left them were intentional. Typical thinking for a race that cried at the feet of childlike gods while my own fathers feasted upon the flesh of a Titan."

Tussilx, the other white-haired priest, had returned. He spoke to Bisseth in the sibilant Slitheren language. The ratman's tail twitched excitedly as he listened, then he turned to his bodyguards and hissed a command that sent Chykri scurrying away into a dark passage at the edge of the grotto.

"We must return for a moment to the gray mantid," explained Bisseth evenly, "For it is important that you realize the honor which is going to be yours tonight. As I said, the behaviors of disease when transferred from one species to another can be quite fascinating, and the mantid is a unique example of that. The slime coating that protects the eggs is relatively harmless, but it mutates rapidly once in contact with a host's blood. Whatever is bitten by an egg-carrying gray mantid almost certainly becomes ill before the larva hatch."

Now the human female was squirming against her ropes once again. It was good to have her attention back on her predicament, instead of her hope for rescue.

"The mutation is what makes these insects an interesting specimen," continued Bisseth, "Because a unique disease is created in the blood of each different race into which gray mantids vomit forth

Tie Your Own Rope

their eggs. Each species' mantid-based illness is distinct and cannot be transmitted to a different species. That means it isn't a case of different symptoms in different creatures but Chern's might breeding a new plague each time the gray mantid's eggs enter a race that hasn't yet been touched by its unclean glory!"

"I find all of this remarkable," Bisseth grinned. His captive's head had drooped, either to look upon the mantids' pool or to hide the sobs that seemed to be wracking her hanging body. "But as I said, this study is Tussilx's expertise, not my own. Perhaps he'll do me the favor of illuminating you to some of the afflictions he's already found to have originated from our little friends here?"

Chykri had returned from his task, and was bearing a bloody skin stretched taught across a large silver ring. It appeared to be human. Worse still, it appeared to be fresh. Bisseth smeared a vial of black liquid on what had been the inside of the skin, hunched over it and began chanting. The other albino spoke to their prisoner for the first time.

"It wass the barrow wormses that I notisssed first," hissed Tussilx. The warren's high priest hadn't had as much contact with humans and other surface races as Bisseth had, and it was noticeable in his use of Common. He smacked his lips between nearly every word. "They don't gets sick muchs. Ssometimes I see ones asleep for days and rolling over isself. The worm doessint notisss me, and its hide feels s soft and hots. Ssoon the mantid larvaes chew theirs way outs."

"And some of the others, Tussilx?" Bisseth had finished intoning the strange Slitheren syllables over the stretched hide. Its surface was now utterly dark, the kind of blackness that seemed more like a pit than a color, and he carefully poured a fine, shimmering powder across it.

"Whens the coal goblinss are bitten, sthey get boils is around their eyes," the priest rasped on, "Sand as the boils pop sthey can spreads to other goblinss. I know, too, that iffs a gray mantid bites a dwarves his fleshes will rots while is still alive. The necrosstic lesions are lovelies, but sadly nots contagious."

"Ah, but what of the humans?" asked Bisseth with a grin. "They are the most prolific of the gods' chosen races. What deliciously foul pox befalls a human when the mantid's eggs mix with its blood?"

"The inssects normally live too deeps underground to meets humans," Tussilx said, "We don't know becausss is hasn't happened. Yet."

The pair of white Slitheren laughed, a high-pitched twitchy sort of laugh that no human mouth could repeat. Then Bisseth turned the silver ring that held the enchanted skin so that their prisoner could gaze into it as well. Tricks of reflected light sparkled across its wet, black surface until an image resolved itself deep within the darkness. It was the mouth of a cave, seen from deep within looking out. Soon her eyes adjusted to looking into the device. She could make out the hooded robes of three Slitheren facing the cave's entrance, hiding from its moonlight. They were aiming bows toward a silhouette in the moonlight, a man in shining chain armor with his

Tie Your Own Rope

sword sheathed and his shield arm hanging relaxed at his side...

"Do you see?" whispered Bisseth, "I knew Girtnu Shav would be here before the holy night of Fleasbirth was over. I find those rare humans who take it upon themselves to bravely set forth against all odds to rid the land of evil so sublimely predictable. I mentioned before that disease is not my particular field of study, but I didn't tell you what is."

The albino turned his eyes down from the bound woman to watch the image of three ratmen drawing their bows simultaneously.

"To put it simply," he said, "I hunt heroes."

He paused at the threshold of the narrow cave. It wasn't that he saw anything, or heard any suspicious sounds. He was fairly certain that the light clinking of his long chain mail tunic would be louder than the sounds of the subterranean creatures he may soon face. It was just that as he'd stepped into the mouth of the cave something occurred to him.

"You know," he mumbled to himself, "If I were going to ambush someone, I'd set it somewhere around he-"

He raised his shield and ducked behind it.

Three arrows embedded themselves into the shield before it had even stopped moving. The face of the large, bronze shield was circular and divided into eight sections. Into each section the symbol of one of the eight gods was carved, because Girtnu had always said that one should take all the help one can get.

Running into the cave without actually knowing what he was charging at, he spared a quick glance around the side of his shield and very nearly caught an arrow in his face for it. He did spot the three Slitheren, however. The nearest one had dropped its short bow and was drawing a thin scimitar. He angled his dash toward that one and reached down for the scabbard hanging at his hip.

Instead of drawing the broadsword there, however, he snatched one of the daggers tucked in his belt. With a quick flick of his wrist he send it flying under the rim of his shield. It struck the scimitar-wielding ratman in the thigh. It had been expecting to meet the human's charge and cross blades. In the moment it took to reach down and pull the knife out of its leg, a bronze shield crashed into its body with all the force of an armored man rushing down a sloped tunnel behind it.

The man shoved the rat backwards before it could catch its breath, throwing it between himself and the other two Slitheren. At least one of them must have panicked and released its bow because when the ratman fell to the cave floor there was an arrow shaft sticking out of its back. He said a silent prayer of thanks to Enkili and drew his sword.

Of the two remaining rats the taller one tossed his bow aside and drew two long, nasty-looking knives. The other stepped back deeper into the cave and nocked another arrow. The human's heavy broadsword arced down in a wide overhead sweep at

Tie Your Own Rope

the approaching Slitheren before it was close enough to use its pair of shorter blades. The swing was slow and the ratman easily sidestepped to avoid it.

The swordsman's momentum carried him past the ratman who'd dodged out of the way, though he felt one of the wicked knives press against the mail below his right rib. He brought his already overextended blade up in a short jab that snapped the string from the bottom of the second rat's bow. In reaching to eliminate the threat of long-range attack, he'd dangerously out-balanced himself and there was now a Slitheren behind him. It didn't waste time in kicking his legs out from under him, and he did the most tactically sound thing he could think of.

He fell.

Just before hitting the stone floor of the cave he flung his broadsword at the ankles of the Slitheren in front of him. The blade tore a gash in the bottom of its cloak but clattered past harmlessly. He kicked blindly at the ratman behind him, holding it off for a few seconds until his left arm was free of the shield's straps. His opponents were closing in, but a clumsy forward roll pushing off of the shield sent him crashing into the legs of one and the bronze disc flying up at the face of the other.

The chain mail armor was too heavy for him to be able to stand up quickly. While still tangled on the floor with the short ratmen he pulled a thin dirk from his boot. With two smooth strokes the creature's hamstrings were severed, ensuring that at least it couldn't get up easily, either.

A dagger bit into the side of his calf, well below the protection of his armor tunic. The Slitheren lying facedown on the ground, though squealing in pain at its own wounds, was not about to let him get away. The still-standing rat rubbed its bleeding mouth where the shield had luckily struck and knocked out a tooth. He knew it wouldn't stall long before rejoining the fray, however. With a twist he freed his uninjured leg from beneath the sprawled Slitheren and brought his boot down hard on the back of its cowled head. It blinked woozily and lost its grip on the dagger.

The tall Slitheren leaped. A tattered cloak flapped behind its elongated, hairy body, which was angled to land knives-first on the human intruder. He kicked again, this time rolling with it so that the blow pushed him to the side. His kick pushed the ratman over the edge of consciousness as well, for it shuddered briefly and then lay limp. The final ratman landed precisely where the man had been a moment before. Its knives chipped on the rocky ground and a mailed elbow quickly dislocated its shoulder.

The Slitheren and the human combatants tumbled over one another in desperate attempts to finish each other off with their tiny steel blades. Unable to reach its knives below the protection of the chain shirt or to the human's uncovered face while they struggled on the ground, the rat soon lost the battle. The best it managed was one vicious bite on a momentarily exposed shoulder before a dirk found its way to its hairy throat.

Tie Your Own Rope

The man in the cave rose to his feet. He bandaged his wounds as best he could with cloth cut from the Slitherens' cloaks and drank a bitter-tasting potion from one a pouch tied to his belt. A Madrielite pilgrim he'd met on the road had told him it would help his body cleanse itself of poisons and diseases. Between the dagger and the bite, he figured he likely had some of both. While recovering his throwing dagger, shield and broadsword it occurred to him that no other rats had came and joined the noisy battle, which must mean the plan was working.

"Of course," he muttered to himself wryly, "Everybody knows that Girtnu Shav never fails." He sighed and ventured deeper into the cavern, deciding that being a hero wasn't quite the deal he'd been led to expect.

"Disappointing," said Bisseth. He looked up from the darkened scrying skin and tapped the side of his elongated jaw thoughtfully. "I had expected much better from a human with such reputation as Girtnu Shav."

"He has sstill killed our brethren," hissed Tailless with a bowed head, "We musts destroy him."

"Remain faithful," Bisseth warned, "We shall, but it will not be by your hand. The Shields of Chern will subdue him if need be, but it is His Breath and Blood that is to strip Girtnu Shav's life away. Be wary lest you become overzealous, my guardians. If you kill Shav before the gray mantid's disease has run its course then the pain I inflict upon you during this life will seem a blessing compared to what Chern sows in your hide throughout the next."

"Girtnu will free me," a quiet, feminine voice spoke out. The albinos turned slowly to face their human prisoner.

"I'm sure he'll try to," answered Bisseth. "That is, after all, the entire point to your presence tonight. We've kidnapped farmers' wives and children for over a month waiting for Wagonsflow to entreat some itinerant local hero to come and save their village. So when the renowned Girtnu Shav, said to be the favored champion of one of the gods, rode into Wagonsflow with a young female in tow I was overjoyed.

"Tussilx and I have been counting on the fact that Shav would come here to rescue you. I knew it from the moment my spies reported the two of you sharing one horse, you behind him with your arms wrapped around him in loving admiration. It wasn't hard to predict his actions so far, nor what he'll do upon arriving to this very chamber. Most humans, particularly the brash sort given to taking up 'adventures', think almost entirely with their loins. You are, after all, a stunning specimen of feminine beauty, from what I understand of human standards."

Actually, Bisseth found the woman's appearance repugnant. Her skin was disgustingly smooth and hairless. Her body curved in ways that seemed ridiculous to the hunched, skulking Slitheren. However, he did know what tended to produce an emotional response in male humans, so when they'd tied her up he'd carefully torn long gashes in her simple white gown and left all of her gaudy jewelry in place. Not that it was worth anything to the rats, mostly consisting of crude woven necklaces and bracelets from which hung various twigs, clusters of leaves and small colored stones.

"We want Girtnu Shav here, obviously," the albino continued, "Because Tussilx is on the brink of creating a plague that's never been seen on Scarn before tonight. He wants it to be a really nasty one, too. Something that can wipe out nations, only slowly, painfully. So he sent for me to lure a champion for his gray mantids. Tonight is Fleasbirth Night, the anniversary of Chern's creation of the first parasite. It's a most holy time for the genesis of a new disease. A god's favored hero, and yourself of course, will make splendid first hosts for the disease as well. It's all certain to gain Chern's blessing and ensure that humanity's version of the gray mantid pox will be a sickness to cherish! Now what do you think about the honor I've bestowed upon you tonight?"

Bisseth's grin beamed at the hanging woman. His elation paled next to the other priest, who was panting fervently. Tussilx had swelled with pride and worshipful exultation when hearing how mighty Chern would sanctify the contagion he'd spent years studying and preparing. Even Tailless and Chykri were nodding eagerly at the idea of witnessing the brand new illness firsthand. Such an opportunity was worth leaving their hated captive unharmed and uninfected for the time being.

"I think," she replied slowly, "That you've gnawed off more than you can swallow this time. I think Girtnu Shav is going to be the one who kills you."

Jubilation turned to fury as three of the four nearby ratmen hissed and spat at her impudence. Bisseth was the only Slitheren who still smiled. He motioned for his Shields of Chern to back down, for they already seemed to have lost sight of the human's importance. Once they were silent he made a point of casually scanning the perimeter of the cavern.

A dark-robed ratman had just dashed into the wide grotto from one of the tunnels. The runner chittered quickly at a group of Slitheren warriors clustered patiently near the passageway opening. Bisseth watched them scurry to take up their assigned positions. Archers sought cover in dark alcoves and behind water-worn rock outcroppings. A pair of crafty rats with long barbed spears climbed to perch on a small ledge above the tunnel's mouth. Two burly Slitheren, almost large enough to be mistaken for Foamers, waited unarmed a few yards to the left of the opening. Finally four Slitheren armed with long, curved swords formed a defensive line between the entrance and the gantry from which the prisoner hung. From behind these four, Bisseth and Tussilx nodded to each other, pleased that their commands were executed so precisely.

Bisseth was particularly delighted. He always loved watching pieces of a plan click into place perfectly, each fitting after the last as proof of the care with which he'd crafted them. Girtnu Shav would arrive soon, rushing in unwisely to save his female. The endgame should prove interesting this time, then the infection made and Chern's great sufferings glorified. The only thing the albino was unsure of was if he could get Shav to be the initial human bitten by the gray mantids or if the woman would have to be dropped into their pool first. She was almost surely his lover though, so she would still make a suitable sacrifice if it came to that.

"No, I doubt that I'll die tonight," Bisseth turned back to face the bound woman. "I've used up far greater champions than your precious Girtnu. Do you know how many of the noblest Coreanic Knights can be killed with a single distressed child and a sufficient quantity of Asaatthi Bloodfang Rum? Three fell to that toxin, but then the little blight pricked himself on the needles concealed in his clothes and was of no more use.

"Once I tricked a dwarven general, a veteran of the Titan's War, into eating a stag tainted with a certain pollen which can be used to mimic death." Bisseth noticed his Shields of Chern shift their gaze from him to the far end of the cavern behind him. Since they said nothing urgent he continued, though slightly louder than before, "For two and a half weeks he appeared completely lifeless, even while on display for the dwarven six-day hero's funeral. The plant acts as if by magic, yet with no signs of enchantment to be detected. They buried him beneath the Keldar Mountains. Dwarves like to put their champions in stone coffins three feet thick, of course. When I scryed on him later, the bones in his hands were worn down almost to the wrists and he must have kept trying after that for his feet were scraped raw, as well. Quite an impressive effort, though he only made it eleven inches through the lid."

"So worry not for my life tonight," he said to the captive. Her eyes were downcast once more, else she may have noticed what no doubt drew the bodyguards' attentions. "If you have worry to spare, I suggest you use it on your hero and yourself."

Tussilx hissed and placed the blade of a spear against the rope that tied the woman's hands and hung her from the gantry. A fair warning, and since there were no sounds of a scuffle, one that seemed to be heeded.

"There is one thing I would like to know about Girtnu Shav, however," said Bisseth, "He is said to be favored by a god. I'm curious which one. Which god so blesses the hero whom we watched barely defend himself against three Slitheren foes?"

"Enkili!" came a shout from far behind Bisseth.

"The Trickster, god of bad luck? How terribly fitting," the albino replied without turning to face the new voice, "Considering the situation you must now find yourself in. I was beginning to wonder how long the heroic Girtnu Shav would stand quietly in the back."

"I wouldn't be very much of a hero if I didn't make a good entrance," he said, "Besides, I'd hate to interrupt my host in the middle of his story."

"I admire your patience," Bisseth said, and pivoted on one clawed foot to see his adversary in

Tie Your Own Rope

the flesh for the first time. "It's something I've found lacking in those of your profession."

The human Bisseth saw standing a few feet inside the cavernous chamber was clad in leather leggings and chain armor common to human warriors. His only hair was on the top and back of his head, and was a dusty blonde color not seen on Slitheren. He held his shield and sword ready, but not threatening. He smirked. All told, these postures showed the arrogance of a young human who had gone out and made a name for himself. Apparently he wasn't too arrogant to notice the spearheads inches from his back and arrows aimed at his chest, though, for he remained still.

"I'm flattered," the man replied, "So I'll do you a favor. If you let that maiden go, I'll leave here without killing you or any more of your followers."

"The renowned Girtnu Shav would leave the villagers of Wagonsflow defenseless against our warren in exchange for his woman? How noble." Bisseth paced slowly in front of the gray mantids' watery pit. "And how terribly human to expect that I'd believe you. I didn't insult your intelligence with promises that if you let us have yourself as a prisoner I'd let the female go free unharmed, after all. We both know what the other wants, and neither has reason to keep his word once we have it. So, Girtnu Shav, in the spirit of your patron I propose a game. If you don't accept, we'll just have to cut her down right now."

"I've never been very good at dice," the male's eyes were locked steadily on the helpless female. How easy to manipulate these emotional humans were.

"No, I was thinking of something simpler," the albino priest stopped and faced his opponent again. "As you've already gathered, if you take a step closer to your maiden, Tussilx here will cut the rope which holds her. She'd fall into this hole, which I assure you, she would find most unpleasant. You'd love to dash up here to clash with us before the rope can be cut, or leap across and catch her as she falls. I'd say it's roughly fifty human paces from you to me, though, and you know you could never make it in time."

"You've thought this through."

"Quite," Bisseth smiled at him. "I propose a series of exchanges. I'll give you distance each time you sacrifice a tool of your warrior trade. For example, if you cast off your shield, you may take ten paces forward. Keep in mind that you can end this game at any time. As soon as you make a rush for the girl or try anything violent, my fellow Slitheren will be free to execute you, and Tussilx will cut the rope. Once you think you're close enough to save her, the real fun can begin."

The bronze shield rang like a clarion when it fell to the rocky floor. The human's smirk turned to a wide grin as he took ten long steps forward. Walking to his own destruction and happy as he went, it was almost too easy with these adventuresome fools. Bisseth made a gesture, and the two bulky rats without weapons in their hands moved up to stand on either side of the man, a few feet behind him.

"A wise decision," Bisseth lied, "Would you hand your sword, hilt first, to one of my large friends, in exchange for another ten paces?"

Tie Your Own Rope

He did so, and the Slitheren tossed the heavy broadsword away to the side of the grotto. The pair then kept pace behind him during his ten steps.

"Girtnu, you're already losing," sighed the albino, "You really should have made counteroffers. Now all that's left of interest to me is your armor and you've got a ways left to go. How many paces do you want me to give you in trade for removing your chain mail and placing it on the ground?"

Human locked eyes with rat-priest for a long, silent minute. When he spoke it was a single, firm, emotionless syllable. "One," he said.

"Well I can't propose anything much lower than that," Bisseth laughed, "So I take it the heroics are about to begin? Very good, place your armor at your feet and take your desired 'one.'"

It took him a few moments to shrug out of the chain tunic. He removed the wool padding as well and set it on the floor beside his armor, leaving only a simple leather vest protecting his sinewy, thin frame. The moment he took his single stride forward two large pairs of clawed hands clamped onto his upper arms, almost lifting him off his feet.

"What's this?" he demanded.

"They're such good sports," answered Bisseth smoothly, "That they're going to take you the rest of the way to the pit, of course. Head first, I should think."

"Didn't anyone tell you rodents," the human growled defiantly, "That Girtnu Shav is a sorcerer?"

"The chosen hero of Enkili is a sorcerer as well, is he?" Bisseth said thoughtfully. If it was a bluff, it was not a very good one. "In that case, I seem to have only one option. Show Girtnu Shav how he failed. Tussilx, cut it."

The warren's high priest sliced his spear through the rope. Bisseth didn't watch though, he wanted to see the hero's reaction to her fall, not the relatively uninteresting plummet itself. The pitiful human squirmed futilely in the grasp of the two hulking Slitheren. All at once, behind Bisseth there was a rush of heat, a frightened hiss and a woman's laughing voice.

"I really do wish you'd stop calling me 'he,'" she said.

Cursing under his breath, Bisseth turned around. The top of Tailless's towering shield was charred. He'd gotten behind it in time to save himself, but it hadn't protected Tussilx. The albino ratman was slapping hysterically at his face and shoulders, where robes and fur blazed like a campfire. The rope had been cut. Its frayed end hung limply from the woman's wrists, but she hadn't fallen. She was floating in the air at exactly the spot she'd been dangling moments before.

Bisseth cursed louder.

Most of the Slitheren were too startled to immediately react, but the burly pair holding the now unarmed human warrior decided to play it safe. They each kept one hand on the man's arms and reached for the daggers sheathed in their belts. They didn't find them until a moment later, however, when they felt the knives not in their sheaths, but stabbing

Tie Your Own Rope

deeply into their bellies. Their prisoner easily slipped away from their dying grasps.

"What took you so long to get here, Piedrim?" Girtnu Shav called to him. Chykri swung his flail at her legs in a low sideswipe. Her simple spell of levitation didn't allow much mobility, but Girtnu leaned forward. Her body tipped at the waist, causing the spiked heads to harmlessly pass through the air under her. Laying flat in the air, Girtnu twisted her wrists out of the rope and grabbed the upper rim of the ratman's large shield. She was already mouthing the arcane words of another spell as she used the shield to pull herself toward Chykri.

Bisseth partly chanted, partly screamed a prayer to Chern. For an instant, Girtnu felt all of her muscles tense up at once, but the unholy magic passed over her, leaving only a strange tingling sensation. Her free hand snaked out and clasped onto the top of Chykri's skull just as her spell was complete. White-orange sparks leapt into the Slitheren's head. Fur singed and skin melted and peeled away. Still pulling herself forward on Chykri, she dropped the spell that held her suspended in the air. Girtnu Shav tumbled to the ground behind the electrocuted Shield of Chern.

"I wasn't carried here by an armed escort," Piedrim answered. The line of ratmen rushed toward him with their scimitars slicing through the air, even as the two spear-rats leapt down from the ledge above the tunnel mouth and advanced behind him. "And have you ever tried hiking in that damned chainmail? Cut me some-"

There was a twang of bowstrings and Piedrim threw himself backwards. Four arrows arced through where he'd been standing. When his back hit the ground he reached out and plucked the daggers from the stomachs of the husky Slitheren he'd already killed. He curled himself into a fetal ball, feeling a little like a taught bowstring himself.

The pair of Slitheren behind him crept up with their long, two-handed spears more cautiously than the four charging rats he was facing. He waited until they were almost upon him, the span of a few seconds, and released himself. With a dive, twist and roll he was suddenly standing behind the line of confused Slitheren, and one of them was gushing blood from a small but precise cut on the inside of its thigh. Another had two daggers thrown into its back before it could even turn around.

Piedrim glanced to the side of the chamber, at a niche in the wall two of the arrows had come from. He spotted it just in time to see Girtnu leap in front of the alcove with a fan of flames roiling from her hands. The two Slitheren archers lit up like candles and slumped together in a smoldering pile. The surviving ratman priest, Bisseth, was chasing after her with a rusty sickle that looked like a large, sharpened hook. Piedrim started to cry out a warning but was suddenly struck by a six-foot slab of wood and steel that seemed more like a wall than a shield.

"This was impressive, woman," snarled Bisseth. He stepped in and took another swing of his sickle. The curved blade passed within an inch of Girtnu's

Tie Your Own Rope

skin, cut through one of her bracelets and scattered the spell components tied to it. "I admit that when I watched your friend's inept fighting in the tunnel I was more concerned that Girtnu Shav wouldn't be an interesting adversary than I was over his fitness as a sacrifice to Chern. But you, Girtnu, you truly do me justice. I almost wish there was some way I could give you to the mantids but still keep you around for some crafty opposition. We could do this sort of thing all the time!"

Bisseth's strokes were slow but continual. The steady rise and fall of his sickle was fairly easy to dodge, but doing so kept pushing Girtnu back. She was always on the defensive and moving further away from Piedrim and the remaining Slitheren.

"You'll soon find once is enough, you stain," Girtnu answered. With a bark of ancient words and some rapid, intricate hand symbols she thrust both arms at the albino's chest. Another torrent of fire blazed from her palms. The flames licked Bisseth's body, dancing fountains of heat that wrapped around his arms and head. In the center of the pyre the white-haired rat-priest stood calm and serene.

"You do need to pay a little more attention to the conflict," he said to the sorceress, "I have been." With that he brought his sickle around in a quick flick that severed two of Girtnu's outstretched fingers.

Nearer the center of the grotto, Tailless had slammed his full-body shield into Piedrim and was running him toward the pair of Slitheren brandishing barbed spears. When he was pushed into range of the nearest one, he kicked off of Tailless's shield just as the ratman thrust with his spear. The edge of the spearhead scraped Piedrim's side, giving him a long gash above his right hip.

Once the head was past him, Piedrim spun along the spear, rolling against its shaft to keep his sense of direction while closing instantly with the Slitheren holding the weapon. His elbow lashed out at the end of his spin and smashed the rat's face. So quickly it seemed part of the same motion, he grabbed the unconscious ratman's spear before it even fell, let his momentum move the weapon with him and brought it in a wide slash at the second spear-rat. His speed alone made the strike successful. The spear's barbs tore the Slitheren's throat from its sinewy neck before it could bring its own weapon up to guard.

Piedrim stopped twirling, steadied himself for a moment, and caught sight of the other two Slitheren archers. They were on the opposite side of the cavern from the pair Girtnu had incinerated, and they were drawing back arrows. Still somewhat dizzy, but lacking a better option, he hurled the spear in their direction. The long spear was a little heavy for throwing and his equilibrium was off, but somehow it drove itself into the shoulder of one of the archers. The other ratman was startled by the accuracy of the foe and severe injury of its companion, but it had already released its arrow.

The Slitheren archer crawled into a small side tunnel and scurried away on all fours. Its arrow pierced Piedrim's thigh, the fletching sticking out the front and the arrowhead sticking out the back. The human considered his luck about even then, and that's when the flail hit him.

Tailless brought the flail down perfectly, its multiple chains and balls spread wide and striking Piedrim's back, shoulder, and head. The man's vision went dark and he staggered a few steps. He could feel hot stickiness running down the inside of his clothes.

"To the hells with this," Piedrim slurred, tasting his own blood, and collapsed.

Girtnu Shav watched Piedrim fall. She was still avoiding Bisseth's almost casual sickle strokes and trying to pinch off the blood flow from her three-fingered right hand. As she stared at the human body lying crumpled on the cold stone, ancient voices and strange shapes formed in her mind. Part of her consciousness could hear Bisseth intoning another prayer to Chern, but from somewhere within her another voice rose. The silky voice spoke in long-dead tongues and told her what the impossible shapes swimming in her vision were, and how they fit together.

She traced her hands through the bizarre shapes. Time seemed to slow down for Girtnu Shav as she recreated the forms of things which couldn't exist. Darkness billowed out of her bloody hand. For a moment, her own palm seemed like a vast landscape of fleshy plains and red rivers, with clouds of purest black rolling overhead. The darkness coalesced into a short shard Girtnu held between her remaining fingers.

The name of a man long dead entered Girtnu's mind as the voice faded away, but she chose to ignore it. She let the shaft of shadows fly at Tailless. When it struck the Shield of Chern in the back he shuddered and convulsed. His eyes rolled back in his furry head and he dropped face-first onto his shield. The spell had destroyed his life without leaving a mark on his body.

"I didn't," Girtnu whispered, staring wide-eyed at the lifeless Slitheren, "I didn't know I could do that."

A single clawed finger touched her forehead, jolting her back to reality. She heard the albino's voice speak the words "...of the Last Great Suffering," and she was engulfed in sensations.

"Didn't you?" asked Bisseth. "I wondered why your own magic would seem to fascinate you so, but I appreciated your distraction." His words screeched razorblades through Girtnu's ears. Her bones pulsed and throbbed as though they'd rip her apart from inside. Every nerve in her body tied into one fat knot, which was ground under an iron boot.

Bisseth grabbed the back of Girtnu Shav's neck and began dragging her floundering body back to the watery hole where the egg-swollen gray mantids swam. Bolts of agony lashed through her lungs with every breath.

"Don't worry," the albino told her, "This torment is only mental. What you're feeling now won't kill you. Rest assured that you'll still be alive when the mantids lay their eggs in you, and you'll be around to enjoy the very real ravages of the new disease Chern will breed within you."

Tie Your Own Rope

The Slitheren's words didn't even register in her mind anymore. Every inch of her body cried out at the ever-mounting and indescribable pain.

"Almost there now, and then the little mothers can have their meal," said Bisseth, stepping over Piedrim's bloody body. He paused and blinked a moment, recalling the battle. "Hadn't he been fighting over-"

The scimitar hilt was jammed against the front of his hipbone. Its blade ran through his belly, inside of his ribcage and the point just barely stuck out behind his collarbone. In the surreal moment before Bisseth the Slitheren Priest and Hero Slayer realized he was dead, he looked at the sharp, glinting scimitar point. And then it twisted.

As the albino's life faded, so did Girtnu Shav's agony. She ached all over and was still dazed from the pain, but she managed to stand. Piedrim shoved the fallen Slitheren's body off of himself and tried to do the same.

"What about the other two," she asked him wearily, "the ones behind the Shield?"

"After you did whatever that was you did to the one without a tail they came over to see if I was dead," Piedrim grimaced. "I wasn't." He thought for a moment.

"You're not mad at me for laying down on the job?" he asked. "I felt like taking a little break."

"If we can drag each other to the healer's house I'll forgive you," said Girtnu. They leaned on each other's shoulders and staggered out of the caverns. It wasn't until they were out in the cool night air and halfway back to Wagonsflow that either spoke again.

"You know, there was a pit full of nasty biting things back there," said Piedrim, "And none of the ratmen fell into it. It won't make a very good tale."

"So we'll tell the bards you pushed the high priest into it and he was killed by his own monsters," she shrugged, "Right before saving the defenseless maiden."

"You mean that you pushed him in?" said Piedrim.

"You know damn well who I mean," sighed Girtnu Shav.

The River's Flow
By Alejandro Melchor

There was a time when Jedem would cast off his clothes and enjoy the fury of the storm; he'd find the highest rock in the grove and climb it, letting the wind buffet his hair and the rain wash his body of impurities, feeling the thunder rumble down to his core.

That time was long past, and Jedem now huddled beneath an outcropping, drawing the bearskin that he used for a cloak tighter, and fueling the small fire he'd build. He coughed as the smoke and the cold ambushed his breath. The storm raged the same as the others before it; year after year, they came down to touch the scarred face of Ghelspad; they were always the same, it was Jedem who was changing.

The druid threw another humid log to the fire. He was old now; any other man would be dead now, killed by the weight of a lifetime. But he was a faithful servant of Denev, the Earth Mother, and her favor allowed him the health of a much younger man. But not even the sole remaining Titan could stop the cycle of life, and Jedem was feeling his body complain.

He would laugh each time lightning struck; now he only winced.

He'd abandoned his grove, left it in charge of his disciple; he'd been traveling for a couple of years, taking one last sight at the world before surrendering his body to Denev. In truth, he'd been wishing to leave for a long time; his duty tending the lands around him grew tiresome with each passing winter. He had no more patience with the men from the villages, always trying to encroach on his forest. Some of them were respectful, and devoutly prayed for Denev's permission before cutting down the trees. He'd have none of it, but he sensed that his mistress was giving her blessing to these loggers and farmers.

He didn't understand it then, and he didn't understand it now. That's why he'd made preparations and passed on

The River's Flow

his duties years before he really felt Denev's call. Was he being irresponsible? Maybe, but he couldn't honestly maintain his position while harboring such strong doubts in his heart.

He was turning his ideas about his head when he heard the steps. It wasn't an animal, since they had more sense than to travel in this weather, and the pacing was clearly human. Loud, trampling... intruding.

The traveler came into view. Jedem's haven was part of a slow-climbing hill, so he could spot the intruder well before he noticed the fire. The figure was covered with a light cloak, so soaked it couldn't possibly serve more than to weigh down its wearer, instead of protecting him against the rain. However, the stranger didn't seem uncomfortable, his steps sure and unwavering. Not even the wet leaves covering the ground presented more than a moment's distraction when they slipped beneath he walker's feet.

Jedem made no noise, but he also made no move to hide or call attention. When he was younger, he'd have invited the traveler to share his refuge from the elements, but now he just wished to be left alone.

No such luck, as the stranger stopped and looked the druid's way. Beneath the hood, a delicate chin revealed the age of the traveler, a young boy barely through his adolescence. The boy greeted Jedem silently before approaching the shelter. Jedem grunted to himself.

"Greetings, old one." The boy spoke, still outside in the weather. "May I share your fire in this rain? I have food to share."

"Do as you will, child." Jedem answered. He'd really have liked the newcomer to keep on his way, let him catch his death of cold for his foolishness in defying the storm.

Only when the new arrival put the cloak aside did Jedem realize he'd been mistaken; it wasn't a boy, it was a girl. No older than twenty springs, she dressed in a rag tied together with tattered scraps of fabric; her hair was cut short, in a style that would've strengthened the false impression about her gender. The druid realized his visitor was female only because her soaked clothes clung to her body.

"I was caught in the storm." She said simply. "I didn't expect it to hit so suddenly."

Jedem grunted, looking away from her. A girl traveling alone, dressed like a boy. She'd have to worry about more than the weather.

"You're a druid, aren't you?" She asked as she got something from the sack that hung from her shoulder.

Jedem eyed her suspiciously. He had cut his beard just after setting out of his grove, and he had changed his ironwood staff for a more plain-looking walking cane. There was nothing in his appearance that would reveal his nature except to the prejudiced, who thought any old man in the woods just had to be a druid. He remained silent.

Her answer unsettled Jedem; instead of pressing the point, she just smiled at him and remained silent as well. She offered a handful of dried fruits, but Jedem made no move to accept or reject them. She shrugged and let her offering on the ground between them.

By the time the storm turned into a drizzle, it was already sunset, which meant that traveling would have to wait for the next day. In all that time, neither girl nor old man had uttered a word.

She got up without warning and without hurry, stepping out of the shelter of the rock and into the rain. He didn't ask anything; soon it would be dark, and she hadn't taken her things with her. She came back minutes later, and set some firewood on the ground.

Jedem wondered at the reasons behind her being there; it wasn't normal for a human her age to be traveling, and she seemed completely at ease with a complete stranger.

The River's Flow

But the most intriguing was her silence. He'd been dreading an evening ignoring a youth's chatter, but instead he who grew increasingly uncomfortable by the lack of words. He fell asleep shortly after she did.

The next morning, the rain had turned into a fine mist, with droplets falling and mixing with the dew. Jedem opened his eyes and found that the girl was gone. Good riddance. The moist air played havoc with his legs, and he rubbed them to ease the light cramping he was feeling. He stretched and prepared to resume his travel. With mixed feelings he discovered the girl's cloak and sack near the smoking remains of the fire.

He heard something slide in the mud, then the wet sound of a foot coming down. He peered around the rock and, sure enough, there she was. Dancing? The druid leaned on a tree; the slippery ground made it difficult to stand, and he wanted to analyze what she was doing. She stood with her legs spread, her arms moving in circles in a slow and graceful pattern. One step after another, she moved as if the ground was dry and firm. She kept this on for a few minutes before standing straight and pushing her hands down at the same time she exhaled audibly. She opened her eyes, which Jedem hadn't noticed were closed during her dance. She smiled again, and started walking to their rocky shelter.

"Yes, I am." The druid answered her question from yesterday.

"I'm glad I haven't forgotten to recognize Denev's touch." She nodded. "My name is Essery."

"Jedem."

She bowed lightly.

"We should be on our way, Jedem." She continued.

He nodded; though he wasn't in any hurry about getting anywhere, there was the danger of mudslides after a continuous rain. He returned to the road, and Essery caught up with him seconds after, fastening her cloak.

"You don't mind a companion, I hope." She said. "There is safety in numbers."

"An old man and a young girl are better targets then either alone." He answered from experience; he'd crossed paths once with a band of brigands who wanted to set base in his forest. It was a fine lesson in human nature when he failed to save a farmer and his granddaughter. He chuckled, what irony that this time it was him who was the old man.

"Ah, but then I can count on your help in fending off any attacker." She spoke with such assurance that he nearly believed it. The druid only shook his head and continued walking.

The remainder of the morning passed as last night had: silent. He had ample chance to measure up his uninvited companion. In his long years of service to Denev, he'd learned to recognize the strength and weaknesses of all living creatures. He could even adopt the form of some of them, but he'd never seen together in one place the great cats' grace, the stag's speed and the bear's strength, until now. Even he, used to walk in the wilderness, was having a hard time dealing with the muddied road, but the girl's steps were sure and steady.

Just when he thought he understood nature's mysteries, she presented him with another.

By early evening they reached a small town, a logger town as far as Jedem could see. There were some farming fields, but the remains of cut trees that stretched around the periphery was a telltale sign of the town's true source of income. With a perverse glee, Jedem noticed that some of the farmland was flooded, and there were makeshift dams on the river's shores. Such is the defiance of humans against Denev, and such is their punishment.

The River's Flow

There were no peasants tending to the fields, and they reached the town proper without meeting a soul.

"Hello?" Essery called, raising her voice but not actually yelling. "It doesn't look like a ghost town."

"Indeed." Jedem looked around. "But we may yet find some information." He walked over to where he'd seen some movement. "Come here, little brother..." He whispered, and seconds after a dog peered around the corner.

"Yes, we are just travelers." The druid explained, attuning his soul to the animal's, sharing one meaning. "Where are the big two-leggers that make their dens of wood?"

The dog whimpered and grunted. He heard Essery's steps behind him, but he kept concentrating on the divine gift that allowed him to understand the dog.

"What's he saying?"

"All the people are upstream." He said after a few moments of talking with the mutt. "The old and the young are praying at a nearby shrine to Madriel."

"Flooding." She stated simply. "The townsfolk must be trying to keep the river from overflowing."

"Without much success." He pointed at the fields they'd walked past. "It's folly to even try and constrict the river. Ah, well, provisions will have to wait until next town."

The druid walked off, in the direction of the town's end.

"Wait, don't you want to talk to the villagers?"

"What for?" The druid turned to answer the girl's question. She was absent-mindedly petting the dog he'd just talked to.

"Well, for once, to ask them where we can cross the river." Her smile was knowing, in a mischievous way.

Jedem frowned.

"If there's been a flooding." She continued. "It's a good bet that any bridge this town had was washed away, and we can't possibly swim across a river that overflows. The choice is to go back where we came from... but it looks like another storm is coming."

She spoke matter-of-factly. With another grunt, Jedem cast his soul upwards, uttering a prayer to his patron Titan. He was the clouds and the wind pushing them. He felt laden with water and about to burst. He felt lightning crackle around his limbs as they moved against each other. Essery was right, another storm would hit very soon.

"Travelers!" Someone shouted, waking Jedem out of his casting. A woman with a child trailing her was walking hurriedly, while waving a crude greeting. "My apologies, travelers, I'm Decha, my husband owns the general store and inn, but he's away with the rest of the men."

"Hello!" Essery waved back, then bowed as she'd done before.

"Why, such a pretty girl! Too bad about your hair, would you and your grandfather wish for someplace to pass the night?"

"Oh, we're not related." The girl cleared the issue, stealing Jedem's words from his mouth. Of course, he had intended to be more biting.

"Oh, dear..."

"We're not married either." Essery's laughter was like a crystalline waterfall. "We're just traveling companions, and for merely a day too."

The woman looked puzzled, less able to accept Essery as a lone traveler than Jedem was the night before.

"His name is Jedem." The girl started their introductions, leaning closer and speaking with a loud whisper. "He's not very friendly."

The River's Flow

Jedem heard her, as she probably wanted. He decided to ignore her.

"And I'm Essery, from Hedrad."

"Hedrad?" The woman was shocked; the druid hid his surprise. "You're all the way from Hedrad?"

"Not really." Essery answered. "But I started my travels there. But you're right; the road's been hard and we need a place to dry our cloaks and eat something warm."

"Of… course…" The woman doubted before breaking into a grin. "Lerin! Go fetch your father!"

The boy ran off, and Decha guided them towards what passed for an inn in this town. It had only four tables and the bar was barely enough for three patrons, but the fireplace was solid, and the place was well kept. Decha served them a cup of hot tea and, a few minutes after the two travelers had settled, the smell of cooking reached them.

"The town does well." Essery commented, leaning back on her chair. "Or else they're very hospitable."

"They cut down trees." Jedem said. "They rape the land. Of course they do well."

"Oh." She looked at him seriously.

The old druid looked back, staring into her eyes, ready to show her a lifetime of witnessing humans' abuses of his beloved land. He found himself blinking an instant later. She looked back, beyond sadness and pity, with an infinite understanding.

"How old are you?" He measured his words carefully.

"Now, now; that's very rude of you!" She laughed again.

"Answer me, girl. I'm very serious."

"Fine. My mother bore me nineteen summers ago." She rested her chin on her hands. "How about you?"

"I reach my sixtieth winter this year." He answered, still suspicious. He felt around her; trying to find traces of any magic. He found none.

"It's rude to stare too." She interrupted his scrutiny.

"Are you human?"

"As they come. Ah! Supper!" She cheered as the woman arrived with two bowls of stew. "My deepest thanks! I don't mind trail rations, but I certainly missed a hot meal!" She received their hostess with a wink. "It's one of the small sins I simply can't get rid off."

"Dear girl; what's so sinful about a nice hot bowl of stew?"

"That's what I always told my teacher." Essery dug into her bowl with enthusiasm.

Jedem ate without taking his eyes of his young companion. The broth was good, he had to admit, and he admitted waiting too long for something warm to put in his stomach.

"What are all the menfolk working at?" Jedem asked Cheda.

"River blocks." The woman answered from the bar. "We've had very strong rains this season and the river is overflowing. My husband says no more crops will be ruined once they finish.

Essery eyed him intently, then pointed her eyes to the sky. The next storm. The druid huffed; let it come and wash away the houses and fields, the tools and the furniture. If it was Denev's will to clean the face of the land, who are humans to dare try to stop Her?

"Cheda!" A man entered the room, followed by the child they'd seen before, surely the innkeeper. "What…? Oh, I'm sorry, travelers; I welcome you to my humble inn… if you'll just wait a moment… Cheda!"

The River's Flow

The man took his wife away to a corner and began arguing as quietly as he could.

"It's over us." Essery informed, her head cocked in the villager's direction. "He wants us to leave."

"I'll be happy to oblige." Jedem commented.

"No, it's not because of hospitality… it's… he's saying the town is not safe."

"You have keen ears."

"Ah… good folk…" The innkeeper approached them, hands clasped together and with an apologetic smile. "I'm afraid I must ask you to leave. Don't be mistaken, we receive all visitors with open arms…"

Essery turned to Jesem.

"It's just that it's not safe tonight; the river is overflowing…"

"So we've noticed." Essery said. "Would you be needing some help?" The man paused to digest her words.

"If you have a way of bringing several strong men to help with the blocks; certainly." He answered. "The rains have been bad, already a nearby farm was buried by a mudslide; we lost our bridge two days ago, and we fear we may not contain the river for much longer if the rains keep up."

"Are… are you a wizard, sir?" The boy asked Jedem.

"No." he said bluntly.

"Illhem! Don't bother our guests!" The woman chided her son.

"The boy's heard too many stories." The man said. "But magic would certainly give us a much-needed hand."

"Don't worry." Essery said, and smiled softly when Jedem glared at her. "We can't travel either in this weather anyway. Jedem here is too old, but I'll gladly give you a hand for your hospitality."

"But…"

"I'm stronger than I look." She beamed at him, Jedem was disgusted by the way the girl easily disarmed any argument from the innkeeper: she just smiled reassuringly.

"Can you look after my things while I'm gone?" She asked the druid.

"No." He rose. "I'll go too."

"Dear guests... it's too much to ask!" The innkeeper complained. "With all respect, but an old man and a young girl will only get in our way; please accept my gratitude and turn back, while you still can."

"Rest easy." Essery put a hand on the man's shoulder, like a father who's trying to inspire confidence in his child. "When my companion deigns to speak, his words bear a wisdom of their own. As for me..." She patted the innkeeper's shoulder. "I'll show you once we get there."

They followed the man, who later introduced him as Gareth. They walked a path covered in mud. Jedem slipped twice, the innkeeper three times as many. Only Essery seemed like she was actually enjoying the scenery and not worrying where she stepped.

"So, why did you come?" Essery asked the druid; Gareth had gone ahead once the path upstream reached higher ground.

"Curiosity."

"About the villagers' efforts?"

"About you."

"Oh, Jedem. What's there to see? I'm a simple girl." Her reply was jovial.

"What are you?" He asked. "You're not fey, and I sense no magic around you."

"True enough."

With those two words, she told him he knew what he was asking, and she also dared him to find the answer on his own.

The River's Flow

There were around two-dozen people gathered among scattered sacks and logs, arguing loudly.

"Here they are!" Gareth pointed at them. Another villager, covered in mud, walked over angrily, wielding a shovel. He pointed at the two of them with the metal end.

"You shouldn't be here!"

"We know." Essery answered calmly.

"You're in danger, you fools!" The villager shouted. "I don't know what this idiot and his wife told you, but the river will flood soon, and drown everything in this valley."

"Then why are you still trying?" The girl asked with complete innocence, hiding Jedem's low chuckle.

"Wh…what?"

"I ask, why do you try, if you know you'll lose in the end?"

"It's… we…. Look, little girl…" He pointed the shovel at her and stared in amazement at his now empty hand.

Jedem was looking at Essery. Now she had disarmed the man with an ease that spoke of a warrior's training; she now held the shovel, and was leaning on it.

"It's rude to point, specially with a sharp object." She said.

"Er… sorry."

"All right!" She gave the shovel back. "Now, Jedem, is there a way in which you can help these people?"

Of course there was, Jedem thought. He could conjure the incoming storm away, he could harden the peasants' crude blocks into hard barriers of ironwood and stone; he could even have the trees still standing help build the blocks, or invoke a wall of stone that would serve much better than their inappropriate bulwarks. But he wouldn't; Denev had decreed the storm, and if a human settlement was washed away, it was because it was built where it shouldn't.

"No." He answered finally; Essery just shrugged.

"Figured as much." She turned to the villagers. "Right, people. Give me something to do!"

The druid spent remaining hours until dusk watching the girl intently; she didn't lie when she said she was stronger than she seemed. She was also tireless. No matter how hard the task was set upon her frail-looking shoulders, she finished it without complaint, and with the good cheer to joke around. The men's morale increased a thousand fold, and by the time the sun hid behind the horizon, they had made great progress.

The men themselves were amazed at how far they've built their blocks. Jedem faded into the background, letting his presence be forgotten. He looked at everyone work hard at a completely futile task. It reminded him of ants.

They all returned to the town in good spirits; several buildings had light coming from inside, but none of the farms did. The druid supposed that they were being cautious, keeping all the people in the settlement together in case of a disaster. The fools didn't realize that they stood a better chance by scattering; the flood would take them all out in one swoop.

"Gods, I'm beat!" Essery crumbled on one of the inn's chairs; the room was packed, with all the men and some of their wives and daughters.

"You realize you worked for nothing." Jedem talked low.

"Yes." She answered.

"Why, then?"

"Look at them, Denev's son." She gestured toward the peasants. "They too know they face their death and that of their loved ones; yet their spirits are high."

"Sheer foolishness." He grumped. Already someone had taken out some musical instruments and they were all singing.

The River's Flow

"They tried to turn us away." The girl leaned closer to him; he could smell her, sweat and mud and dried leaves. "They wanted to spare us the fate they fear. You know of the coming storm; probably they know too."

"Except I know exactly how strong it will be." Jedem wanted to prove how Denev favored him, not these people that abused her.

"Why haven't you left yet, then?"

"Because…" He hesitated; it was an excellent question. "I have ways to survive, and I'm still curious."

"I hope your curiosity can outweigh your conscience." She was uncharacteristically serious. "You have these people's salvation in your hands."

"Only by the power Denev grants me." He hissed. "And who am I to go against Her will?"

"You know Denev's will?" She countered.

"Of course! I've served Her for longer than you've even been alive!"

"Humans have trouble understanding the will of the gods, and they're here with us." She looked at the townsfolk. "You think you can understand the will of a Titan?"

"You speak nonsense, girl."

"Maybe." She got up. "But consider this, mighty druid: If Denev believed as you do… would she have helped the gods in the Titanswar?"

She walked into the mob, leaving Jedem scowling. He left the room angrily, shutting the music and laughter from his ears. The last thing he heard from the annoying girl was her rejecting a marriage proposal.

He saw lightning in the distance, and felt the wind. The storm would be here tomorrow, if not tonight.

He was tempted to raise his hands and bring the storm over. Have it hit now and be rid of all this nonsense for good.

"Jedem?"

"Go back to the room, girl." He grumbled. "You have a good chance of catching a husband in there. Of course, you wouldn't be able to consummate the union once both of you die tomorrow."

"Dear gods…" She approached, bringing with her a pair of steaming mugs. She handed one to him, but he crossed his arms. "Well, Nard is a sweet young man, but I won't marry in this life, I took a vow of chastity upon entering the order."

Jedem looked at her intently, mulling over the bit of truth she'd dropped on his lap.

"I'd never been outside the monastery until last year, when it was my turn to serve the priests at Hedrad. I took the chance to explore the world, see the land, meet the people… It's another one of my sins. I grow too attached to persons and places. Mostly persons."

"You… defied your masters?" Jedem was shooting in the dark. If this girl was a monk, as her words implied, it would explain many things; from her appearance to her solitary travels."

"Such a strong word…" She smiled again. "It was more like a philosophical disagreement on methods of spiritual improvement."

"You're a rogue, then."

"Miss Essery?" The innkeeper's wife came out. "I've arranged quarters for you and your friend. You'll be sleeping at my house, of course; can't trust any of those louts to keep their hands off such a sweet and pretty girl."

"Don't worry about them." Essery smiled. "They'll get to keep their hands. Good night, Jedem."

He ignored her again. She had managed to leave the cup she brought him on the ground, near the hem of his tunic. He kicked it over.

The River's Flow

The storm was considerate enough to announce itself with a drizzle that started a little before sunrise, and that midmorning had grown into heavy rain. The men scrambled to check the blocks they'd built yesterday, and some of the women went with them. Essery went with the men, but Jedem opted to stay in the town this time.

The old, the females, the young... prey for nature's unforgiving cycle. They piled more wood, from shattered barrels, tables and chairs; he spotted the remains of a cart, even. He walked to the river; climbing over the barricade the peasants had built first, the one protecting their homes. The river wasn't too wide here; twenty feet at the most, but the water was brown, carrying the mountains' dirt in its fury. The water level was still two feet below the top of the mud barricade, but it wouldn't hold for much longer. Already he could spot stress points where the river struggled to break free, and the level was rising.

He should leave. He didn't care for these people's future, but he wasn't one to relish their pain either. He knew they would all die today, drowned and crushed. Here, a young mother helped her son carry off a piece of what once could've been a bed to the pile, where the men would pick it up and use it to reinforce the blocks.

An old man was trying to calm down a pair of wailing children, speaking about how the heroes of the Titanswar didn't cry.

How could he know what the War was like? How could any mortal? Even one who remembered the battles didn't truly understand the scope of what was being fought over. A man might lose his family and suffer a great hurt. But a god who lost followers felt the loss intensely.

And what of Denev? Jedem remembered Essery's question; why did she fight with the gods? She didn't feel the mortals' pain, she was a Titan... but she could feel her siblings' ravages on the face of Scarn. Then again, she could've remained neutral; why did she fight.

The sky wept for an eternity, and Jedem was fascinated by the slow increase in the water level. He heard a roar from upstream. He sighed. It was the sign of this town's doom. He walked away from the river and in the direction where the men were hard at work. Maybe he wanted to ask Essery her thoughts about the Titanswar. For one so young, she already had proven wiser than him in many of life's ways.

He felt the pressure in his bones seconds before the river came thundering down, splashing over the barricades and threatening to wash them over. He hurried his pace. If the river were like this here, it would be like a wild beast broken loose upstream. His feet splashed on water running down, less than an inch deep, but it meant that the blocks had given in. He heard the shouts before he could see the men, trying to pry loose a tree that had washed down and was now making a dam. He looked for the girl, and found her standing amidst the men; apparently, the tree had trapped one of the villagers in its branches as it tumbled down. The men were trying to lift the trunk, but it was too thick and too slippery, and they were loosing their handhold. The part of the tree that was on the river budged; if they didn't rescue the snared man, he'd be carried down river, to his death. He saw Essery move her hands in a slow, wide arc and, with a short yell, struck at the log. There was a loud crack of wood, and she struck again. She began hacking at the branches with her bare hands, until two more men could maneuver their neighbor out of the deadly trap.

"We must go back!" One of the farmers yelled. "There's nothing more we can do here!"

"No!" Another tried to make himself heard over the rain's and the river's din. "If we hold fast here, the river…"

The River's Flow

"The river is already breaking through!" The druid surprised himself. "You must release the pressure from here if you want your town to survive!"

"But what about the crops!?"

"You must choose!" Jedem cried angrily. "Your crops or your families!"

An anguished silence followed the old man's words.

"Let's use the tree!" The young man who had asked for Essery's hand in marriage shouted. "If we break the barricade from the other side, it won't flood the farmlands!"

"Right! Let's push!" As one, the men ran over to the tree that had almost claimed the life of one of them.

"You came." Essery approached the druid as the peasants got in position.

"I liked you better when you didn't speak." Jedem grumbled, watching the men work. "They're still doomed."

"Yet you gave them a glimmer of hope."

"Wait! No! Stop! Damnation!"

Both of them turned to see the felled tree slide off the barricade's edge into the raging waters, leaving an opening where water was spilling through.

The strong current pushed the old tree down, making it twist and bump against the blocks, weakening the packed mud constructions.

"The town." Jedem realized aloud. "The barricades near the town are already weak."

"What? How do you know?" Jedem was too preoccupied to notice that, for the first time, there was strain in Essery's voice.

"I was there. I saw. I felt." He answered, finally turning to see her.

"Men! Back to the town!" She shouted, and no one questioned her authority.

The villagers started to run, but it wasn't easy for them, with water running faster than them under their feet. The terrain's inclination didn't help their balance either. Essery gained ground, barely touching the ground in her hurry. Jedem was doing all he could to keep his breath; healthy he was, but years pressed on his chest and robbed him of his former strength.

"Damn you, girl…" He panted, seeing her figure become smaller, until he lost her in the small forest that grew between the town and their position. At that rate, maybe she would outrun the floating tree. "And damn my years."

He stopped to rest, letting the peasants pass him. He concentrated and prayed; he asked forgiveness for his doubts, and closed his eyes. He begged to Denev to grant him the stag's speed and vitality; he needed them now if he was ever to reach the town in time.

In time for what? He asked himself. The answer came likewise: to save that stupid girl from her own altruism.

He completed the prayer and felt the heat run from his heart and extend to his limbs. He was now the stag, and no human would ever outrun him. So he ran downstream, not noticing when he left the villagers behind or when he discarded his cloak and bared his torso by abandoning his shirt. All he cared now was to reach the town.

"Sir! Please help us!" Cheda, the innkeeper's wife, called for him once he arrived. He paid no heed to her summons, instead checking the barricade's soundness. They were holding, with the efforts of old men and children, but they were holding. However, water was trickling from the points where the river found an opening. There was no sign of Essery.

"Sir!" The woman now reached his side, with urgency streaming out from her very pose.

The River's Flow

"What is it, woman!?"

"It's young Essery! She's trapped!"

"Take me." He stated.

"One... one of the children." The woman explained as she guided him towards the river, there were several women shouting, doing nothing in desperation as there was nothing to be done. "He... he fell in the river when reinforcing the block. The dear girl dove after him and managed to catch him, but then, then..."

They arrived, and Jedem didn't need an explanation. The tree had gotten there, despite Essery's speed, and had knocked her down. Now it was stranded on the opposite shore, and had the girl and the boy she tried to save pinned in the middle of the river. She was holding the kid high with both arms, and trying to stay afloat kicking with one of her legs, the other snared by the branches, probably broken. The boy was crying as if he'd just been born.

"Essery!"

"The child!" She yelled. "Take... the child!" She was exhausted; the work on the blocks and her frantic run had surely depleted her strength. Her head went under, but surfaced again with an agonized expression: she'd had to twist her trapped leg further.

Jedem stood motionless. He'd sworn he wouldn't interfere in this disaster, and already he'd done too much. Nevertheless, he cringed when the tree nudged a bit, threatening to take both it's victims down.

He heard the men arriving, still indecisive.

"Bring rope!" One of the men shouted. "Tie me, I'll dive after them!"

"That's insane!" Jedem faced the man, the farmer Essery had disarmed yesterday. "You will all drown!"

"Do you have a better idea, old man?" He retorted, tying a rope someone had fetched around his waist. As if following a secret order, all the men ran upstream. They meant to let the current do part of the job of helping them reach the trapped children.

Jedem was grinding his teeth; it was useless. Even if they reached Essery, they wouldn't be able to free her from the tree. They could save the boy, but she would be helpless. And if he did try to free her, it only increased the chances of the tree freeing itself from its moorings and tumble downstream, killing all of them.

He saw as the farmer dove into the brown stream, fighting to gain some ground inward as the current pushed him forward. The rest of the men held the rope and tried to keep their footing in the mud, wiping the still falling rain from their eyes.

All the women screamed when the log turned on its axis and sank Essery and the boy. The farmer tried to swim harder, but if the others released more rope, he'd only go past his target. Jedem extended his hand; but closed it in a fist. This surely was Denev's will; why would he defy Her?

The child surfaced suddenly, holding Essery's free leg with the strength only fright gives. She had kicked the boy up and was now holding him afloat with her leg, keeping her balance with her arms. Soon, she would drown.

The farmer reached the tree, but he was on the wrong side of the trunk.

"Swim under!" A woman cried.

"No! He'll be trapped too!" Another argued.

Essery's leg flexed, and shot upward; she kicked the boy upward and over the trunk. He fell within the brave farmer's reach. The man grabbed the boy with one arm, and tried to climb over the tree in a desperate effort to get to the drowning girl. The tree rocked again. For a second, Jedem thought he saw her head surface and take a big breath, then sink again. The tree was loose.

The River's Flow

The men on the shore began pulling on the rope, while the farmer made a last attempt to rescue Essery.

Why? Jedem asked in silence. Why is this man risking his life for a child that's not his own? To save a girl he only met yesterday? What had made them all act as one when one of their numbers was in danger? Essery's suitor dove in as well, holding onto the rope. The first farmer handed him the child and went back to the tree, but it had turned more, sinking the girl under it. Now there was no chance; she would die.

Jedem felt blood on his hands. He'd stayed true to the ways of Nature: impartial, centered. When had his disinterest turned into apathy? When had he begun to believe only in Denev's destructive face? He was witness to man's best aspects here; the farmer had everything to lose by trying to save Essery. All the other's efforts would be better put to use by strengthening the barricades and saving the whole town, instead of only one girl.

He felt it then, the feeling he had lost years, decades ago. The women's anguish was his own anguish; the relief at seeing the boy saved was his too, as was the despair of the farmer who couldn't find the girl he was risking his life to rescue. The druid had blamed the humans for forgetting their ties to the land. Meanwhile, he'd forgotten his own ties to the rest of humanity.

He understood Essery's riddle now. Why had Denev fought alongside the gods against her brothers and sisters? Because She was linked to the land, and felt it's suffering. Because She was maybe the only Titan able to feel the lesser creatures' pain. How would She not ally with Her children?

Jedem extended his will; he felt the tree's branches, he saw the dimming light of Essery's life. He was now one with river and mud. He gnarled his fingers, and the trees' branches gnarled in response; roots grew and fastened to the riverbank and the wood twisted. His soul cried to Denev as his mind shaped the tree to hold the girl aloft. He felt the pulse of a far of lightning, and he made its energy his; he laughed at the raw power coursing through his fingertips.

Essery woke up in bed; the sun was high in the sky, a deep blue sky. Her leg was fastened to a straight stick. Jedem watched her, unmoving, from the room's corner. With the cloth removed from his eyes, he could now recognize the joy of life in her every movement.

"Well, it seems Hedrada will have to wait some more." She said.

He rose and kneeled next to the bed, now echoing her smile.

"You idiotic, impulsive…" He didn't finish; she put a finger on his lips and caressed his wrinkled face.

"You remembered." Her eyes were a pool with unfathomable depths.

"And almost too late." He said, feeling now his connection to her. He took her hand between his.

"I was ready to die. It didn't matter." She looked at him. "I would come back, as I've done before, and as I will do again, until I feel the time is right to join Hedrada."

"As you said, he can wait." The druid stood up. "There is little sunshine in this world, girl. Who am I to let even a single ray be extinguished?"

Thief's Mark
By Carl Bowen

Carl Bowen

Camouflaged in leaves and scraps and castoff clothing, the half-orc highwayman known as Kaltaag lay silent on a thick oak branch that hung over the forest path. Two more men had taken similar positions in the nearby branches and underbrush, and the three of them formed a loose ring around a dark and narrow pass in the nighted woods. Kaltaag's mismatched articles of clothing and the leafy branches he'd added to them made him almost invisible against the forest canopy, and his companions were equally camouflaged. The others held unstrung short bows and waited with arrows ready in bristling quivers. Kaltaag himself lay in wait with a heavy crossbow braced between the branch, his shoulder and his outstretched hand. Shadows draped over him and caressed him like Drendari's amorous hands as he peered up the path.

The path was a seldom-used stretch of a trade route that ran from the Heteronomy of Virduk through the northeastern corner of Zathiske, southeast through Ankila and on into the outlying territories of Calastia itself. It joined up with many major Hegemony trade routes, but not for dozens of miles in either direction, so Calastian patrols of this particular area were few and sometimes days between. What kept the locals from letting the path become overgrown and fall into disuse, though, was the fact that it skirted the Calastian old-growth forest known as Geleeda's Grove and poachers from that forbidden forest used the route to transport their illicit goods. The existence of these poachers (however few) warranted the infrequent Calastian patrols, which,

Thief's Mark

in turn, provided desperate (or simple-minded) peasants from the Heteronomy, Zathiske or Ankila the illusion that the path was relatively safe as long as one moved with purpose and left his fellow travelers alone. Yet, the force that undermined even the shred of security that the locals felt in relation to the path lay in the hands of rogues such as Kaltaag and his cohorts.

Today, however, few travelers had availed themselves of these bandits' predations. The three thieves had been biting their thumbs and waiting since the late afternoon when they'd taken their positions, and not so much as a wagon or trader cart had come by in all that time. This drought particularly agitated Kaltaag today, for it was the day before the Thieves' Festival in the city of Gnersh in the country of Zathiske, and he had promised himself that the next raid he and his men pulled would be the last for the week. When it was over, he'd decided, he would send his men home and go to the festival, just as he did every year.

Yet, it was not until late evening that a covered wagon finally came creaking and bumping west down the path unescorted. It was alone and small, but it was in good condition, and the two horses pulling it were fine, healthy geldings. The wagon's owner might be wealthy enough to be carrying something of value, even if it wasn't King Virduk's royal hoard of gold and gems. Kaltaag could feel the other bandits peering at him, waiting for the whistled birdcall that would signal the attack, and he gave it gladly. Waiting for a suitable target on a busy travel day was one thing;

waiting for *any* target at the end of an already long day was torture. Especially when he had plans in the offing already. Kaltaag's men strung their bows in silence and took practiced aim on their quarry.

When the wagon came into view and entered the encircled pass, it had no chance to escape. The driver — a pale woman in a fine, hooded cloak — sat blithe and ignorant on her bench, without so much as a bow or even a dagger in sight. She flapped her horses' reins idly, watching only the road as the wagon rolled along. She didn't even have any hired guards. She might be carrying passengers who might be armed, but they'd still have to get some warning from her and pile out of the wagon before they could be of any help at all.

However, Kaltaag's men did not allow for that possibility. Almost as a single entity, the two of them drew their bows and let fly. They fired only noisemaker arrows at first, but that was enough to stop the wagon. The heavy wooden heads on the arrows whistled and shrieked like demons as they spun through the air, and the sudden noise made the horses stop and rear in terror. The men let fly with several more shots apiece in different directions so that the driver couldn't tell where they were coming from. Like a good mark, the woman driver yanked back on her reins and looked around wildly.

Snug in his vantage, Kaltaag held his fire and watched. His men did an admirable job confusing and frightening the wagon-driver until she was too upset to decide which way to flee. She only clung to her reins and sat paralyzed, hoping that the next arrow

Thief's Mark

she heard wasn't the one that was pinning her to her seat through the guts. Kaltaag read this expression on the woman's face and made ready to drop down from his hiding place and address her. He always did the talking when he led a raiding band, and, for effect, his weapon was loaded with a deadly, steel-tipped bolt that could punch through full plate armor. He also carried a length of heavy spiked chain, which he could use to entangle the legs of a fleeing victim or disarm a brave fool who challenged him once he showed himself. He didn't intend to kill anyone, but he knew as well as the next bandit that putting a good scare in a victim's heart worked wonders for one's reputation and made that victim all the more willing to cooperate.

So, swinging by one arm like a great and powerful ape, the half-orc dropped from his hiding place and landed beside the carriage with his weapon at the ready. Behind him, he could hear his men slipping down from their hiding places and sneaking off into the woods beside the path to retrieve their arrows.

The wagon-driver, Kaltaag saw, was a human woman of about 20 years. Her clothes were light and loose in deference to the fast-approaching summer, and they were of a fine, moderately expensive weave. Her hair was wavy and brown, and her skin was fair and smooth. As full humans reckoned things, she was quite attractive. As Kaltaag reckoned things, however, she was too tall and fine-boned to stoke any warmth in his lower belly. More to the point, she was too bird-hearted to be much fun. As soon as Kaltaag, in his crude forest camouflage, pointed his crossbow at her and demanded that she surrender and cooperate, the woman gasped, fainted and tipped over sideways across her bench.

Glad that that had at least been easy, Kaltaag took the wagon's reins and settled the horses with soft shooshing noises. When the beasts were quiet, he climbed up beside the woman and looked under her bench for any valuables she was carrying. Between her feet and pushed against the backboard of the bench, he found a black oak chest that made him very happy that he hadn't gone on to the Thieves' Festival already.

It was twice the size of his head, and an experimental tug on the side handle revealed that it was packed full of something heavy. Its lock, an ugly iron thing that was made for function rather than form, hinted at the importance of its contents, as did the carved ensigns that intertwined on the box's lid. One ensign was the dragon-and-ram's-head sigil of Ankila; the other was a more elaborate family crest that Kaltaag didn't recognize. The box might just be full of the unconscious lady's luggage for her trip, but Kaltaag doubted it. He'd robbed enough carriages all throughout the wilds of the Calastian Hegemony to know what a noble's strongbox looked like. The lady's luggage was probably what was filling up the covered wagon.

Deciding to find out for sure, just in case she happened to be carrying any more easily portable valuables, Kaltaag left the woman where she was and eased the tension out of his crossbow's string. He pulled the heavy strongbox to the ground where one

Thief's Mark

of the bandits rushed to pick it up. That man, a well-muscled human who had smeared cool mud on his exposed flesh and into his hair as well, all in order to help him blend with the surroundings, hefted the strongbox and disappeared into the forest toward where they had left their horses. The other bandit had still not finished retrieving his noisemaker arrows. Kaltaag waited for his fellow thief to return then decided to go ahead and see what other fancy cargo the rich woman was carrying.

He cut away the lashings from the front corner of the wagon's cover and yanked back the loose flap to reveal what was inside. He expected to see finely worked trunks of luggage or a handful of sleeping servants or perhaps even a rare caged animal of some sort, but the wagon's actual contents came as a surprise. A tall, middle-aged man lay flat on his back in the center of the wagon, snoring deeply, and the wagon was otherwise empty. In sharp contrast to the unconscious woman on the driver's bench, the man wore mismatched clothes that were ill suited to the weather, and which hung on him like rags. The man's white shirt was unlaced and half untucked, his deep burgundy vest was wrinkled and filthy, his gray pants looked to be made of threadbare wool and patched with sail canvas, and his boots were scuffed and coming apart at the seams.

The man himself was in no better condition than his clothing. His cheeks were sunken and sallow, and his eyes were set very deeply in his head. His thick, reddish-brown hair was tangled and matted, and he appeared to have burs caught in his beard. He was

Carl Bowen

tall and thin like a scarecrow, and his lips were cracked like the hardpan floor of a desert. His eyes rolled beneath their lids as if the man felt some internal pain that was yet too soft to wake him, and he murmured beneath his uneven breaths. Time and the elements had run roughshod over this man, then they'd kicked him once for good measure, Kaltaag judged.

What was truly inexplicable about the man's appearance, though, was that he seemed to have been bound to the floor of the wagon by someone with an odd sense of humor. A wide purple ribbon — of all things — had been run through an iron ring at the front of the wagon and then looped around both of the man's arms and legs as steel shackles would be wrapped around the limbs of a Calastian prisoner. The ribbon was not tied or clipped at any point (except where it was knotted to the iron ring), but it was looped firmly enough to raise the man's flesh at the edges.

Furthermore, despite the growing dark outside and the lack of illumination in the wagon, Kaltaag could make out a series of symbols painted in silver along the entire length of the ribbon, further adding to the mystery. The symbols didn't look important individually, and in series, they were nothing but gibberish. Kaltaag could read Common, and he knew magical ideograms when he saw them, yet these symbols were just scribbles and scratches, added purely for mad decoration.

For all Kaltaag could tell, the man bound in the wagon appeared to be either the victim or the impetus

Thief's Mark

of some unfathomable Thief's Mark prank. Curious, and vaguely annoyed that such a strange thing had captured his attention when he had better things to fill up his time, Kaltaag lifted a section of the ribbon with two fingers and ran his thumb along the painted side. When he did so, some of the silver paint flaked off onto his skin, smudging three of the symbols and eradicating one of them entirely.

Adding madness to strangeness, the disheveled man sat up straight with wide-open eyes the instant the symbols were gone.

"Hold and speak," the raggedy man commanded. His voice did not creak or falter as the voice of a man who'd just been asleep would. "If you are friend, then say name so that I may bestow proper and due thanks. If you are foe then speak regardless for the sake of good form and courtly gentility."

Kaltaag blinked in stupefaction and stood silent. Any minute, one of him men was going to jump out from behind him and shout, "Thief's Mark!" Any minute.

"I know that you're no immaterial shade or other ethereal being," the man continued, "although you have affected the aspect of some mad druidic enchanter's living golem. If you are not some false creation of my waking mind, then speak."

Again, Kaltaag could think of nothing to say. This barrage of words spewing from the mouth of one who had been sound asleep mere moments ago was overwhelming. The way the man spoke confused Kaltaag even more. His delivery was that of an atavistic nobleman, but his nasal accent and rolling drawl marked him as one of the port folk of the southern peninsula of Ankila.

"Perhaps," the man went on, "you simply have no affection for high-born speech. As my eyes welcome this dim light after my long and painful slumber, I am able to mark your heritage. Could it be that you understand me not? Perhaps the language of your rougher parent is more pleasing."

Before Kaltaag could reply that, no, he understood the Common language perfectly — though less so for the way this man entangled it — the man scrunched up his face and said in ugly, halting Orc, "You is name? We will fighting?"

Kaltaag rolled his eyes and said in Common, "That's enough already, Mister. No, I don't want to fight. What's the matter with you?"

"Then you are not my enemy," the man said, clearing his throat and switching back to his brand of Common. "And unless my eyes deceive me or some grudge-bearing illusionist has created you in order to torment me with false hope, then I must thank you for setting me free."

"What? Setting you free? Are you kidding?"

"Good soul, do not assume that I seek to rob you of glory by saying 'set free' instead of 'rescued,'" the man said. As he spoke, he untwisted the purple ribbon from his wrists and began to rub his forearms as if to work circulation back into them. "My choice is purely semantical in nature. One rescues maidens who are under attack or children who have been entrapped inside dank dungeons. When one is a prisoner aboard

Thief's Mark

a demonaic ferry driven by an unhallowed harridan who would take him to a pernicious fate that only the truly debased and evil could devise for one of the righteous, that one is merely set free rather than rescued. You see, I intended no slight. Except to impugn your grammatical mastery, of course — although only in jest."

After that alleged "jest," the man smiled a crooked, gap-toothed smile at Kaltaag. The expression livened his face with youthful energy, despite the age lines that creased the skin beside his eyes like streaks of gnarled lightning. Kaltaag was grateful for the pause, because it allowed him a moment to pick the kernel of meaning from the chaff of the man's rambling.

"You think you're some sort of prisoner?" he asked, hoping in vain for a simple yes or no. "Is that it?"

"Yes," the man said, "although you have set that compounded tragedy aright. The world owes you as much thanks as I."

Kaltaag tugged on the purple ribbon that he was still holding as the man unwound it from his bony ankles. "And this is your prison chain?" He looked down at the ribbon then wiped off the silver paint that had smudged onto his thumb. "Right. You're about to say 'Thief's Mark' and run off laughing at me, aren't you?"

"Be not fooled by its harmless seeming, nor that of this grounded carriage, which, I divine, has now assumed this mundane aspect," the man said. "Were it not for you, this fetter would have held me unto

Doomsday — when the titans arise once again to challenge the gods — and this conveyance would have disappeared with me out over the sighing swell of the Blossoming Sea."

"But you're nowhere near the Blossoming Sea," Kaltaag cut in, unable to stand the rambling any longer. "You're in the woods of Ankila, more than 200 miles from even the coast."

"Two-hundred miles?" the man said with a disturbingly heavy sigh of relief. "And I am in northern Ankila you say? If that is so, then I am still favored by my patron deity, Enkili. Doubtless, he has sent his storm winds to help me make up ground that I had lost and placed me here on this sylvan path so that my holy quests might continue where I left them off. In which direction lies Zathiske? I have much to do there."

"What?" Kaltaag said with bubbling frustration. "It's west." He pointed. "That way. Did you hit your head or something?"

"Friend, I apologize for my seeming rudeness and evident haste, but I have neither world enough nor time to explain. Accept instead my assurance that I am not a madman but a valorous soldier sorely tested. Yet, even now, I remain pious and upright. My name is Goraidin, and I am a paladin soon to be sworn into the service of the god, Enkili. I am born to Scarn in this dark age in pursuit of noble quests that are of utmost interest to the god himself."

"Enkili? Scarn? Friend, you've got—"

Thief's Mark

"I have no more time for speeches," the man said, "and for that, I am most humbly unworthy in the eyes of the very one who set me free. I would ask that you hold my friendship and gratitude in trust until such time as I can return to see it bear fruit."

With that, the man stood and leapt to the ground next to where Kaltaag was standing. He landed ungracefully and nearly stumbled into the ditch beside the road, but he somehow managed to keep his feet. He then turned back to Kaltaag and took the half-orc's long gray hand in his.

"Fare thee well and gods be with you," he said. "Although we must now travel separate paths to our gods-appointed fates, I will not forget you or the service you have done me. Now I go."

The scarecrow man then turned straight toward the woods, in the direction that Kaltaag had pointed him, and hurried away. At first, he made more noise in his flight than a boar through winter brush, but then his steps began to grow silent, and his outline began to grow indistinct, although he had not gone very far. At about the same time, Kaltaag's remaining bandit — who had finally returned from picking up his noisemaker arrows — rushed to Kaltaag's side with a real arrow drawn and aimed in the direction of the noise, although he couldn't make out where it had been coming from. Kaltaag put a hand on the archer's arm and told him to relax.

"Was that someone hiding in the wagon?" the archer asked, eyeing Kaltaag uneasily. "He'll have a Calastian patrol out here before the night's up if we let him get away. Where'd he go?"

"Don't worry," Kaltaag said with an annoyed sigh. "He's harmless. It was just a paladin for Enkili."

"What? A paladin! I didn't know Enkili had paladins, but even still—"

"Relax," Kaltaag said with a grin. "It's okay to let a paladin for Enkili go. He's a madman. He's no danger to us."

"Oh," the archer said, easing the tension out of his bowstring at last. "A paladin for Enkili. A madman. I get it now. And I actually believed you, too, Kalt. I'm a Thief's Mark. Good one."

"Yeah. Thief's Mark."

"So what was it really? A deer? A fox? Some kind of pet wolf or something?"

"More like a pet fox," Kaltaag said with a shrug. "Who knows? He took off before I could make any sense out of him."

"What kind of person keeps a pet fox in a wagon and doesn't expect it to run away as soon as the wagon stops?"

"Rich people," Kaltaag said, looking back over his shoulder at the unconscious woman sprawled out across her bench. "Rich Thief's Marks. Now get your stuff, and let's go."

Once they'd tidied up the site of the raid — which mostly included binding the unconscious woman where she'd fainted and tying off the horses' reins so they wouldn't take off into the forest unguided — Kaltaag spent the next day and a half making his way into his home country of Zathiske for the Thieves'

Festival in the city of Gnersh. His fellow highwaymen (humans both) had opted to ride on and divide up their share of the past several weeks' haul at home, which left Kaltaag to go to the festival alone. Zathiske, they claimed, was too crowded with Calastian troops and Calastian spies for their tastes.

Kaltaag, of course, was hardly bothered by soldiers of the Hegemony, so he parted company with his men at the Zathiske-Ankila border and headed southwest toward Gnersh while they rode on northwest toward their sylvan fastness in the Heteronomy of Virduk. He sent them ahead with his crossbow and his share of the haul as well, trusting them not to steal from him. He knew that he could do so partially because these men had been loyal to him for years already, but mostly because they knew that Kaltaag's money had bought them food and weapons and other supplies that made their lives easier ever since they'd joined him. They also knew that any coin they stole from him would be one less coin that he could use to bribe the local authorities to stay well clear of their sylvan fastness. Years of experience had taught Kaltaag's men that their long-term prosperity and security outweighed any short-term itch that might develop in their pockets where Kaltaag's money was concerned.

As he sent his men home, Kaltaag kept with him only a small purse full of the silver coins that bore the generic crowned-dragon stamp of Calastia. He took more money than he specifically needed for the entertainments that the Thieves' Festival made available, but only because he expected to lose a large portion of it before his brief holiday was done. Yet, he was not afraid of being assaulted or having his purse cut, even though he planned to be alone amid a veritable sea of criminals. The thieves who attended the festival in Gnersh developed an odd professional respect at this time of year, and they didn't commit "base" crimes against one another while the festival was going on. They would lie to one another or try to cheat one another out of whatever they could — and the festival's Scavenger Hunt was nothing more than an officially condoned burglary contest — but such crimes as mugging, rape, arson and vandalism were considered simply antithetical to the spirit of the affair.

Regardless of that romanticized notion of why the attendees of the Thieves' Festival had developed such an understanding, though, Kaltaag knew that the truth was far more sensible. The locals and the festival-regulars knew that more new Thief's Marks came to the festival each year and that such violent displays would only drive them away again. The marks wouldn't hang around if they felt that they were always on the verge of being accosted, and the loss of potential customers would drive away those businessmen who didn't cater solely to Zathiske's contingent of Calastian soldiers. However, if the marks could have a good time at the festival and even enjoy the act of losing a few loose coins to a charming swindler, they would return like flocks of birds the next year and all the merchants would be happy.

The city authorities — both local shin-breakers and Calastian troops — had long since given up trying

Thief's Mark

to put a stop to the festival. Although King Virduk had abhorred the idea of an army of thieves descending on any city in his Hegemony, Lord Satrap Virduk Olem of Zathiske had finally managed to convince the king that the festival improved the local economy, lowered the crime rate (for a time) and gave Calastian spies a chance to infiltrate various illegal organizations whose representatives were in attendance. Now, law-enforcement during the festival was minimal as long as the thieves practiced relatively good behavior and didn't mock the laws *too* openly. The arrangement had resulted in an immediate improvement in relations between the locals and the Calastian soldiers, and the tradition of the post-festival riot against the soldiers had ceased altogether.

As Kaltaag entered Gnersh, he felt himself relaxing at last after weeks of planning and raiding and hiding from Calastian patrols. He had come here only to enjoy himself, rather than practice his trade, and here was one of the few places at which he could do so. He and his band were notorious for their raids against soldiers and noble families of the Calastian Hegemony along most of Calastia's major trade routes. Their particular specialties lay in setting traps or ambushes, and the band's reputation had grown in direct proportion to the bounty placed on its members' heads. But here, Kaltaag was one of hundreds of thieves, and as long as he kept himself out of trouble, he could do as he pleased. And to get started doing just that, he headed down the main thoroughfare of Gnersh toward the city's Thundershrine.

The main street was a wide, stone expanse that separated the city's inns and alehouses from its metalworkers and trade shops. The division between the laborers who crafted the tools of war that supplied King Virduk's Calastian war machine and the more relaxed businessmen who looked after the soldiers' less professional needs was sharp all throughout Zathiske, and Gnersh was no exception. Most of the time, the main street was a tense no-man's land between warring economic sensibilities, in which a loose word in the wrong ear could start a free-for-all brawl or even a riot.

Today, however, and during the entire Thieves' Festival, the place was as packed and energetic and loud as a Veshian street market. Wooden booths, leaning tents and simple curtained boxes dotted the street like the walls of a maze, and all sorts of people massed at each one. Kaltaag passed fortune-telling booths, gimmick apothecaries, rigged games of chance, puppet shows and people selling hand-drawn "authentic" treasure maps. In the middle of the long street, Kaltaag watched an illusionist make volunteers from his audience disappear, then charge that volunteer's traveling companions a hefty sum before making him reappear. Farther on, a troupe of white-faced beggars who pretended to be blind or partially crippled or ill tripped over each other, knocked each other down and dropped heavy boards and tools on each other as they tried to build a booth in which they could sit and beg for money. This display — which had been a standard at the festival for years — so amused the nearby crowd that a short rain of coins

Thief's Mark

had already started to fall. Amusements of all sorts filled the road from curb to curb, and there was no shortage of marks to take part in them. And over it all, stood the Thundershrine, Zathiske's largest temple devoted to the god Enkili.

Kaltaag smiled in appreciation of the hand-made spectacle of the Thundershrine — an enormous tower shaped like a war scepter and crowned in iron to receive offerings of lightning — and he headed in its direction. Although he was partial to the goddess Tanil, he respected Enkili and was a firm believer in the value of making offerings to Enkili's daughter, Drendari, before every raid. Therefore, he thought it best to stop in at the Thundershrine and say a quick prayer of thanks for all the luck he'd been having recently. By the time he had reached the steps, however, he realized that he was being followed.

He heard the rhythm of it first, and it drew his attention to other, more obvious details from which the sights and sounds of the festival had distracted him. Two quick, darting steps fell after each one of his, and now that he was listening, he could hear it despite the general noise all around him. Next, he noticed a flash of color that appeared just at the edge of his peripheral vision and stayed there. He switched directions abruptly, jarring a short woman who was carrying a basket and making her curse under her breath. Two seconds later, the woman cursed again, louder than before as Kaltaag's pursuer bumped into her as well. Kaltaag veered to the right, stepped over a large puddle and cut a corner behind a large locksmith's booth into one of Gnersh's alleyways. The sounds of the festival were still close and pressing, but he was removed enough from the press of the crowd that he could deal with his pursuer in relative solitude if the situation demanded such a thing.

Like most knowledgeable people, Kaltaag was not worried about being victimized by any rough sort of thief. He was savvy enough at infighting and strong enough that he could defend himself against any single opponent. Should some gang of toughs surround him, the length of spiked chain that he carried was more than enough to even the odds. Regardless, though, such things just weren't done at the Thieves' Festival. Kaltaag knew that just as any self-respecting thief in attendance did. The reason, then, that this unsubtle pursuer put Kaltaag's back up was because he might be some bounty-hunter who had recognized him or even a Calastian spy sent to mark him and trail him back to his sylvan fastness for King Virduk's benefit. Kaltaag had heard tales of other bandit gangs that had been broken and rounded up for the Calastian dungeons in just the same way at Thieves' Festivals in the past. Therefore, once Kaltaag was sure that he was out of sight of his pursuer, he dropped into a shadow, made ready his spiked chain and waited.

Five seconds after he'd hidden, he heard a splash in the puddle he'd stepped over. A second after that, Kaltaag's pursuer stepped into the mouth of the alleyway, paused, then continued down the alley all alone. In that slim second's pause, Kaltaag materialized from the shadows behind the person, wrapped his chain around the person's middle with a backhand cast and yanked him off balance. Kaltaag then spun his pursuer around to hit the wall back-first, and disengaged his chain with the same motion. The pursuer — a human woman, oddly enough — tripped over her feet and landed hard on her rump with her back against the wall. The breath whooshed out of her, and the look on her face made it clear that she didn't want to fight.

Kaltaag might have let the matter go at that, but even in the alley's shadows, he suddenly recognized the woman from a certain carriage he'd visited in the Ankilan woods just two short days ago. Trying not to roll his eyes in frustration or show that he recognized her, he grabbed the woman by the front of her light, travel-worn dress and lifted her against the wall to face him. Her wet shoes dangled above the ground.

"Why are you following me?" he asked her, putting more grunt and growl into his voice than was strictly necessary or natural. "What do you want?"

The woman gasped, clutching Kaltaag's hairy wrists instinctively. "Let me go," she yelped. "I won't make trouble for you, I promise."

"You?" Kaltaag snorted, giving the woman an awful smile. "Lady, I could eat you." Maybe if he scared her enough, she'd forget whatever dreams she might be having of vengeance or vigilante justice and go bother someone else.

"No," the woman said, holding back the fear in her eyes and trying not to squirm in Kaltaag's grip. "I know who you are. I saw you on the street, and I recognized you. I need to talk to you."

"Right," Kaltaag said. He dropped the woman back on the ground, making sure that she didn't tip over or hit her head on the wall when she landed. As she straightened her dress, Kaltaag gathered up his chain. "You're lucky I didn't break your skull in for sneaking up on me. Forget it."

"Wait," the woman said with quivering lips as Kaltaag began to walk away. "If you don't listen… I'll scream. I'll scream that you're attacking me and doing all sorts of awful things to me. Every Calastian soldier on this block will come running when they hear that, and when they catch you, I'll tell them you robbed me on my way here."

Kaltaag flinched at that last and stopped walking. If the woman raised a big enough stink, the local shin-breakers would haul him into a Gnersh prison cell for the night while they searched through their hand-drawn wanted posters for his likeness. Considering how busy his band had been lately, Kaltaag had no doubt that they'd find it and that he'd be in for a great deal of trouble when they did.

"What do you want?" he grumbled, turning around to face the woman.

"I want to find my brother," the woman said. "I want to know where Alonso is."

"Who?"

"Alonso, my brother," the woman said. "You know who I'm talking about. You let him out of my wagon, I know you did. The last thing I saw that awful night was you with your crossbow, and the next thing I knew, my brother was gone!"

Thief's Mark

"Oh, I see," Kaltaag said. "You're talking about Goraidin."

"His name isn't Goraidin!" the woman said, stamping her foot in a frustration that was not young. Kaltaag could see water shimmering in her eyes. "His name is Alonso Keyhost, and I'm his sister, Maria. Our father is a wealthy harbormaster on the southern peninsula of Ankila, and Alonso is his only son. Unfortunately, my father is on the brink of death and I'm not married, so everything my father owns will go to Alonso when my father dies, even though Alonso isn't fit to take care of it."

"What's wrong with him?" Kaltaag asked in spite of himself.

"You must have seen," Maria said. "For weeks, he's been going mad thinking he's a paladin for the storm god. He claims to be a hero like they had in the Divine War, and he demands to be taken to this city's Thundershrine at once to be recognized and ordained. When I don't agree and hitch the horses for him right away, he steals away into the night, forcing me to come out looking for him. One night, he even stole a boat from Father's harbor and tried to sail it up the coast. Every time he disappears, I have a harder time bringing him back, and he makes me even more worried than the last."

"Worried?" Kaltaag grunted. "The last time I saw this fellow, he was tied up in the back of a wagon."

"If you saw that," Maria said, "then you saw how well he was tied. Looped ribbons aren't prison shackles."

"Then he must have been sickly and weak already," Kaltaag said, "because he couldn't move, and he looked awful."

"Those ribbon bonds were so effective because he believed that they were parts of a mystical spell designed to hold him," Maria said. "And he looked awful because he refused to eat anything I gave him. I told you, he's gone mad. I hired an actor to pretend to be an enchanter and put a spell on him when I caught up to him this time, and he believed that the enchanter paralyzed him. I was finally trying to take him where he needed to go all along, and for once, in his madness, he was cooperating."

Kaltaag narrowed his eyes and scratched his head in deep thought. In a way, he wanted Alonso Keyhost's fancy to be true rather than his sister's explanation story. The fancy was certainly more heartening than this depressing tale of delusion and folly.

"Now you've gone and ruined that," the woman went on, wearing an expression of sadness and desperation that was stronger than her earlier fear. "I had intended to take him to a temple of Madriel in central Ankila, and that money I was carrying was going to pay off the priests there to cure him."

"I see," Kaltaag murmured. "I didn't know that."

"Now what can I do?" Maria said. "With Alonso cured, he could have come home and taken care of our father's estates. But now my brother's gone, and some Calastian moneylender is going to seize everything Father owned because no one in the

Thief's Mark

family is fit to govern it under Ankilan law. Oh, what can I do?"

"I'm sorry to hear this," Kaltaag mumbled, looking away from the woman and scratching the back of his neck. "But there's not much you can do. There's nothing I—"

"Oh please, sir," Maria said, clinging to the front of Kaltaag's tunic in desperation. "You must help me. Help me find my brother. If I can't get him cured, I can at least take him back home before Father's health gives out. After the trouble you've caused me, you owe me that much."

"I don't owe you anything," Kaltaag grumbled, although he still couldn't look the woman in the eye. "Maybe you don't understand what thieves do, but—"

"You do owe me, and if you don't cooperate, I'll turn you in right now, like I said," the woman said, raising her voice dangerously high. "You must help me!"

"Look," Kaltaag said, "just be quiet and listen. Even if I wanted to help you find your brother, how would I even start? He could be anywhere in the wilderness of the Hegemony right now. I don't care what you think I owe you, I'm not going questing all over Ghelspad for a single madman."

"But it won't come to that, I'm certain," Maria said. "If I know my brother's madness, he'll be coming here to Gnersh. He thinks he's Enkili's paladin, you see, and what better place for such a one to come than to this, the biggest temple of Enkili in the country."

"Fair enough," Kaltaag said. "He's coming here. But if you know that, you don't need my help finding him. Wait out here for him to show up, then take him home. Hire some mercenaries or Calastian soldiers to help if you need it, but leave me out of it."

"But no, I do need your help," Maria said. "My brother is convinced that I'm some monster determined to take him away to an afterlife of torture and misery. He runs away every time I get near him, and he always manages to escape when I think I've captured him. I can't do this on my own.

"But you... I think he would trust you. He believes you set him free of my 'trap,' and if I know my brother, that act has made you his friend for life."

"Wonderful," Kaltaag grumbled.

"You, then, could lie in wait for him and speak to him when he arrives. You could play up to his madness and convince him — somehow — to return home to Ankila and stay there. If you could get through to his addled mind, he would do as you said and even be happy about it. I know he would."

"But why should I?" Kaltaag asked. "What's to keep me from leaving right now and going where you'll never find me? I've been escaping Calastian soldiers for years, and I doubt you can put on a better chase. Even if you call for the shin-breakers right now, I'll just lose them all in the crowd and disappear."

"Maybe you can," Maria said, "but I think even still that you're going to help me. I can see in your eyes that you're not so cold-hearted as to leave me stranded with no hope. And I think that even though you don't want to, you like my brother. You'll help, I think, because you care and you want this sad tale to end well."

"Is that so?" Kaltaag grumbled the words, but his grumble had no spirit left in it. Down inside, he realized that the woman was probably right. "All right, listen," he said. "You forgive the money I stole from you and count it as lost, and I'll talk to your brother *if* I can find him."

"You will?" Maria said, clapping her hands and forgetting her earlier fear, sadness and desperation. She took Kaltaag's hand in hers, just as her brother had done in the forest, and kissed it right on the knobby, gray knuckles. "That's wonderful! Thank you so much. Thank you. The theft is forgiven, I swear."

Kaltaag retrieved his hand and stepped away from the woman. "Thanks," he said, rolling his eyes and trying not to groan. "Now stop that and go find yourself a comfortable room at the Levin-Sword Inn at the far end of this block. You can have a few coins, but when they run out, you have to get in your wagon and go back home." He fished a small handful of coins — enough for a week in a small room or a night in a large one — from the purse on his belt and handed them over. "You can come by the Thundershrine once a night, and if I can do what you want before my own money runs out, I'll leave you a message with the Minister of Alms. Do you understand?"

"Yes," Maria said. "And thank you again. Thank you, thank you."

"Sure," Kaltaag said. "Now go on. Beat it. Get to Levin-Sword, and don't spend those coins on anything except a bed and food."

Continuing to thank him and almost sobbing in her relief, Maria agreed and left down the opposite end of the alley from which she'd entered. When she was out of sight and out of earshot, Kaltaag shook his head and whispered after her, "Little Thief's Mark. You'll learn some day."

He wasn't sure, though, if he was referring to Maria or to himself.

For the next two days, Kaltaag could not enjoy the Thieves' Festival, try as he might. Everywhere he went, everything he saw or heard reminded him of the madman, Alonso, and his sister, Maria. When he sought to catch up with old friends whom he saw only at the festival a conversation about everyone's latest exploits inevitably got started, which Kaltaag had to participate in. When he gambled in the local alehouses, every deck's Fool card reminded him of Alonso's motley attire. When he listened to human storytellers (one of his favorite pastimes), their way of telling stories reminded him of the outdated way Alonso spoke. When he listened to half-orc storytellers, the way they told stories only reminded him of the miserable way Alonso had tried to speak Orc. And when he tried to simply lose himself among the crowds and just enjoy the feel of the Thieves' Festival itself, the Thundershrine seemed to loom over him expectantly, reminding him of what he'd said to Maria and of the agreement he'd tentatively made.

Therefore, it was something of a relief when Alonso finally arrived in Gnersh and — just as his sister had predicted — made his way straight for the Thundershrine's front gates. Kaltaag was in the street watching a pair of dancing pickpocket girls beguiling (and robbing) a knot of lascivious off-duty Calastian troops, when he saw the madman on the opposite side of the road. The bedraggled man moved through the swelling and ebbing evening crowd carelessly, bumping into people and being jostled in turn without even noticing. With head erect and shoulders back, Alonso marched forward with eyes for nothing but the Thundershrine. He walked under an arc of knives between two jugglers and passed inches from a practicing fire-breather without so much as slowing down. The man's mad reverence for the temple had transported him to some ecstatic inner realm and blinded him to everything that was going on around him.

Kaltaag pushed off into the crowd after Alonso and hurried to get ahead of him. The going was more difficult for him because he preferred to dodge the obstacles around him rather than ignore them, but he was not moving in the slow, dreamlike way that Alonso was. He darted between people or around them, tracking and staying ahead of Alonso as if the man were a raid victim in Kaltaag's home forest. Kaltaag wasn't exactly certain what he would do when he actually confronted Alonso, but whatever he did, he thought it best that he did it before Alonso actually entered the temple and started causing serious trouble. Likely, the acolytes and templars inside the Thundershrine would not appreciate Alonso's claim to be a paladin for their god, and they wouldn't hesitate to throw him out on the street. Naturally, Alonso wouldn't stand for that, and the noises he would raise in protest would earn him a working-over from the local shin-breakers or some easily amused Calastian soldiers. The least Kaltaag could do, he decided, was warn the madman off and make him promise to wait for his sister to come to the Thundershrine to check after him. If he did that, his conscience would be clear, and he could get back to enjoying himself. Or better yet, he could just go home and try to relax there.

Yet, Alonso seemed determined to confound Kaltaag intention to intercept him well before the gates of the Thundershrine. As the madman drew closer to his goal and the crowd around him began to shy away from him, he started moving faster. First his steps grew longer, then his pace picked up, and then suddenly he was running in long, ungainly strides. Kaltaag — who had been only a few steps ahead when his quarry was walking — was caught off guard, and he had to drop all courtesy and start running himself. However, the people who dodged out of Alonso's way just happened to dodge into Kaltaag's way, and the half-orc had to push and shove to make any progress.

Unlike the surly brutes of his half-breed race, Kaltaag was built more like a runner than a warrior, and the progress he made was slow indeed. He was tall enough to see over the crowd, but he lacked both

Thief's Mark

the muscle mass that would help him toss impediments aside and the intimidating snarl that would open a path for him on its own. Unwilling to actually knock anyone down and thus move ahead faster, he had to watch as Alonso finally reached and practically crashed into the gates of the Thundershrine. He actually climbed several feet up the wroughtiron barrier and hung there like a monkey, much to the astonishment of those closest to him in the crowd.

"I beg your permission to enter!" the madman cried, which drew the attention of even more people. "After epic hardships and many onerous trials, I, Goraidin, have come to be ordained a paladin in Enkili's service!"

Some Calastian troops who had been stationed near the temple gates rushed up to investigate this commotion, and when they found Alonso, they shouted for him to hop down right that instant.

"I have come in answer to my patron's call!" Alonso proclaimed over his shoulder for all the world to hear. "I will not be denied by the likes of you at his threshold!"

These protestations carried even farther over the general noise of the festival, and people began to take interest in what was happening. Several groups and at least a score of individual gawkers began to move in the direction of the disturbance, and that small migration made Kaltaag's progress a great deal easier. He sprinted the last short distance and tumbled out into the bubble of distance that had opened up between the curious crowd and the Calastian troops who were busy trying to pull Alonso down from the Thundershrine's gate.

"Unhand me!" the man cried, trying to climb even higher, despite the efforts of a soldier who had a solid grip on his jacket. "You know not what you do! Release me at once!"

A second soldier and then a third all added their might (and weight) to that of the first, and the four people tumbled at last to the ground. The crowd laughed at the spectacle, and a few people actually cheered Alonso on.

Although he'd come down hard, the madman hopped to his feet and danced away from the grabbing arms of the soldiers on top of whom he'd landed. He squinted and made ready to rush the lot of them in a new (and likely doomed) charge on the gates, but this time, Kaltaag reached out from behind and stopped him. The crowd murmured at this new development, the Calastian soldiers got to their feet angrily, and Alonso whipped around to see who had accosted him this time.

"Who dares... Why, it's you, my new friend! Enkili's providence has thrown us together once again!"

"Right," Kaltaag said, not liking at all the looks that the soldiers were now turning his way. Fortunately, though, they had not yet drawn weapons or called out for reinforcements. "Something like that."

"When we first parted, when you set me free from that demonaic ferry that had captured me," Alonso said, "I was sure that our paths would cross again!"

Thief's Mark

"Sure," Kaltaag murmured. The feeling of so many eyes watching him made his throat want to close up, but somehow he pushed even more words out as he took Alonso by the arm and tried to tug him back into the crowd away from the soldiers. "I guess they did, at that. Now why don't we just go over—"

"It must then be Enkili's will that you and I be compatriots!" the madman interrupted, holding his ground.

"If you say so. Now how about—"

"And," Alonso went on, pulling away from Kaltaag altogether, "since we compatriots are reunited by Enkili's will, it must also be Enkili's will that we stand together against these foes who would keep us from his holy temple!"

"I don't think that's exactly—"

"Come, brother!" Alonso bellowed, waving a fist at the Calastian soldiers, who had begun to look back and forth among themselves and loosen their swords in their scabbards. "Let's punish these heathen lickboots together! Let's show them what power our god lends the righteous!"

Tired of fooling around, the Calastian troops drew their weapons and stepped into a loose formation before the temple gate. The crowd hushed when the soldiers' blades rasped into open air, and several people pushed back away from Kaltaag and Alonso in haste.

"Friend," Kaltaag said, taking Alonso's arm again. "This is a *bad* idea. Let's just—"

"Yes, draw, cowards!" Alonso shouted, ignoring Kaltaag completely. "Savor the false security that your paltry blades afford you! But know this! Your weapons are nothing compared to mine, for I wield—" and at this point, Alonso retrieved something from beneath his jacket "—the levin-flail of Enkili!"

Although dramatic lightning failed to flash and ominous thunder failed to crash when Alonso drew his weapon, the crowd gasped collectively anyway. That gasp turned into embarrassed and mocking laughter, however, when everyone got a good look at Alonso's weapon. It was technically a flail, just as the god Enkili supposedly carried, but if a sorrier weapon existed in all the world, no one present had seen it. The haft was a crooked stick around which thin leather had been wrapped for grip. A hole had been punched in the top of this stick, and a length of cord had been looped through it and tied to a smaller block of wood, through which a similar hole had been punched. This attached block was the flail's head, and the only thing that made it and the weapon dangerous at all was the fact that long nails had been driven through it at irregular intervals on all sides. The object was flatly ridiculous, and to claim that it was a divine instrument only made it that much more so.

Neither the soldiers nor Alonso saw any humor in the situation, though, so Kaltaag knew that he had to do something before this farce became a tragedy. Both he and the soldiers could tell that the tension in Alonso's lanky frame was a precursor to violent action. Even though Alonso wouldn't likely do any

Thief's Mark

of them much harm, even with his preposterous weapon, the soldiers were trained to kill quickly and efficiently when presented with an enemy who threatened them. So, fearing for the madman's life as well as his own, he moved before the soldiers did. He grabbed Alonso's weapon arm at the elbow and wrist then jerked it sharply up and back. The madman cried out, and his weapon popped over his shoulder into the dirt behind him. The crowd bubbled in astonishment, but fortunately the soldiers backed off.

"What treachery is this?" Alonso shouted, pulling free of Kaltaag's grip and whirling to face him. "I'm betrayed at victory's gate! And by my own compatriot! You're a blackguard, sir! A rogue and a villain! Why have you done this?"

"Because you were about to get yourself killed!" Kaltaag shouted back, surprising himself with how loud the words came out.

"Nonsense!" Alonso shouted right back. "My faith in Enkili gives me the strength of a dozen soldiers! A hundred! Any paladin of my stature could defeat schoolboys such as these with his eyes shut!"

The soldiers grumbled at that, and some comedians in the crowd began to heckle them from the safety of anonymity.

"A paladin, maybe," Kaltaag said, ignoring the crowd and the soldiers "but not you. You're not a paladin." Then, as much to his own surprise as that of that the crowd, he added in a low and taunting voice, "Not unless I say you are."

"What?" Alonso said, voicing the dumbfounded shock that ran through the crowd like a wave of water.

The outraged expression left his face, but he said no more. No one in the crowd spoke either. Even the soldiers froze in puzzlement.

"You have trained hard and come far to be ordained a paladin," Kaltaag said, hoping that his nervousness didn't freeze his tongue or make his voice crack. "You have righted wrongs and spread the good word of Enkili wherever you went. You have been pious and forthright and valorous in all your days since Enkili called you. Is this not so?"

"It is so," Alonso said. "I have done all this."

"Then you have passed every test that our storm god, Enkili, has set before you," Kaltaag went on, trusting his wits and trying not to overthink what he was saying. If he thought first before speaking, he might realize just how ridiculous he sounded and stop talking. "All except one. You have not bested his gatekeeper and proven to the god your martial skills."

"His gatekeeper?" Alonso said. Doubt had begun to cloud his features at last. "But what of these three here? Surely when I vanquish them…"

"These three aren't worthy of a paladin of Enkili!" Kaltaag snapped, dismissing the Calastian guards with a contemptuous wave. "And they're heathens besides. No, one who would be a true paladin of Enkili must face down a true opponent before he may be ordained and recognized in the god's eyes."

"Then who is it?" Alonso demanded, getting his confidence back as Kaltaag spoke. "Who would stand between me and the glory that is rightfully mine? What poor soul has Enkili chosen to administer this, my final test? Only show him to me, and I shall break him like a handful of sticks! Yet even then, I shall spare his life, for he is but a servant of my patron as am I."

"You are ready to face this final challenge, then?" Kaltaag said. "Here in front of so many witnesses?"

Having finally caught on to Kaltaag's ploy (or simply deciding that this entire scene was being staged by clever street performers after all), the crowd came to life and began to cheer Alonso on. The Calastian soldiers even sheathed their weapons and waited to see what would happen. Alonso looked around him briefly, but although he appreciated it, he did not need anyone's encouragement.

"I am ready!" he declared, looking Kaltaag in the eye. "Who is my last enemy? Where is Enkili's gatekeeper?"

"He is here," Kaltaag said, drawing himself up to his full height and speaking with a thunderous grandiloquence that would have done any street storyteller proud. "I am Enkili's gatekeeper!"

The crowd was really getting into the performance now, but Alonso was not immediately convinced. Over a rumble of applause, laughs and whistles, he said, "You? That can't be."

"But it is," Kaltaag declared, hoping that he didn't look too ridiculous. "I have been watching you from the beginning. I know that your name was once Alonso Keyhost and that you came from a port city in southern Ankila. I know of your sister, Maria, and of your father whose health is failing.

"I also know of your exploits in coming to this place. I know about the time you stole a ship and braved the Blossoming Sea to come here. I know of your lone expeditions to reach this place and about the enchanters who arrayed themselves and their arts against you to turn you back time and again."

"I have been plagued by enchanters," Alonso said. "And I did sail the Blossoming Sea just like you said. And those names you spoke, though secret and known only to me, are exactly right."

"And it was I," Kaltaag said, hoping that Alonso was thoroughly fooled at last, "who appeared to you and set you free when you'd been taken up on that demonaic ferry, headed for an afterlife of torture and misery."

"And when you did," Alonso said with the wide, wondering eyes of a child, "your shape was different than it is now! I mistook you for a druidic homunculus, when all you had done was change your shape to be as one with your surroundings! You *are* a servant of Enkili! And I accept your challenge!"

"Then retrieve your weapon," Kaltaag said, "and get ready. This is your final test."

Alonso bent to retrieve his ridiculous flail from where he'd dropped it, and he and Kaltaag paced off a suitable space in which to have their single combat. The crowd began to cheer and chant and place bets, and Alonso closed his eyes to say a short prayer of devotion to Enkili. When he opened his eyes and held up his weapon, he was ready to begin. For his part, Kaltaag had made ready as Alonso prayed. He'd retrieved his weighted chain from the leather satchel he carried it in, and now he held it casually in his hands. The two stared at each other until someone in the crowd (possibly even one of the Calastian soldiers) lost his patience and shouted, "Fight!"

The actual fight lasted only about ten seconds. Alonso ran forward with his flail held high, and Kaltaag made him pay for it. The spiked chain whipped around his body in long-practiced arcs, moving in a blur that the eye almost could not follow. One weighted end hit Alonso in the fingers, knocking the flail into the air, and the other came down on the pit of his elbow, folding his arm up neatly in the middle. Kaltaag then twisted the chain around in another fluid movement that entangled Alonso's bent arm and pulled him off balance backward as it wrapped around his neck above the apple. Finally, Kaltaag kicked Alonso in the back of the knee, toppling the two of them to the ground with Kaltaag kneeling astride. The crowd gasped collectively again at the efficient brutality of the thing.

"Yield!" Kaltaag demanded, pulling the free end of his chain straight up and putting pressure on Alonso's throat. "You're beaten!"

"I can't be," Alonso croaked, reaching around wildly for his flail. "How can this be? I've slain great sea dragons and vicious jungle cats with my bare hands."

"Yield," Kaltaag said again, more quietly this time. "You're brave and strong and pious, but you're still beaten."

"Kill me, then," Alonso moaned. "You deserve that honor. I have disgraced Enkili and all who serve him."

"I won't," Kaltaag said. "And you haven't disgraced anyone. Failing a test is different than being vanquished in combat. You've only proven that you're not yet ready to be a true paladin for Enkili. You haven't disgraced anyone." Kaltaag then looked up at the faces of the people who were standing nearby and said, "Has he?"

Still somewhat stunned by Kaltaag's rapid victory in the fight, no one in the immediate vicinity spoke.

"Well?" Kaltaag said again. He looked around wishing that someone, anyone, would answer him.

"No!" someone finally cried out behind him. "He's no disgrace at all!"

Kaltaag turned and saw Maria, Alonso's sister, pushing her way through the crowd toward them.

"He was very brave! He almost beat you!"

"I did?" Alonso said.

"Sure," Kaltaag said, loosening the chain around Alonso's neck and relaxing the part that was cutting off blood flow to his arm. "It was very close. But in the end, I still beat you. Barely."

"But that means that I am not ready to be a paladin," Alonso murmured. "I failed your test."

Kaltaag stood, unwrapped his chain and helped Alonso to his feet. "Yes," he said. "But only this one. In all other ways, you are ready and able to stand and answer your god's call. When the time comes, I will visit you again, and you may test your might anew."

"I can?" Alonso asked, rubbing his neck and his shoulder where light bruises were starting to form. "When?"

Kaltaag could feel Maria glaring at him, so he scratched the back of his neck and said, "In ten years' time. Enkili demands that his paladins spend ten years between failed tests so that they can reflect on why they failed and try to think of ways in which to succeed in the future."

"Ten years," Alonso said, obviously crestfallen. "That's so long. How can I wait for ten years? What am I supposed to do until then?"

"You will do as your god wishes," Kaltaag said, glancing once again at Maria. "You will go back to your family's home in Ankila and wait there for my return. You will take the name you had when you last lived there, and you will act in all other ways as you did before Enkili called you to serve."

"That's a harsh penance," Alonso sighed.

"But it is fair," Kaltaag said. "And I know you can bear it. You're strong and healthy as you've always been, and ten years will go by before you know it. And if you've decided by that time that serving Enkili isn't your calling any more, well then, you'll always have your family to protect and take care of. Maybe you'll even be married and have children by then."

"Maybe..." Alonso said. "But it's been a very long time since I've lived that kind of life. How do I know that my family even wants me back?"

"Oh, we do!" Maria said, rushing up to her brother from the crowd at last. "We've waited so long for you to come home! We've been so worried! Every time you disappeared, my heart broke in another place from missing you."

"I know you," Alonso said softly as he gazed at his sister with sane eyes for the first time in months. "Maria. My sister, Maria. Is it really you?"

"It is," Maria said, throwing her arms around her brother's neck and washing his face in joyous tears. "And you're my brother, Alonso. I've missed you so much!"

"And I you, Maria," Alonso said. "And Father. I can't remember clearly, but he was ill the last time I left. Tell me he hasn't died since I've been gone."

"He hasn't," Maria said, "but you're right, he's very ill. Alonso, you must come home with me before it's too late. It would break Father's spirit if you didn't return with me this time."

"Then I will," Alonso said. He then turned to Kaltaag and said, "And I'll wait there for Enkili to call upon me once again when he's ready to test me a second time. And that time, I will not fail him."

"I believe it," Kaltaag said. He then turned to address the crowd and said, "So ladies and gentlemen, as you stand beneath the Thundershrine, bear witness to what has come to pass. I give you this faithful family man, who will be a true and noble paladin one day in Enkili's service. His name is Alonso Keyhost, and this is his sister, Maria."

At that, the crowd was finally convinced that this was, indeed, a practiced performance, and the people burst out in wild applause. Some even threw coins,

Thief's Mark

which Kaltaag dutifully scooped up. The cheers went on for several minutes, and the brother and sister stood in the center basking in the joy of their reunion. Then, like all acclaim, the cheers faded away and the crowd dispersed bit by bit until only the Keyhost siblings and Kaltaag remained. Even the guards drifted away, certain that they'd been played for Thief's Marks, but none too resentful regardless.

Kaltaag, himself turned to go when both Alonso and Maria stopped him.

"Wait, friend," Alonso called. "Don't leave yet."

"Yes," Maria said. "Stay a while. I want you to know my brother as I know him, not as the man you met in the forest."

"I don't think so," Kaltaag said, taking a step back and holding up his hands. "I really should leave."

"But why so fast?" Alonso said. "This street festival isn't even over yet. Won't you at least stay until then?"

"Not this time," Kaltaag said. "I've had enough excitement in this city for a while. Now I've got my own home and family to get back to. Here, why don't the two of you take this money I've got left in my purse, and enjoy yourselves. It should see the two of you through until the end of the festival. Then get home and take care of your father. And each other."

Alonso took the purse from Kaltaag's reluctant fingers and dropped it down inside his shirt where a pickpocket couldn't get at it easily. He then took Kaltaag's hand and gave it a vigorous shake, in which Maria joined in.

"At least do us this one favor before you go," Maria said. "Even though I know you've already done so much."

"Yes," Alonso added. "I think I know what my sister's going to ask."

"All right," Kaltaag sighed. "What is it?"

"Tell us your name," Maria said.

"Yes," Alonso echoed. "Tell us so that we can tell everyone back home the name of our new friend and Enkili's gatekeeper here in Zathiske."

Kaltaag thought about it for a moment then finally shrugged. "Sure," he said. "It's Kaltaag. And if you don't recognize that name, someone back home will."

"Kaltaag," Alonso said, gargling the word into a mess. "I'll remember that, my friend. And in ten years, I'll call you that when you've come to test me again."

"Right," Kaltaag said, backing away again. He waved one last time and started to walk away into the milling crowd toward a street that would lead him out of the city. "Ten years," he called over his shoulder. "In ten years, we'll meet again, and maybe then you'll be ready."

Then, in a voice pitched just low enough for his own ears, he smiled and added, "You Thief's Mark."

And this time, he knew exactly who he was talking to.

SWORD & SORCERY
PRESENTS
DEAD GOD TRILOGY
FORSAKEN

The elves of Scarn remember a time when the lands were whole. They remember when sympathetic gods protected them from the thoughtless titans who dominated the earth. They remember the wars that raged when those titans fought to destroy the usurpers. The divine battles shattered the landscape, decimated many races and left gods dead — including the god of the elves. The titans have since been overthrown and imprisoned and the world has moved on, but without their god, the bereft elves of the Scarred Lands are dying out.

Scarred Lands

AVAILABLE JUNE 2002

www.swordsorcery.com

SWORD & SORCERY

the largest independent publisher of d20 material

>...a compilation of exciting material to include in your game... that cannot fail to make them more diverse and challenging.
> — **Gary Gygax**
> creator of D&D

>...will have a lasting impact on many campaigns and the D20 landscape...
> — **RPGnet review**

>These Sword and Sorcery guys are good...Wizards of the Coast might have real competition...
> — **Monte Cook**
> author of D&D's 3rd edition DMG

Tribe Novels 5: Children of Gaia & Uktena

THE RAGE CONTINUES...

The Garou, the bestial werewolves who fight to save the natural world, have their backs to the wall.

In Tribe Novel: Children of Gaia, the storyteller Cries Havoc, robbed of his memories by the Wyrm, fights to become whole again.

In Tribe Novel: Uktena, another songkeeper named Amy Hundred-Voices comes face to face with Lord Arkady, the Silver Fang accused of conspiring with the Wyrm. Can she turn him from his destructive path?

March 2002

White Wolf is a registered trademark of White Wolf Publishing, Inc. Werewolf the Apocalypse is a trademark of White Wolf Publishing, Inc. All rights reserved.

WEREWOLF THE APOCALYPSE

EXALTED

Trilogy of the Second Age™

Before there was a World of Darkness®, there was something else.

It was a land of turmoil in the Second Age of man.

It was a time of high adventure and heroes re-born.

It was a setting of savage peril and sprawling decadence.

It was the world of Exalted™.

Book One
Chosen of the Sun

Available Now!

Richard E. Dansky

Book Two
Beloved of the Dead

April 2002!

White Wolf is a registered trademark of White Wolf Publishing, Inc. Exalted is a trademark of White Wolf Publishing, Inc. All rights reserved.